***Straining to hear any sound, I stepped into the room.***

A glint of metal caught my eye. My racing pulse kicked up another notch. Was that a canister like the one that had released the virus?

I was rushing forward when I sensed motion to the side. I whirled but caught a glancing blow to my head. Stars exploded and I fell forward, losing my grip on my gun. It skittered across the floor.

Legs clad in black pants stood before me. I reached out and gripped my attacker's ankle as I lowered my internal guard.

Contact.

Hatred seared through my body, overwhelming me with painful intensity. Gasping, I released my grip and instinctively curled up in fetal position.

Another set of legs appeared and through a haze of emotional and physical pain I heard the grunts of people fighting. Then my vision blurred and darkness claimed me.

Dear Reader,

I believe in destiny. After all, I've been an action-movie addict all my life and just *knew* that one day I would be writing my own tales of danger for a fabulous line like Bombshell.

I believe in karma. Fortune blessed me when it allowed me to become part of the most amazing group of writers: THE MADONNA KEY authors. Imagine writing an adventure spanning Western Europe! Not only could I write about places I've been to, such as Lake Como and Milan, Italy, but also places that I wish I could visit, such as Switzerland, Spain, Austria and France. Imagine exploring the thirteenth century, the Cathars and the Third Crusade in a contemporary thriller!

Like my character Eve St. Giles, I believe in redemption. If one is willing to believe and to sacrifice, there will be an opportunity to undo the damage of the past. Flu hunter Eve certainly needs all the chances she can get in her race to stop a monster pandemic. Especially since she has to join forces with her sexy ex-fiancé, Nick Petter. After all, who could resist a former Swiss guard who once took a bullet for the pope?

Seven women. Unthinkable danger. A lost history waits for those who dare.

Eve St. Giles is one of those women. Join the adventure! And for more exciting Marian insights, be sure to visit www.madonnakey.com.

Carol Stephenson

# Carol Stephenson

# SHADOW LINES

Published by Silhouette Books
America's Publisher of Contemporary Romance

THE MADONNA KEY series was cocreated by Yvonne Jocks, Vicki Hinze and Lorna Tedder.

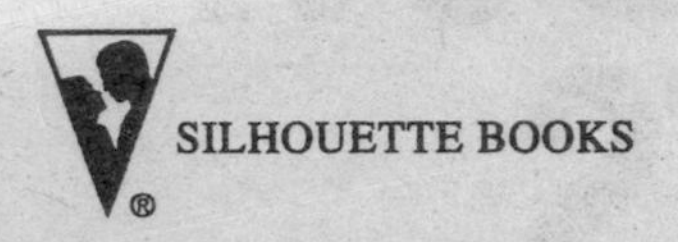


ISBN-13: 978-0-373-51424-3
ISBN-10: 0-373-51424-7

SHADOW LINES



This edition published by arrangement with Harlequin Books S.A.



www.SilhouetteBombshell.com

**Printed in U.S.A.**

**Books by Carol Stephenson**

Silhouette Bombshell

**Courting Danger* #51
*Shadow Lines* #110

Silhouette Special Edition
*Nora's Pride* #1470

*Legal Weapons

---

## *CAROL STEPHENSON*

credits her mother for her love of books and her father for her love of travel, but when she gripped a camera and pen for the first time, she found her two greatest loves—photography and writing.

An attorney in south Florida, she constantly juggles the demands of law with those of writing. I-95 traffic jams are perfect time oases for dictating cutting-edge thrillers. You can drop Carol a note at P.O. Box 812034, Boca Raton, FL 33481-2034.

To my fellow Madonna Key collaborators—
Cindy Dees, Vicki Hinze, Sharron McClellan,
Jenna Mills, Lorna Tedder and Evelyn Vaughn—
thank you for sharing your creative energy on this
fabulous project! It was a magical journey for
me to be part of this special continuity.

# *Prologue*

Once there lived a woman whose beloved hills were alive with the sounds of death.

Thirteenth-century crusaders led endless lines of religious martyrs, singing their last defiance, to the burning pyres in southern France.

So much fear, so much agony. Too overwhelming for a healer to bear.

The Inquisition's swath of devastation extended far, even reaching a sacred temple, long hidden. As the healer and her fellow Marians raced to dismantle and hide their precious source of power, her assassin, aided by a traitor, drew close.

Betrayal had sealed the fate of one ecliptic. Only the dawn of a new age could bring redemption.

With no hope for herself, the healer sent off into the

chaos her most precious treasure of all in the belief that, one day, one of her descendants would help save the world....

# *Chapter 1*

I was elbow deep in cow udders when my cell phone rang.

Hopefully, the caller was my veterinary friend returning the message I'd left. My face was pressed against warm quivering cowhide. I managed to say, "Dr. Eve St. Giles," into the voice-activated headset without getting a mouthful of hair. I ran a swab along the udder wall and placed it in a test tube.

"Eve?" My sister's strident voice came through loud and clear, causing the cow to shift away from me.

"Shhh," I whispered to the nervous animal. "Everything's going to be all right."

Actually, the situation here in Yorkshire was anything but all right. Constables in yellow slickers and armed with rifles stood outside the barn, ready to slaughter this and every other cow on the farm if my verdict was mad cow disease.

"Did you just tell me to shush?" Yvette demanded over the receiver.

"Not unless you've developed hooves and are chewing your cud since I last saw you."

Silence.

So much for that admittedly poor attempt at lightness. My sister had never understood our physician father's need for humor in tense situations either. I swore Dad was a walking encyclopedia of every poor joke in the world.

I capped the test tube and sighed. "I was kidding, Yvette. I'm checking out a cow at the moment and she's a little skittish."

"Really, Eve. Your fascination with germs is bad enough when it pertains to people, but must you also muck about with animals?"

Life in any form was precious as far as I was concerned. That belief was what kept me going. "Animals get sick, too."

No point in explaining animal-borne diseases could easily mutate and become transmitted to people. Yvette always left the room whenever Dad and I engaged in medical shop talk at family gatherings.

Because the barn was closed up tighter than a coffin, the air felt stuffy and heated. A bead of sweat ran by the corner of my eye. I nearly wiped my brow before recalling where my hand had just been.

Occupational hazard of being an epidemiologist. I swiped my face against my shirtsleeve.

"Yvette, what's up? I'm slightly busy."

"So what else is new? You never have time for the family."

Normally Yvette's discontented tone meant she was

between men and needed a shoulder to cry on. I sought to sidetrack her with my favorite topic after microbes.

"Where are Laurel and Phillipe?" I adored my niece and nephew and would gladly suffer through Yvette's gripe session if it meant I got to speak with them, remote as that possibility was. Yvette didn't exactly encourage my contact with her children.

"I sent them back to their grandparents in France. Everyone seems to be sick here," Yvette complained with a slight cough.

I tried to squelch the disappointment that welled up in me. When was the last time I had gotten to speak with them? One month, two months? I knew it had been way too long since I'd heard their voices.

"Where's here?" I ran a soothing hand over the cow's haunch as I rose from the three-legged stool. To my left, the gaunt-faced farmer and his wife didn't move, didn't react to my movement. Resignation lay like a dark shroud over the barn.

I had read the case study on my helicopter ride in. Following an urgent call from a friend with Great Britain's health department asking me as a favor to come, I had flown into London from Stockholm for a briefing before coming here.

Like so many British farmers, the owner had almost lost his farm with the first devastating outbreak of mad cow disease. Over the years, he had rebuilt his herd only to have a dozen cows fall ill and die over the past few days. Stepping out of the stall, I nodded at the couple as I moved to the other side for privacy.

In the quiet I realized for the first time that my sister's breathing sounded thin, wheezy. "Yvette, are you all right? Where are you?"

Along with a sizable fortune, my sister had come into

several estates when her husband, a French aristocrat, had been killed water-skiing. A drunk on a jet ski had run into Jean-Pierre Fouquet, leaving in his wake the death of the sole heir to the Fouquet vineyard in Languedoc-Roussillon, a shell-shocked widow and two grieving children.

"I'm in Damassine. I was going to take in the festival and ski, but I think everyone in the whole damn town is sick. I never should have come here."

Damassine. While the little village tucked off the beaten track in western Switzerland wasn't on my sister's top-ten list, even its name resonated within me.

I gnawed on the corner of my mouth as I mentally ran over the last computer updates I had read before leaving my office at the European Centre for Disease Prevention and Control—the ECDC—in Stockholm. No mention of any influenza outbreaks in Europe.

"What are the symptoms?"

"Damn it, Eve, I'm not some lab rat for you to quiz." While our father was Boston proper and we had been raised in his hometown, our very French mother had left a strong stamp on both her daughters' temperaments and language.

I also suspected that Maman had bestowed an extra little gift on her youngest, aka me. However, her psychic powers paled in comparison to mine. In which case, if such powers expanded with each generation…

*No, don't go there. You've already made your decision to ensure that doesn't happen. The risk has been contained.*

"I didn't call to be part of your freak show," Yvette continued.

My sister didn't take kindly to my special talents. "Then why—"

"I need you to watch Laurel and Phillipe next week."

Delight sped through me. She must be truly desperate to call me, her babysitter of last resort. I kept my voice light. "Hot date?"

"Someone of interest. But it's too early in the relationship to introduce him to the children."

My BlackBerry was in my bag, which was outside where constables stood ready to slaughter a herd of cows. I didn't think it was the time to check my calendar.

"I don't have my schedule—"

"Fine. Let me know as soon as you can spare me a minute of your precious time."

"Yvette—"

Click.

So much for advising her to drink plenty of fluids and rest. I removed the icky latex gloves, stuck them in a baggie and took out a fresh pair. Nothing like a sibling guilt trip. I would have to make amends later.

But right now, I had a puzzle to solve.

I left the barn with the owners close on my heels. Immediately the local authorities pressed around us. Although I had my field kit in my bag, I didn't need to run any tests to know something about the situation didn't square with a diagnosis of mad cow disease.

*Wrong,* whispered my inner voice.

As if I would ever listen to my sixth sense again. Not after that disaster in Brazil. Focus on the science, as I had promised myself. Listening to the woo-woo would only lead to failure.

I removed my hat and ran my fingers through the short, damp waves of my hair. "Would you please run over the chronology of what happened?" I asked the couple, expecting the man to answer. But it was the wife who spoke.

"It wasn't at all like the first time this area had that outbreak." She shot a defiant look at the men with guns.

"How's that?" I walked toward the pyre built to burn the cow carcasses stacked in the pasture. The odor of diseased, rotting flesh hung heavy in the air. I hated death and the grotesque effects it had on bodies. However, the reason I became a field epidemiologist and not a lab rat, as my sister so fondly put it, was so that I could *prevent* death. Only by confronting its ugliness face-to-face could I find the necessary answers.

But death always took its toll. I could feel the blackness smothering the light of energy in me.

I planted my foot on the lower rung of the wooden paddock fence and gazed around the pasture. It was a typical English winter day—gray, overcast sky with drizzling cold rain and a raw chill that seeped into my bones. I flipped up the collar of my field coat.

The farmer's wife stood next to me, her hands stuck into the pockets of her wool, hand-knit cardigan. "When the blight hit this area years ago, it was gradual, like a cancer. First one cow fell ill."

Cow Zero, I thought. The first victim who had become the carrier in turn.

"Then another and another until most of the herd had to be destroyed." The woman swallowed hard but pointed at the dead cows. "That wasn't the case this time. They were all sick at once."

Interesting. Were we dealing with a new variant of the virus or something else?

A man's rough voice spoke behind me. "Cripes. Enough of this bloody waiting. Sorry, but I have my own herd to protect. Let's get it done."

I turned. A man in a yellow slicker and mud-covered

Wellies strode toward the barn. “Hey.” I stepped forward, cutting off his path. “I haven’t finished.”

“You go play with your test tubes, Yank. We have a job to do.” The other men shifted, but when I glared, didn’t follow.

I fisted my hands on my hips. “The chief health administrator personally asked me to investigate.”

Although animal viruses weren’t my specialty, in conjunction with these cows falling sick, there had been reports in the area of an increase of people with flu symptoms. My cachet as a field epidemiologist for the European Centre for Disease Prevention and Control had led the British health officials to invite me to join in the investigation. If gene-swapping was going on where a nonhuman flu virus was adapting and becoming a human virus, the health organizations needed to know. It was easier to stop a contagion in its infancy before it grew into an epidemic.

“I have complete authority here. Not a shot’s to be fired unless I say so.” I had long ago learned in potentially dangerous situations to maintain the appearance of control.

However, my order didn’t faze the man. He gripped the rifle’s muzzle and butt and thrust it at me, aiming for my chest.

The one good thing about having a Swiss Guard as a former lover is that you learn moves in and out of bed.

I grabbed the rifle, giving it a sharp twist, and wrenched it free from the startled man. I handed the rifle to a stunned constable. Small wonder. I stand about five-four in my boots, while the disarmed man had to be six foot and outweighed me by a good seventy pounds.

I wagged my finger at the officer. “I say when and I say how. Clear?”

The constable nodded. "Yes, Doctor."

"Good." I returned to the paddock fence and climbed over. I walked the perimeter paralleling the drive. I didn't know what I was looking for, but my instincts told me the answer was here. The farmer trailed close behind.

I found remnants of a bale of hay in the corner facing the house. I kicked aside a few strands and spotted flashes of green.

*There.*

Ignore the voice, I warned myself, and concentrate on collecting data.

Still, curious, I knelt and picked up a branch with flat needles and a few red fleshy berries. I held it up.

"What's this plant?"

The owner shrugged. "Dunno. Looks like it's from one of those shrubs my wife planted along the drive last year."

I rose and looked at the bushes on the other side of the fence. Although the row was straggly, several branches shot toward the paddock. Here and there were patches of churned dirt, exposing the roots.

I hit the speed dial of the phone clipped to my belt. When I reached my agency, I asked for the resident plant expert. After describing the bushes, I had my answer. I rang off and went to the farmer. Clapping my hand on his shoulder, I pointed toward the group of men milling by the barn.

"See them?"

The owner nodded.

"Give them shovels and have them dig up every one of those plants and burn them."

Hope lit his eyes. He swallowed, hard. "Why?"

"Because your cows got into your wife's yew bushes. Lack of coordination, nervousness, sudden collapse.

All signs of alkaloids affecting the heart. Very toxic. And very much contained in the yew."

The man blinked rapidly and then grabbed my hand. "Thank you. Thank you so much."

A sense of rightness filled me. "You're welcome." I stuck the yew in a bag and then paused.

"By the way, that last cow I examined in the barn."

The farmer's mouth tightened. "My children's favorite. What about her?"

I winked. "She's expecting twins."

"You felt them when you examined her?"

"In a sense." During the time I'd been in physical contact with the expectant cow, I'd seen in my mind's eye two embryos stirring.

I smiled. "A male and a female. Congratulations."

I headed toward my equipment by the barn, whistling all the way. After a long cold streak, life finally had come out the victor.

However, the triumph was too little and too late, as my transfer request was signed, sealed and only needed to be delivered to my boss.

Hours later I was more than ready to head to Heathrow Airport and camp out until my return flight to Stockholm where the ECDC was headquartered and I kept a small flat.

While the obvious career path for me should have been the Atlanta-based Center for Disease Control and Prevention, during my epidemiological studies at Harvard, I had attended a lecture by guest speaker and ECDC director, Dr. Frederic Lutz. Inspired by his talk and the meeting with him afterward, I'd applied for a position and had been put to work as a field epidemiologist. Fortunately, my pragmatic French mother had insisted her daughters be more than bilingual. My proficiency in several languages combined with my pediatric medical degree had proven invaluable in my work.

So my home base was now Stockholm and my work here in Great Britain was done. I had met with the Yorkshire authorities and overseen lab testing that confirmed my assessment the cows had died from yew poisoning. But while I ached with exhaustion, I needed to make one more stop. Otherwise, I'd never hear the end of it.

When her mind was set, my friend photographer-journalist Scarlet Rubashka could pursue a person to the ends of the earth and beyond.

I paused for a moment in the entrance of the pub just off of Hyde Park Corner. Since Scarlet lived in Paris, it wasn't a coincidence that she was in London at the same time I was and had given me a call to meet her for a drink.

Something was up, but then again, something always was with Scarlet. She was a moving force field. When not on assignment, she was pursuing her latest interests, researching either the coming Age of Aquarius or those priestesses she'd recently begun talking about.

I checked my watch, wondering whether I should try calling Yvette before being swept into Scarlet's latest project. I pulled out my cell phone. A rosy-cheeked elderly man brushed against me. "Excuse me, luv," he apologized.

A shock wave pulsed through me, followed by a ripple of sickness. Despite the man's facial coloring, a pale ash-gray light surrounded him. I sighed, knowing the reaction I would get, but the healer in me couldn't ignore the situation. I pocketed my phone.

"Sir." Urgency tinged my voice.

He paused, giving me a polite smile.

Now that I had his attention, how could I warn

him without sounding like a wacko? I mentally snapped my fingers. Of course, fall back on being the voice of authority.

"I'm a medical doctor."

"All the way from the Colonies, eh?" he teased.

"Yes. Do you have a family doctor?"

He must have attributed my very personal question to my being a brash American for he shrugged. "Sure, duckie. At my age, not everything works the way it used to. I have high blood pressure."

"Do me a favor." I pulled out a notepad from my pocket and jotted down a few medical terms and symbols. "Go see him tomorrow and give him this note. He may need to…ah…" I cleared my throat to cover my white lie. "There's something about your skin tone, and I think your dosage needs to be adjusted."

The man gave me a puzzled look, but he took the paper and tucked it into his tattersall vest pocket. He thanked me and said good-night as he left the pub.

I released a long breath. I had done what I could. If the man called his doctor, maybe the cancer he had could be treated in time.

After all, I couldn't exactly proclaim that I was an empath who could absorb other people's emotions and medical conditions. Psychic detectives may be the accepted norm on television, but reality was another matter.

My personal albatross began when I was a young girl. On a trip to visit her relatives in France, my mother had taken me to the Musée Cluny. I'm sure poor Maman had simply wanted to expose me to European culture before America's pop version corrupted my soul. However, the visit had backfired, introducing me to what I fondly called my "woo-woo" factor and why my sister branded me a freak.

As Maman and I had wandered through hushed hallways teeming with medieval tapestries and art, I'd been fascinated. While Maman had studied one tapestry, like any curious child told not to touch, I'd been compelled to touch a statue of an angel.

Screams had bombarded me from all directions followed by waves of pain. I'd collapsed, unconscious. Although doctors had found nothing physically wrong, I'd continued to wake up screaming from nightmares. After one really bad night, a woman had come to me in my dreams. Maman, I thought. She'd taken my hand and said that, although I had a special gift, it was time for me to let go of the pain of people long dead.

Let go of the pain, perhaps, but not the drive to learn what had killed all those people. Through research I'd learned the statue had been made during the black plague epidemic of the 1300s and had come from a central European church.

Maman had found an empathic psychologist who had shown me how to shield myself so that I wouldn't fry to death emotionally whenever I was in large groups of people.

Centering myself, I zigzagged through the crowd to the booth at the back. I plopped onto the bench seat opposite Scarlet and stretched out my booted feet in her direction. Her delicate nose wrinkled.

"Phew! What is that smell?"

I smiled. "Eau de Bovine."

"Eve, you're incorrigible! How an attractive woman like you can dress like that..." In a gesture purely French despite the fact Scarlet was Canadian, she pointed with amusement at my outfit.

I glanced at dirt smears on my khaki shirt and pants and then at her bronze silk tunic. "What, you don't like my taste in clothes?"

Sighing, she tucked one side of her bobbed hair behind an ear. Scarlet's hair color du jour was red and it suited her fine-but-strong beauty. When she leaned forward, curiosity glinted in her brown eyes.

"So was it mad cow disease?"

Signaling the waitress, I ordered a shepherd's pie and a shandy. When the young woman left us, I answered, "No, thank God. Plant poisoning." I explained about the yew bushes.

"So did you figure this out based on pure science?" Scarlet looked a tad too nonchalant.

"Absolutely."

"But of course." My friend leaned back and toyed with her wineglass.

The waitress returned with my beer. I sipped the chilled shandy and sighed with pleasure. "The good news is that there wasn't any reason to destroy the herd, and the children's pet cow is having twins."

Scarlet's lips twitched. "Oh? Did the farmer tell you that or did you feel it?"

I squirmed. Scarlet and I had met three years ago when she had been taking pictures of women scientists for a magazine article. As we'd shaken hands, a strong current had snapped between us, linking us together. I had known that the startled look of recognition I'd seen in her eyes was also reflected in mine.

My friendship with Scarlet had come so easily and naturally that I knew it had to do with what Scarlet called the "Marian" aspect of myself that being empathic didn't explain. Despite our both constantly being on assignments, we maintained quite an e-mail correspondence, getting together whenever our schedules meshed.

At times I thought Scarlet did hold the key to why we were drawn to each other in a relationship, closer than the one I had with Yvette. My friend readily accepted the unexplainable whereas my sister chose to ignore it. But I still had trouble dealing with being an empath. My Boston blood, which cooled my Gallic sensibilities, wasn't ready for yet another woo-woo chapter in my life.

So what if I was a descendant of a band of once-powerful priestesses as Scarlet claimed? Ancestors were merely a pool of genes. Who we were as women was up to us.

Impatient with my continued silence, Scarlet shook her head. "Oh, Eve. Your psychic abilities are like any raw talent. You must use them in order to learn how to understand and control them. You've had some success with using auras to diagnose, haven't you?"

Unnerved by my run-in with the elderly man, I was not going down that conversational rocky path. Not tonight when exhaustion had replaced my earlier exhilaration. With Scarlet, the best way to throw her off the track was to go on the offensive.

"So what brings you to London? Escaping earthquakes or power outages?" Western Europe certainly had experienced a rough patch of phenomena, from shakes to blackouts to freak thunderstorms.

"I know, it's the fish and chips." I indicated her barely touched plate of food.

Now it was her turn to look slightly uncomfortable. Or…scared? "I'm researching certain antiquities."

As I took another sip of my drink, I realized there was something different about her tonight. Now that she had raised the topic, I couldn't help but notice the rosy aura edged with gray that surrounded her.

Stunned, I lowered my glass. "Scarlet, are you in love? I mean, I know you said on your blog that you're in love, but…are you in *love* love?"

Confusion and wariness darkened her eyes before she smiled and broke out into that infectious laughter so uniquely hers. "What is this, Eve? Are your abilities expanding into being a love barometer?"

"Yeah, right. I'm such a whiz at love." I couldn't keep the bitterness out of my tone, even as I wondered whether she was hiding something.

She leaned forward and covered my hand with hers. Once more I felt that tingle of connection to her as if we were linked on an ancient plane stronger and deeper than blood. "Eve, you need to embrace who you are. When you can do that, you'll be able to open up. I still think you owe Nick an explanation."

I shrugged. "Don't see why. Our relationship is history. I did the right thing by breaking it off. The last thing Nick needed was to be involved with a freak."

Scarlet's slender fingers tightened on mine with surprising strength. "Eve, is that how you see yourself? Because you're so wrong. When I look at you, I see you as having the light of day."

I would not cry, I would not… My eyes misted, damn it.

The waitress arrived with the steaming platter, causing Scarlet to break her grip. I inhaled a sigh of relief. During the contact, I had experienced concern for me and her giddiness of being in love. The wariness I'd seen must have been for my sake, not her own. A sense of loss filled me, for once I had experienced that thrill of being in love, really in love. Now I wasn't sure if I could ever have it again.

But as I forked a bite of shepherd's pie, I realized that I could be happy for my friend. If anyone deserved love, it was this woman with a heart of gold.

"So details, please. I want to know all about this hot new flame of yours!"

She smiled, but a shadow seemed to pass through her expression. She tapped the glass face of her watch. "Don't you have a plane to catch?"

Glancing at my own watch, I cursed. "I have to go or I'll miss my flight." I fumbled in my pocket for money and tossed a few bills on the table. "That should cover my tab." I rose. "I'll call you later. I want to hear every detail."

"Eve."

I looked down at Scarlet's earnest expression.

"There are other women who are Marians like us. Remarkable women. I would love for you to meet them."

Others like me who might understand and have the answers to my nightmares?

For a moment the prospect tempted me, but I drew back. It had taken me years to come to grips with my intuitiveness. I wasn't ready to venture down a new path of self-exploration.

"Thanks, Scarlet. Another time." I leaned down, hugged her and kissed both her cheeks.

She shook her head. "When you're ready, Eve. Come to Paris."

"I'll think about it." I couldn't promise anything more.

"Eve, I may be out of contact for a while. There have been certain events recently…" Her voice trailed off.

"Anything wrong?"

"It's a long story, one I'll tell you another time when I have more facts."

"It's a date, then." I took a step and then paused. "Scarlet, I hope your man is good enough for you. You deserve the best."

Her eyes watered and she gripped the key on her necklace. "Thank you, Eve. That means a lot to me. Be safe out there."

"You bet." I felt her watching my progress through the pub. There were times when our hit-and-run get-togethers weren't enough. Next time I would make sure that we would spend a whole day together, kicking back with girl talk.

At the door I turned and gave her a final wave. She smiled, returning the goodbye. I was really lucky to have her as a friend.

It was nearly midnight when I unlocked the door to my flat in Stockholm and stumbled inside. While I had catnapped on the plane, what I really wanted was a good eight hours in bed. I dropped my flight bag on the floor.

I didn't need a light because my apartment was so sparsely furnished that there was no danger of tripping over anything. When your job took you around the world on a moment's notice, it didn't make much sense to collect possessions.

Shrugging off my coat and letting it drop on the floor, I unbuttoned my shirt as I walked toward the bedroom. A red light blinked in the darkness. The answering machine. I hadn't turned on my cell since leaving the plane. Maybe I'd better check my messages…and maybe I should forget about it until after a good night's sleep. After all the Centre could always beep me if there was an emergency.

At the bedroom entrance I paused and with a sigh, turned and went to where my phone sat on a small end table. I pressed the message button. A hideous wheeze filled the flat.

"Eve..." The voice was so weak I could barely make out that it was Yvette's. "Call...please. I'm so sick."

Fear flooded through me as I heard a death rattle as the message ended. I grabbed the receiver as the phone rang.

"Yvette!"

"No, Dr. St. Giles. It's Sylvia from the Centre."

Blood pounded in my temples. "Sylvia, I need to call you back. There's an emergency—"

"That's why I'm calling. There's been an outbreak. Hundreds infected and dying from the initial report."

I wet my dry lips. "Where?"

"Damassine, Switzerland."

# *Chapter 2*

My team flew into Geneva, where a military helicopter was on standby. Joining our group, a local Swiss health authority agent briefed us as we donned our protective gear, boarded the helicopter and took off. While the professional side of me listened to the Swiss agent's concerns about women's biathlon teams, who had been housed at Damassine for an international competition, the personal side heard an internal refrain in time to the whop, whop, whop of the copter blades.

*Too late, too late, too late.*

What was the man saying?

"The reports are that people are dying less than twenty-four hours after falling ill."

*Too late, too late, too late.*

Whop, whop, whop.

Before leaving my flat, I'd called my parents, fortunately reaching my father, a retired cardiologist.

Between us we could share a medical detachment, allowing us to discuss a course of action. Dad would tell Maman and then call Yvette's in-laws, the Fouquets. Until I reached Damassine and could contact Yvette, nothing was to be said to her children. Still...as sensitive as my niece Laurel was, I worried that she would pick up that something was wrong.

The Swiss military officer signaled our arrival, and I tucked away the images of my family. The moment we touched down, I was at the doors with my field bag in hand. As the doors were being opened, I performed the mental exercise of shielding myself from whatever might lay ahead. Observe, don't absorb, I warned myself.

Before the crewman cleared us to disembark, I jumped out and hit the snow-covered ground, running bent over. I faltered and blinked to clear my vision. What on earth?

Everywhere I looked were black lines, vibrating like three-dimensional holograms above the ground. The burst of energy that had propelled me from the helicopter seeped away as exhaustion oozed into my very pores. Taking a step forward was like trying to walk against the ocean tide: useless.

Then the waves of an insidious invader rolled through me like a freight train.

Seething red clouds engulfed me, with the sickness intent on pulverizing my organs to mush. Caught off guard by the virulence of the attack, I tried to amp up the psychic shield but my mental controls sputtered, too drained to function. I heard a soft *click* as if a switch had been thrown on deep inside me.

*Help us!*

As the agonizing cries of hundreds of dying people echoed in my head, I accepted the beckoning blackness as an escape hatch.

I floated in a safe place where the images of death were shut out, but voices intruded, calling my name, asking me to emerge. Reluctantly I swam upward from my harbor to the rocky shoals of consciousness. I cracked open an eye.

"Eve! Thank God!" Relief flashed across the weathered face of my assistant, Johann. "You scared the shit out of me." His voice rasped through the respirator mask he wore.

I opened the other eye. Several members of my team formed a circle around me.

"Can you get up? We need to check your suit to make sure there is no breach. I have Olaf's unit setting up the detox chamber just in case you had a rip."

Woozy, I crawled to my knees. From that position Johann helped me to scramble to my feet.

What the hell had happened to me? Lines. I'd seen black lines. Cautiously I scanned the field but saw only glistening white snow. I took a steadying breath.

Ok-a-ay.

"I was right behind you when you cried out and collapsed," my assistant said as he examined my suit. "I don't see any damage."

"Thanks." I adjusted my helmet and noticed the worried looks of my colleagues. I had to do something. Although I couldn't explain the vision of black lines, I did know from my empathic experience we were about to confront an unknown vicious killer. My team's attention needed to be on their jobs ahead, not on me. While we were too late for many stricken people, we could—no, make that *would*—save many.

And maybe, just maybe, I was in time to save my sister. I had to hold on to hope.

"Johann, next time we get a late-night call—" I

placed a hand over my stomach "—remind me to eat an energy bar before suiting up. The change of altitude on an empty stomach did a real number on my blood-sugar levels."

Everyone's relieved expressions told me they had bought into the explanation. Good.

I picked up my bag. "Let's get to work."

"Are you sure you're all right?" Johann put his gloved hand on my arm.

"Stop worrying. I'm fine." I stepped away and gestured to the others. "Come on, we have an outbreak to contain."

Trailers that would operate as our lab and base of operations were on the way from Geneva. Olaf's team was making good progress setting up the portable containment unit. Other members unloaded extra equipment from the helicopter.

In our work we often dealt with nasty bugs in primitive conditions, so we automatically packed for every contingency. What horror awaited us in Damassine we didn't know, but our team's safety came first and we had come prepared.

Since I knew the area from previous visits, I led the way from the landing site. While I wanted to run to Yvette's house, I knew that doing so would throw the others into confusion and possibly panic.

Stay calm, I ordered myself. You have science and every vaccine known to mankind on your side. Yvette would be all right. After all, it had been less than ten hours since her last message. The pathogen may be fast acting, but no bug was that fast.

Our party entered the village. No matter what the season, Damassine normally evoked quintessential

Swiss charm. Given its proximity to the western border, French was the principal language spoken here.

Steep cobblestone streets bent and curled around wooden chalets with low-pitched slate roofs. Fountains with religious to fanciful statuary decorated courtyards everywhere. From the Baroque town hall with its clock tower to the flamboyant Gothic church with its flying buttresses and stained glass windows, the sun-drenched village blended all the eclectic Swiss styles with an added dash of Gallic grace. Even in the dead of winter, Damassine would normally be bursting with life as everyone from the locals to sports enthusiasts to tourists filled the streets and markets.

Not today.

The scrape of our booted feet echoed on the empty streets. A gloomy pall of clouds blanketed the town, hiding the mountainous backdrop. From building after building, white towels and pillowcases flapped in the bone-chilling wind.

Sickness. Death.

My crew walked in silence. Protocol was that whenever a government imposed quarantine, white cloths were to be hung from a house, signaling someone was ill and needed to be picked up. So damn many. What could do this? Tension stretched as tight as a tourniquet inside me.

I swallowed and looked at the Swiss health official to my right. His face was ashen behind his face mask.

"My God." His voice was hoarse. "Nearly every house has infection. Is anyone left?"

For his sake, I prayed he was made of tougher stuff. Puking inside your suit was not a great experience. I had done it with my first Ebola victim. What hemorrhagic fever did to a human body was not a pleasant sight.

The official must have caught the worried speculation in my glance for he grimaced. "If you're worried about me, don't be. I'm a Serb. There's very little in terms of death that I haven't seen."

I nodded.

He pointed. "I was told that the hospital was set up in the town hall and the field beyond."

I spoke to Johann. "Take the others and get set up. I'm going to check on my sister."

"If I see her at the hospital, I'll call you," he promised.

As quickly as my cumbersome biohazard gear would allow, I made my way to the western side of the village. Yvette's chalet was a large, two-story building with gables and a slate roof. Each side of the square structure had a balcony enclosed by carved wood railings. A lacy camisole top fluttered from the balcony on the street side.

Despite my anxiety, I had to smile. Only my sister would call for help with silk lingerie.

I tried the panel wood door and it swung open. "Yvette, it's Eve!" I called out as I stepped inside to the dim interior.

No answer. Just silence. Has she already been picked up…or was she too ill to call out for help?

My heart pounding, I quickly searched the first floor of the chalet, which was constructed on a typical square plan. The living and dining areas, other than being in the usual Yvette disarray, appeared to be normal. The kitchen was another matter. A chair was turned over on its side. On the trestle table was a plate of uneaten food and a cup of coffee.

Photographs, many of my niece and nephew, covered the refrigerator. Realization punched the breath out of me, so I gripped the edge of the countertop.

Ohmigod. Up to a few days ago, Laurel and Phillipe had been here in Damassine. What divine providence had caused my sister to send her children away from this place of sickness?

Or *were* they safe? For all I knew, they could have been ill when they left. Fear sliced through me like a scalpel.

"Yvette!" I cried out as I ran from the kitchen and took two stairs at a time up the wood staircase to the upper levels. In my sister's bedroom, I found chaos.

Clothes littered the floor while the vanity bench lay overturned. The bedding was twisted, and on the gold silk duvet I saw dark splotches. Horrified, I stepped closer and saw the spots were dried blood. A buzzing sound drew my gaze to the end table where the phone receiver dangled from its cord. Piled high on the table were lace handkerchiefs, all stained with blood.

*Oh God, no.* She was bleeding internally.

I raced down the stairs and out onto the street, not bothering to close the door behind me. I ran to the center of town past the fountain where a statue captured St. George slaying the dragon. I went up one of the town hall's double-sided staircases and entered the main hall.

Stunned, I halted. Row after endless row of cots filled the room, with barely enough room for several men and women in white coats to pass. The sounds of wheezing, coughing and cries merged into a dark chorus. Although I'd locked away the empathic side of me, deep inside my soul it shuddered.

So many sick, so few to tend. We needed more medical personnel.

I pressed the call button on the cell phone clipped to my suit even as I weaved toward the nearest man, presumably a doctor, from the stethoscope looped around his neck.

Someone at the Centre answered and put me through immediately to the director, Dr. Frederic Lutz. Speaking into my headset, I wasted no time on preliminaries. “Frederic, we need help. Now.”

I swear the director could be dropped into the center of a hurricane and remain calm. “Yes, Johann’s already called. We’re sending more people, and the Swiss have put out an emergency alert as well. Medical personnel from Bern should be arriving shortly.”

“The sooner the better. It’s bad, Frederic. Nearly every house has someone infected.”

“Have you found Yvette?”

“No.” I choked back the panic that swelled inside me.

“The others can handle the initial setup and processing. Don’t worry about anything until you can locate her.”

“Listen, Frederic. I need a favor. Can you call my father? My niece and nephew were here until a few days ago.”

“Do you think they could be infected?”

“I don’t know, but they need to be checked out.”

“I’ll call your father,” the director said.

“Thank you.” I disconnected and went up to the man wearing a face mask. “I’m Dr. Eve St. Giles, epidemiologist with the European Centre for Disease Prevention and Control.”

“I’m Dr. Charles Dubuffet. I can’t say what a relief it was to see your team here. We’re overwhelmed. One moment we’re getting ready for the biathlon, the next, people are dropping like flies.”

“More help is on the way, Dr. Dubuffet.” I reassured him. “They’re bringing in doctors and nurses from Bern.”

He swiped the back of his hand across his forehead.

"Thank God. Those of us who aren't ill are exhausted. I've never seen anything that's acted so rapidly. Within hours of falling ill, people are dying or dead. Women and girls in particular seem susceptible to the infection."

I asked him about the symptoms, matching them in my mind with known agents. The infection rate suggested airborne but what, how?

Dr. Dubuffet gestured. "I'm sorry, but I need to get back to work."

I held my hand out. "Before you go, do you know Yvette Fouquet? I'm her sister."

His gaze softened. "Yes, I know Yvette. She was brought in this morning. The last I saw she was placed in a cot at the rear."

Relief filled me. My sister was still alive. I would move medical heaven and earth to cure her and everyone here.

"Thank you, Doctor." We parted and I threaded my way to the back of the room. I wished that I could pause by each cot, to assess, help and comfort, but the numbers were overwhelming. Once I had found Yvette and stabilized her, I would make a more thorough round through the sick. Dr. Dubuffet's observation about the patients' gender appeared to be dead on. Nearly every cot contained a sick female.

Hearing a weak cry of "Maman!" from one billet, I went to its side. A blond-haired girl, close to my nephew's age, looked up at me with a tear-stained face. She clutched a small stuffed teddy bear. Dried and fresh blood stained both her nightgown and the toy. When fear darkened her blue eyes, I realized that my gear was scaring her.

"Hi, I'm Eve," I spoke soothingly in French. "I'm a doctor, sweetheart. I guess I must look pretty scary, huh?"

"*Oui,*" she whispered.

"Ever seen a picture of an astronaut?" I knelt beside her.

She nodded.

"Well, this suit is like theirs, allowing me to do my job."

Too sick to question my explanation, she twisted fretfully in the cot. "Maman." She dragged in a breath of air and I could hear the rattle in her chest. "I want Maman."

I touched her arm. Despite my glove, the contact sent a weak but familiar tingling through me. Dear God, she was a Marian like me and Scarlet.

"What's your mommy's name, sweetheart? I'll look for her."

More tears filled her eyes. "She's 'Maman.'"

"Madam."

I looked up at the middle-aged man standing at the foot of the billet. He gestured at me. I smiled at the child. "I'll be right back."

I rose and stepped to the side. "I'm Dr. St. Giles," I said in a low voice. "Do you know her mother? The child's very sick."

The man whose makeshift badge identified him as a nurse shook his head. "Her mother died this morning."

Sadness filled me. "Can you find someone to sit with the girl? She shouldn't be alone."

The man's mouth twisted with weariness but he nodded. "I'll see if someone can cover for me so I can be with her."

"Thank you." As I turned around, I saw the darkness surrounding the girl and knew she was beyond help. Gently, I stroked the matted curls from her forehead. "Honey, your mother's waiting for you. You're going to be together again."

She turned her head slightly toward me. A strange gleam of light filled her eyes as she stared unseeing at me.

"Maman...I see her," she said on a last rattle of breath. The teddy bear slid to the side of her body. Then she was gone.

Fighting back tears, I caressed her cheek before lightly pressing her eyelids closed. I tucked the bear under her arm again and whispered goodbye. There was nothing more I could do.

In the midst of an outbreak, you learned to move on from those you couldn't help to those you could. Later I would grieve for her and all the others we lost.

In a numb mode I went from cot to cot, looking for my sister. Despite the din in the room, I could hear the sounds of distant sirens. At the rear two men stood talking in low voices.

As I approached, one relief worker shook his head. "I heard that poor Kurt Schmidt lost his mind over the deaths of his wife and daughter and set fire to his house. Claimed the devil was there."

I wondered what else would happen before this was all over. In an epidemic, fear-generated paranoia inevitably took hold of people, adding to the chaos.

I stopped in front of the two men. "I'm Dr. Eve St. Giles. I'm looking for my sister, Yvette Fouquet. She's about my height, five-four." I gestured. "Has dark wavy hair but wears it long."

The taller man shook his head. "I know Yvette, but I haven't seen her."

"But Dr. Dubuffet said she had been brought in this morning and placed in a cot in this area."

"I'm sorry, Doctor." He made a helpless gesture. "There are so many..." His voice cracked. "But I have not noticed her among the dead if that is of any comfort."

I hadn't seen Johann yet. He could be collecting data about the deaths. "Where are the dead being taken?"

With a sad expression, the shorter man pointed to the

back door. "Out there. Now if you would excuse us." In unison both men moved away.

I knew that the rear exit led to a picturesque alpine meadow framed by distant mountains. Normally it served as a gathering place for summer concerts when the grass was vivid green and the air laden with the scent of blossoms. But in November that open expanse would be snow covered and bitter cold from winds whipping across.

Dread slithered and wound into a sick ball in my stomach. With my heart thudding, I went to the door and opened it.

I swayed and desperately clutched at the handle to steady myself.

As far as the eye could see the bodies lined the ground. Makeshift shrouds of sheets, blankets and coats billowed as a sharp gust of wind off the mountain swept across the clearing.

At the far end I saw uniformed men placing corpses into body bags and stacking them in a flatbed truck.

Hundreds and hundreds dead. What silent killer had attacked this town?

"Excuse me, mademoiselle," a man spoke from behind me. He carried a small covered form.

I staggered to the side. As he walked down the stairs, a teddy bear fell to the ground.

"Wait!" I hurried after him. Picking up the bear, I placed it on top of his bundle. "Please, she needs to have this with her."

His eyes deeply shadowed with shock, the man nodded and carried the little girl down one of the long rows.

I could see members of my team moving among the dead, doing their jobs. Angry clouds of smoke rose over the roofs of the other buildings along one edge of the meadow.

My God, were they burning the bodies? Then I heard the wail of sirens and remembered the house fire.

Numbly, I walked up and down the rows. Not all bodies were covered, and the clinical side of me registered the ravages of the disease. I saw women in parkas bearing sporting companies' logos. Most likely the athletes who had come here to compete in the biathlon only to lose in death. I saw countless wives, daughters, sisters and mothers contorted from violent death.

Johann caught up with me in the tenth row. "Eve, I've never seen anything like this." His face was white behind his mask.

"What have you noticed about the victims?" I pointed at one row.

"Rapid onset of symptoms, internal hemorrhaging followed by death." He ticked off the findings. "Possibly airborne. Females at higher risk."

"Beyond high risk, Johann. Look around you. The dead are almost all female. While there are sick men, very few of them are dying."

He scanned the bodies and sucked in a breath. "My God, Eve. You're right. Is there any woman left alive in this village?"

"I want the lab work-up to focus on the linkage between the agent and women's chromosomes."

"Eve." Johann gripped my arm. "What are you thinking?"

The answer welled up from that awareness deep inside me. No, I would not listen to the voice again. Yet I heard myself say, "We're dealing with a bug altered to strike down women."

"Biological terrorism genetically targeting women?

Is that your training talking or your sixth sense?" I didn't blame Johann for his skeptical tone. He had been with me in Brazil when I'd stepped beyond the bounds of epidemiology and had flexed my empathic abilities with hideous results. I had been tragically wrong then. Was I wrong now?

*No.*

"We're doing this investigation by the book. You count the dead and then tell me if I'm wrong, Johann." I stepped away and paused. "For now, though, let's keep my hunch between us."

"Sure, Eve."

Slowly I walked down the row. With every step the anger built inside me. Although the consequences were horrifying, one could accept the occasional outbreaks nature threw out. Life evolved and so did the new strains of diseases.

But I knew this was man-made.

I found Yvette at the end of the row. The wind had blown the sheet away from one side of her body, leaving her hand uncovered. I recognized the glint of the diamond heirloom ring Jean-Pierre had given her upon their engagement.

I dropped to my knees. My hand shaking, I lifted the edge of the cover. Like all the others, the disease hadn't been kind to Yvette. Her hair was matted, her nightgown bloodstained, her once beautiful face ravaged. She hadn't been dead long.

*Too late.*

Too damn late to save her, to make amends, to start over. I slid my arm under her shoulders and held her. Whatever we had been to each other, she was my sister, my blood.

I brushed an icy lock of hair from her face. "I promise you, Yvette. I'll find out what happened to you."

As I cradled her, I stared at the black smoke filling the sky and saw the image of a woman holding a child. The Madonna. If I was having a religious revelation, it, too, was late.

I looked away, tears streaming down my face. I had no faith, only guilt eating away my soul.

# *Chapter 3*

"*Non,* Aunt Eve. It is not necessary for you to come see us. Phillipe and I are fine with Grand-père and Grand-mère."

Two days into the outbreak and exhaustion, grief and guilt had already taken their toll on me. However, my niece, Laurel's, distant formality was like a hammer driving a stake through my heart.

"I'm sure you are, Laurel." I slumped back on the wrought-iron bench I'd sought out in the safe zone.

When there had been no new reported cases this morning, the safety perimeter had been reduced to the length of a football field around Damassine, much to the relief of anxious relatives and the delight of reporters. Along with the Swiss authorities, I had already conducted several press briefings, always careful to speak in short sound bites to reassure the public. Phrases such as "the outbreak appears to be contained" or "no indication it has spread."

I tried again to break through the indifferent reception I was getting from my niece. "Honey, if you and Phillipe need me, I can get a leave of absence."

"We're fine."

Oh sure, she was fine. Then how come beneath her shield of manners I could sense deep currents of grief? Ten years old and her childhood stolen by the death of both of her parents.

Considering my next option, I stared unseeing at the milling groups of press, soldiers and medical personnel beyond the guard posts. There were times when the constant wearing of respirators, face masks and gowns got to you, and this was one of them. I had needed a break from the disease trenches, after spending a fitful night of sleep in the crew's trailer.

I had already called my parents on my cell phone. My director, through the magic of his connections, had not only secured a coffin but cut through any red tape to ship Yvette's body. When the all-clear came for normalcy to resume here in Damassine, she would be transported for burial beside her husband in Languedoc, France.

Next I had phoned Scarlet, only to experience acute disappointment when her answering machine had picked up. As Scarlet's photography assignments didn't normally run to the nitty-gritty, I didn't expect her to be sent to Damassine to cover the outbreak.

However, I really needed to speak with her. Only Scarlet could listen to my account of the Damassine landing when I had experienced the flu attacking people and not think I belonged in a loony bin. Only Scarlet would understand these currents of intuition that had been rippling through me nonstop as if my woo-woo On switch was stuck.

Was I developing a new psychic dimension? Once Scarlet had mentioned that a person could have more than one psychic ability. I hoped not.

And what had been the deal with those black lines?

"Aunt Eve? Are you all right?" Panic edged Laurel's voice.

"I'm fine, Laurel." I hurried to comfort her…or was I merely trying to reassure myself? "Just tired."

Another worry. Normally in a disease crisis, I could run twenty-four/seven, but since arriving here it was as if the very earth was sapping my strength. Even now, I felt run-down.

Focus.

"Sweetheart, I promise you. I will find out what killed your mother and I will stop it."

"That's all right, Aunt Eve. It is already too late for Maman."

"Laurel—"

"I have to go. Grande-mère is calling me."

Defeated, I closed my eyes. "All right, Laurel. I'll either call or e-mail you and Phillipe."

"That will be nice. *Adieu.*"

"Bye, sweetheart."

I thumped the cell phone against my forehead. I could unravel the DNA of a new virus, but I couldn't get through the defenses of a ten-year-old girl. Despite the lukewarm reception I would get from my niece and nephew, maybe I should just catch a flight to France. I rolled my neck.

But who in my place would hunt the man-made flu? All modesty aside, I had worked hard to be the best in my field.

And this bug was personal. It had killed my sister.

My gut told me that someone had created a microbe to exterminate women, but proving it was going to be another matter.

We had already tested every rodent, bird and beast for animal-borne disease. Nothing. We'd checked the water and samples of food. Again nothing.

With the biathlon event, the town had experienced a flood of tourists and athletes, but so far we had not located Patient Zero, the first person who fell ill. We had interviewed many townspeople, but nearly every account indicated dozens had fallen ill, almost simultaneously. That was strange in and of itself.

Fortunately, the quick quarantine appeared to be working. There were no reports of any cases outside Damassine. Perhaps the villagers had stayed close to home for the influx of visitors. No, I didn't buy that explanation for one moment.

Restless, I rose and walked, prepared to skirt around a group of men talking. For there to be no Patient Zero, the whole population had to have been simultaneously contaminated. That meant airborne or aerosol.

If so, why here? How had it been disbursed? A courier. For that type of disbursement, there had to be a courier who introduced the pathogen to Damassine. Who?

I kicked a clump of ice. The new factor introduced into this community was the international sporting event, but so far no group had claimed responsibility, if it had been a biological attack. With over a thousand dead and national press, the rats should have been crawling out of their holes to claim the limelight. Killing in secret didn't further their agenda, which would be to promote fear and chaos.

The female victims were the key.

I needed to find out the why and the who and track it to its source. First step, hunt down the carrier.

I froze at the sight of two men talking by a barricade. No, it couldn't be. Why him, why now?

My empathic psychologist had shown me how to shield myself from others' negative emotions. Perhaps too well, according to some who accused me of being distant.

But she hadn't shown me how to protect myself from my own foolish heart. While my mind rushed to reassure me I had made the right decision, my heart ached with longing.

The taller man, wearing a black ski jacket and dark sunglasses, turned toward me, his alert stance indicating I'd been spotted.

No place to run, no place to hide.

Besides, the decision as to whether to avoid a public meeting was not mine to make, it was his. After all, twelve months ago I had been the one to break off my engagement to Nicholas Petter. By phone call from Brazil no less.

I hadn't had the decency to do it in person, but I had been in such a panic that I hadn't thought I *could* do it in person. From the moment I had met Nick while attending a health symposium in Rome, I'd been a goner. To fall so quickly, so deeply in love had been…terrifying.

Without hesitation, Nick walked toward me, only a slight hitch in his stride evidencing the bullet he once took as a Swiss Guard protecting the Pope. No, some things never changed. Nick had always been one to tackle a problem head-on.

I let out a quick huff of breath and lifted my chin. When cornered, my mother always said to fall back on manners and pride.

"Hello, Nick."

"Eve, how are you?" But there was his husky voice that even now caused my toes to curl.

"All right. I've had better days."

He pushed his shades up atop his head so that I could see the sharp scrutiny of his blue eyes. Some women might describe his features as harsh, but I'd always admired the strong planes of his face.

Warily we studied each other. The past year had added several silver strands to his close-cropped black hair and perhaps carved a few more lines to his face. Otherwise, he looked the same—vibrant and sexy as hell.

Me, I thought ruefully as I self-consciously ran fingers through my mashed down hair, I probably looked like a bedraggled lab rat.

A stray curl fell onto my forehead. In a blink of an eye, Nick's hand shot out and he brushed the hair away, the rasp of his callused fingertips sending a shock wave to my core.

He flinched as if he too felt the surge, letting his hand drop.

Guilt consumed me. On Nick's last visit to Stockholm before I had gotten the call to go to Brazil, we had argued about having children. Afterward, Nick had been making love to me when my erratic empathic power had connected to his feelings: swirls of anger, hurt and disappointment.

Angry with himself? Disappointed in me? Hurt by my refusal to consider having a family?

I hadn't been able to ask what his feelings meant. How could I and let him know I had invaded his privacy? How could I stay with him if I couldn't control my abilities?

Nick stuck his hands in his jacket pockets. "I'm sorry about Yvette."

"Thank you." What else was there to say? An ocean

had separated us when I had ended our engagement. However, an even wider gulf now separated us.

"Your niece and nephew are still fine? When I called your folks, they said the children didn't have any symptoms."

"You called my parents?" I hadn't realized he still spoke with them.

He hunched a shoulder. "I wanted to make sure you were okay. I knew you would rush into the hot zone."

He called to ask about me? My astonishment grew along with confusion. A person didn't call unless he was concerned, right?

Suddenly I didn't know what to do with my hands and mirrored Nick's action of sticking them into my pockets. But I had a job to do and I had a new variable standing six foot two in front of me.

"What are you doing here? Although we're past the crisis level of new cases, the outer area remains cordoned off."

He shrugged. "My client, Janssen Pharmaceutical, has a contract with the Swiss government to develop various vaccines and to respond to outbreaks."

My internal antenna went on alert. His injured leg had forced his early retirement from the Swiss Guard. When we had first met, he had been setting up his own security company headquartered in Vienna. From what I heard—and I'd kept close tabs—his agency was doing quite well.

"Really. And your client requires your security presence here?"

Nick wore his professional mask. "We understand there's a possibility that this was a bioterrorism attack."

Hmm, touché. My turn to be inscrutable. "We haven't come to any conclusions. We're still investigating, collecting evidence."

"As I'm sure you will understand, I need to make sure the situation is safe for my client's personnel. However, I'll try to stay out of the way of your crew."

"You do that." Then I let out a huff of breath. We were being ridiculous, tiptoeing around each other with formality. Our relationship was dead and buried. I was an adult. I could handle him.

"Well then…" I pulled free a hand and gestured. "I need to get back." I started to turn.

"Eve."

"Yes?"

"Perhaps we can get together while we're both here. I'm sure I can find coffee for us."

That was being a little bit too civilized too quickly. "That would be nice, but I'm really tied up. I was just taking a break."

With his serious gaze studying my face, he nodded. "We'll play it by ear, then."

"Fine." He moved away and I turned toward the hot zone.

Then I paused. The man Nick had been speaking with remained by the barricades. He looked familiar. I had probably seen him on my previous visits to Damassine. It wouldn't hurt to find out what they had been talking about.

I approached the man. "Hi, I'm Dr. Eve St. Giles. Aren't you a town resident?"

He nodded. "Yes, I'm Paul Hodler. I own Sky Cruisers."

The name clicked. "Your place is outside town. Right? You sell parasails and hang gliders?"

I shucked in a breath of the ice-cold air as excitement thrummed in me. A glider could have carried the flu.

"Yes."

"Did you sell or rent any equipment in the past week to a tourist?"

He smiled faintly. "As I just told that man, with the biathlon I've had a brisk business. I keep records of all my sales and rentals so you're welcome to look at them."

"Great." I considered the sky. A skilled operator might be able to make several circles before having to land.

"Switzerland still doesn't allow motorized gliders, right?"

"That is correct. As I told that security agent, that's what was so strange."

"What was strange?"

Hodler gestured in the direction of Lake Neuchâtel. "A few days ago a man operating a powered glider buzzed the town. It was a beautiful day, pristine sky. All my equipment had been rented out. I thought that he was either a private operator daring the authorities or," he shrugged, "he flew across from France."

Damassine was close enough to the French border that a very determined individual could fly into Swiss airspace.

Although the wind was brisk, it wasn't dangerous. I'd discovered the joy of this type of flying in college and had indulged in parasailing and hang gliding wherever I'd traveled in my job.

"I need to rent a glider."

Hodler frowned. "Do you have a license?"

I pulled out my identification badge and held it up. "This is an official investigation."

His mouth tightened. "I lost my niece in this outbreak," Hodler said, then he hesitated, glancing about. He said in a low voice, "I have a personal glider, much like the one seen earlier. You can use it."

A motorized glider. Illegal or not, I could cover a larger area. "Then let's get going."

* * *

An hour later I was airborne. For an instant I enjoyed the rush of this Peter Pan moment. To be free of the earth and fly like a bird, with a whole new world calling to me. Nothing's more thrilling than to defy the law of gravity and breathe the sky. Energy flowed through me so I no longer felt fatigued. How could I be when this region was simply breathtaking against the backdrop of the Jura Mountains?

I was tempted…oh, so tempted…to keep flying toward the horizon and beyond. To fly beyond past mistakes and relationships. To fly toward understanding and accepting who I was.

Yet the drone of the engine and the crackle of the glider owner's receiver reminded me of my mission. Another time I would drink in beauty without a care. How many times had I promised myself that and failed?

Once my sister had remarked that I couldn't experience life beyond the microscope. She'd been wrong. Because those microorganisms I saw on a slide could cause death, I appreciated life so much more and fought to preserve it. So I turned the glider toward Damassine.

From above I could only see the picturesque charm of Damassine, not the horror that had swept through it. Even the blackened ruins of the burnt chalet didn't mar the beauty of the scene below me.

No tall structures and a condensed layout. Perfect target for an aerosol attack.

Depending on the method of dispensing, the courier would have had to make only a few passes to ensure total coverage.

Once more anger churned inside me. While innocent people had gone about their lives, death had been disbursed from above them. They'd never stood a chance from this attack.

But even motorized, the glider needed a launch and landing site. I swung in a curve and headed in the direction Paul Hodler had indicated earlier. Soon the winter blue waters of Lake Neuchâtel glittered below me. More charming villages lined the lake's edge, certainly as accessible as Damassine.

Then I saw western Switzerland's major spa resort, Yverdon-les-Bains, and the massive towers of the castle Château d'Yverdon. Known as the Thermal City for its hot sulphurous springs, Yverdon-les-Bains was this canton's second-largest city. Judging from my gas tank gauge, this town was well within a round trip for a glider. Large enough population with tourist traffic for a stranger to blend in. Spotting an airfield, I debated whether I should land and make a few inquiries.

*No, not there,* my inner voice whispered. Ever since my arrival in Damassine, my psychic control had been almost nonexistent.

Should I trust it? What did I have to lose? If I didn't find anything, I could always turn back.

Right now, with the tingling in my blood, I felt like one of those divining branches. Casting logic to the wind, I flew past the town. Beyond the northern suburbs, I saw it, a glint of metal outside a Neolithic stone circle.

*Yes, land there.*

Spotting a suitable clearing, I swung in a curve and swooped downward. I winced as my feet hit the ground. Frozen earth wasn't the softest landing bed. After I freed myself from the harness, I sensed that I wasn't alone. Someone was watching from the line of trees separating me from the stone circle.

I crouched and pondered my options, which weren't many. Given all the hassles of carrying a gun from country to country, I'd given up packing one for protection a long time ago. If I couldn't talk myself out of a tense situation in an outbreak situation, I wasn't worth my salary.

However…I twisted, opened my pack and pulled out a flashlight. It wasn't much, but if I got close enough to that dark shadow behind the tree to my left, I might inflict serious damage.

"Eve?" Dressed in his usual black, Nick stepped into the clearing. "What the hell are you doing here?"

I rose. "I could ask you the same thing."

We met halfway. Amusement flickered across his face as he glanced from me to the glider and back again. "I see you spoke to the owner of Sky Cruisers."

I wasn't as amused, and glared at him. "Obviously, we both came to the same conclusion that the bug was spread by air. Why are you really here?"

When he hesitated, I stabbed a finger into his chest. "I want answers, Nick. I lost my sister among those thousands who died."

Regret flickered in his eyes before the inscrutable look returned. I pressed my advantage. "And don't give me the line about protecting your pharmaceutical client from harm. You know something about the bug itself. Did your client develop it?"

Blowing out a breath, Nick nodded toward the woods. "Why don't we take a look at the remains of the glider while we talk?"

Remains. "It crashed?" I started across the snow-covered field toward the woods with Nick matching me stride for stride.

"No, more like it was intentionally burned."

I thought about the nearby airfield. "That makes no sense. Hodler said the operator appeared to be an experienced pilot. Why didn't he land in Yverdon-les-Bains?

All he had to do was load it on a trailer and disappear into France."

I glanced at him. "How did you find the glider?"

He winked. "Nothing as adventurous as your arrival. Satellite images picked up the remains."

Hmm. Having a satellite at your disposal sounded pretty darn exciting to me. But now that I thought about it, Nick had worked hard to cultivate his government contacts by feeding them useful information whenever he could.

We reached the other side of the stand of trees where a frozen circle marred the snow. In the center lay the blackened twisted remains of a glider. Sloppy. Had he been in too much of a hurry to stick around or had he been interrupted?

Kneeling outside the circle, I studied the area. "Tracks?"

Nick pointed. "Lead to the other side of the clearing where a car was parked. Most likely an SUV, from the looks of the tire marks. Other than he wore boots, not much I could tell."

"He and every other person in Switzerland this time of the year," I said as I rose and walked around the ruined metal. Something didn't feel right. It didn't feel like the metal I'd spotted from the sky.

"He set a fuse in the gas tank so he was a safe distance away when it blew."

"Any signs of a canister?"

"I was looking for it when I heard your approach, but as you can see, not much is left."

I closed my eyes and envisioned the scene as I had seen it from above. It had been closer to the stone circle. Reopening my eyes, I headed toward the menhirs.

"Where are you going, Eve?"

"Just checking out something I spotted while flying over the area."

I slowed down when I reached the outer perimeter of the semicircle of ancient stones, where trees cast shadows on the snow. Wind gusted through the clearing and the trees swayed. There. Metal.

My heart pounding, I hurried over. A twisted cylinder about the size of a large can of hairspray rested against one pillar.

"Careful!" Nick gripped my upper arm, bringing me to a halt. Despite the layers of clothing, I shivered at his touch.

Irritated by my reaction, I pulled free. "I handle this stuff every day."

"It could be rigged to blow."

Now that was stuff *he* handled. "Okay, you look first. Just don't touch the release valve."

"That reminds me," he said. Ripping open a Velcro pocket in his parka, he reached inside and pulled out a small vial. Next he pulled out a needle and a small packet I recognized as being an alcohol swab.

"What's that for?" I know I'm an epidemiologist, but that didn't mean I liked needles.

"Take off your jacket and roll up your sleeve." He ripped open the package before inserting the needle into the vial.

I stepped back. "Not until you tell me what you're packing."

Nick grinned, the first one I'd seen in a year. Its power was as mesmerizing as the first one he'd ever flashed at me. "Don't tell me you're scared of a little needle?"

I bared my teeth. "I am if I don't know what its contents are."

"Vaccination." He held up the syringe. "Either take

the shot, Eve, or leave. I'm not risking you being exposed to what's in that canister."

"I've been vaccinated against every disease known to mankind."

"Not this one. It hasn't been in existence for over eighty years."

I opened and closed my mouth but rolled up my sleeve, allowing him to clean a patch of skin before administering the injection.

"Ouch! Careful!"

"Don't be a such a baby," he chided. However when a drop of blood welled up on my arm, Nick dug out a handkerchief and pressed it over the puncture mark.

"Spanish flu. You're talking about *the* Spanish flu."

"More precisely, my client's aborted lab project."

"What project?"

"Recreating the Spanish flu."

My legs suddenly didn't seem to have any strength. Snow or no snow, I sat down. Nick kneeled beside me. "Are you all right?"

"Was your client *crazy?*"

He shrugged. "A government was interested in bioweapons. My client was exploring possibilities."

My voice was hoarse. "Oh, I would say a flu that killed more people than World War I was more than a possibility."

Any student of diseases knows about the influenza pandemic of 1918. An American soldier at Fort Riley, Kansas, had reported to the camp hospital just before breakfast on March 11, 1918. By noon the number of sick soldiers had jumped to one hundred and by week's end, five hundred. Spreading like wildfire through forces on both sides of the war, it wasn't long before it struck the civilian population. In New York 851 persons died in a single day. The world had gone from ending the war to combating an even deadlier disease. Before the global pandemic ended, an estimated forty million had been killed in a single year.

"It also ceased to exist," Nick reminded me.

"In that variation, yes, thank God. But you know the bird flu has been linked to the same gene. What gene was the lab experimenting with?"

"The original DNA."

I'd heard that some scientists had gone so far as to dig up bodies buried in the Alaskan permafrost to extract the gene. "Where did they get the original?"

Nick took a clump of ice and gave it a sideways toss. It skipped across the ground. "A victim's body."

I'd also heard that at least ten segments of the DNA strand had been recreated, possibly more. "How far along did the lab get?"

"The entire strand segments."

"Oh God, no."

"When the government got back the test results and realized how uncontrollable the flu was, they canceled the project."

"Why, then, the vaccine you just injected me with?"

"Let's just say the lab's project manager was a cautious person. When playing with dynamite, she wanted to make sure her staff was protected."

My mental file on the symptoms of the Spanish flu had already matched it with those of Damassine. An abbreviated incubation period, beginning with a cough. Head pain, drowsy numbness in the body followed by a high fever. Then, in the throes of the disease, the victim would develop epistaxis so severe that blood would pour from the nose and the mouth.

"Did the experiment include a test—"

"Of course not, Eve." Abruptly, Nick stood. "Look, the lead scientist on the Spanish flu project disappeared along with the notes and a test sample. At first we thought it might be a kidnapping, but when no ransom demand arrived, we had to assume he had been either bribed or killed."

"Who is the scientist?"

"Willem van Velsen."

I recognized the name and knew his reputation as a leading influenza geneticist. "Brilliant, wrote a book on the 1968 Hong Kong flu?"

"You forgot his God complex." Nick rubbed a hand over his face. "Our profile on him indicated he had an ego, but when Janssen put a halt to the recreation of the Spanish flu, Willem initially was furious. Then he seemed to accept the decision and became wrapped up in a new project studying people's immunity. Next thing we knew, he was missing. Then the alert came in on Damassine."

I stared at the ancient stone pillar. It had weathered all the tests of time, but could mankind? Was van Velsen the type of scientist who would recreate a Frankenstein bug and release it one time just to see if it would work?

Or had the Spanish flu fallen into someone else's hands—someone who would use it again and again?

"The genie's been let out of the bottle, Nick. God help us."

# Chapter 4

While Nick examined the cylinder, I called the Centre. The director himself came on the phone.

"Frederic, I may have something," I advised him. "Have the lab compare the Damassine samples to Spanish flu."

He inhaled sharply. "Don't tell me that some madman has released it?"

From his crouched position Nick shot me a warning look. I didn't need to be psychic to know what it meant: do not mention his involvement.

"I have strong reason to believe that Dr. Willem van Velsen stole a recreated strand from a lab."

"There's been nothing appearing on any agency reports. We should have been advised of it immediately."

I glared at Nick. "The lab may have been handling the matter privately to avoid panic." Since the theft should have been reported to Interpol and major disease agencies, that was all the slack I was going to cut him.

"We'll get on the lab tests and let you know. They've been working on your theory about the virus being genetically altered to impact women more than men."

My heart racing, I asked, "And?"

I must not have managed as neutral a tone as I wanted, for Nick looked at me. I turned away so that he couldn't read my face.

"They want to run more confirmatory tests, but the initial results were affirmative."

"Interesting. I may be moving away from the Damassine zone."

"You're my top flu hunter. If anyone can track down the source, it's you."

I smiled. "Thanks, Frederic. I'll keep you posted."

The moment I switched off, Nick asked, "What had you vibrating?"

"What?"

"Whenever you're excited, you radiate energy. Waves of it were positively rolling off you when Frederic told you something."

I dropped into a crouch beside him to examine the cylinder. "Just a hunch I had may be panning out."

"Your empathic abilities getting stronger?"

I kept my gaze fixed on the metal. The first time I had bent over in agony because I'd experienced a passerby's pain, Nick had freaked out. Not that I'd blamed him.

When your life's work is the world of secrecy and security and you've taken a bullet for the Pope, someone who might have access to your private thoughts could be a threat. If he knew I had once connected with him on a nonphysical plane…

The lines between paranormal abilities can be blurred,

and the way things have been going recently, I wasn't so sure where empathy stopped and another ability began. For example, should I point out to Nick that strong vibrations were coming from the standing stones?

Right.

Not willing to go down one of the many paths that had divided us, I pointed to the cylinder. "Is that a marking?"

"Someday we need to talk things out, Eve."

I tensed, dreading any of that spill-your-guts type of personal conversation, but Nick carefully rolled over the twisted, blackened container. "Can you make out what those lines are?"

I squinted at the design. "Two crescents. That jagged mark across them could represent a bolt of lightning." In my travels I came into contact with many cultures and I'd always marveled at the similarity in symbols. The two opposing crescents were fish.

"I think that's the astrological symbol for Pisces." I bent closer. "What's that in the center, a star? The metal's so twisted I can't tell how many points."

Nick withdrew a cell phone and flipped it open to reveal a miniature screen before hesitating. "Are we working together or not? I think we can help each other, but we're going to have to trust each other to share information."

I released a frosty breath. "Work together?"

"I know Frederic's just given you carte blanche to track down the courier and the source. If he told me once, he told me a thousand times you were the best flu hunter he's ever had."

I didn't recall any occasions where Nick and the Centre's director would have had time for social conversation. During our brief engagement, Nick's and my schedules hadn't been conducive to getting to know each other's colleagues. After all, I'd been based in

Stockholm while Nick had been working hard on his fledgling agency.

The time we had managed to be together had been spent in heated sex…in bed…or in the shower…in the kitchen…. Nick had never minded exercising his healthy appetite wherever the mood had struck him.

Not that I hadn't done the same. Aware that the flush I felt spreading across my face had nothing to do with the cold, I cleared my throat. "I didn't know you and Frederic were such speaking buddies."

Nick's smile was savage. "Only when it came to you."

Great, locker-room talk. "What did you two discuss about me?" I demanded in a frigid tone. I swore if it was about our sex life, I was going to bean Nick over the head with the canister.

"Let's just say Frederic's extremely possessive of you, whether professionally, personally or both." Nick shrugged. "However, I was not about to let him stand between us."

Was there a compliment wrapped up in that remark? I opened my mouth and then snapped it closed. Best not to go out on the fragile branch of our past relationship.

"Frederic interested in me? Don't be ridiculous. We're simply work colleagues."

"Really? I vividly recall a conversation where Frederic brought up the topic of my being Catholic and from a large family. He proceeded to point out that between your bugs and my run-ins with criminals it was no kind of environment suitable for raising children. He suggested that I might be happier with someone living a more normal life."

My God. Frederic had made a similar comment to me when I'd been leaving for a weekend visit with Nick. How was I going to handle Nick's desire for a large family? From then on I had obsessed about Nick wanting children to the point that all the joy in my being with him had been destroyed.

When you're out in the field during an outbreak, your coworkers become your family, confidences are exchanged. Perhaps too many. Clearly, the ever-astute Frederic had pushed a few relationship buttons. I was going to have a little heart-to-heart talk with him upon my return.

Meanwhile, Nick was right. Working together was logical. With his security connections, he would have very useful resources. The important thing was to stop any further release of the flu.

"I can handle working together if you can," I said to Nick. "But won't your client object?"

"No, since I already cleared it with Janssen."

"You what?"

"I knew you wouldn't rest until you tracked the source of the outbreak. Given your reputation and Janssen's need to retrieve the flu, it was a natural marriage of interests. I suspect Janssen's already clearing matters with Frederic."

I huffed a frosty breath, but he was right. I would do anything to hunt down the virus.

Holding up his phone to the cylinder, he explained, "I'll send the logo image back to my staff to research and come up with a name."

He made a motion with his free hand. "What about the glider you had? Can you ditch it? The courier would have either headed into Yverdon-les-Bains or Geneva."

"Or Bern or Lausanne. They all are travel hubs," I pointed out. "I'll call and let the owner know where the glider can be picked up." In order to get better reception, I walked into the center of the stone circle.

Everything around me blurred. Death was…

*Everywhere. Once the land of enlightenment, Languedoc now lay ravaged by war. Pope Innocent III's bitter crusade against the usurper religion Catharism was wiping out not only entire towns, but also prosperity for ages to come: torches set to people and the fields alike while barbaric rulers replaced the educated Counts of Toulouse.*

*Slowly but inevitably, the language of culture—Occitan—was being silenced. No more poetry, no more songs, no more texts.*

*The Age of the Troubadour was over.*

*The healer stood on one of her beloved foothills in Southern France. She despaired of ever seeing again the greening of the laurel. The sliver of moon overhead cast the barest of light over the dark landscape, but she only dared to venture out from the cave she called home at night while the warriors slept.*

*Because of her calling, she forsook living with her sisterhood for fear that her work would lead to discovery of their secret meeting place. She didn't see the others like her, not nearly enough. Sometimes the feeling of aloneness nearly crushed her heart. However, since the apprentice had come to her to learn the ways of healing, she no longer felt so isolated. Her joy in company overrode her concern that the apprentice did not have the inner strength to endure the demands of healing.*

*No matter. She mustn't linger here. She needed to replenish her precious supplies of herbs and the red earth of Languedoc. When the proper amount of cave-fed water was added to the dirt, the mud contained amazing healing properties.*

*So many wounded to tend, so many ill from famine*

*and illnesses. She couldn't save them all, but how could she say no to even one in need?*

*Spying the silhouette of a familiar plant ahead, she hurried forward. A muffled sound brought her to a halt, her heart beating with alarm. Had one of the crusaders ignored the superstition of being about at night and prowled, looking for Cathars in hiding or even worse, the Marians?*

*With all her senses on alert, she strained to hear even the slightest sound on the wind. There it was again, to her right. As she had spent her entire life in these hills, she knew the terrain. Carefully she climbed higher and then circled around. Crouching behind a boulder, the healer studied the shadows below.*

*Behind a bush something moved: a man's leg. She circled until she had an unobstructed view. The man lay curled on his side, huddled against the night's chill. Whenever he shifted, he moaned as if in pain.*

*The healer sat back on her heels. Another wounded knight, possibly titled by the quality of his clothes. However, he wore no colors to announce his allegiance. Clever man, she decided. No one could tell if he warred on the side of the Pope or the Cathars. When he moved again, she saw the glint of metal.*

*A very clever and determined man. The enemy would have to draw near enough to check him out, allowing him a chance to deal a mortal blow with his knife.*

*Then he called out in his delirium. Italian. Sacré dieu. He was a warrior for the Catholic Church, who not only sought to eliminate the Cathari but also those who followed the Goddess.*

*The healer wiped her sweaty palms on the folds of her skirt. She should leave him here to die. Why should she save one who sought to destroy her sisters?*

*He called out again. "Oh God, help me!"*

*She pressed her forehead against her knees. Pain was a language that transcended all races and religions. He could be too wounded even for her skills. He would be no longer any danger to anyone if he died, but she could make his passing easier. If he lived, surely he would be grateful to the one who saved him. Redemption began with an act of kindness, didn't it? Didn't she believe that by healing a person she could help to heal the land?*

*Her grotto wasn't far from here. He wouldn't be able to find the hidden passage to the temple and the mosaic the sisterhood guarded. She would make sure her apprentice understood the importance of secrecy.*

*She took a step forward...*

Crack!

The report of a gun being fired echoed in my ears. Bark on a tree not ten feet from me exploded.

Guns? Shouldn't there be swords and daggers? Where was I?

"Eve!" Nick tackled me as snow spat at my feet from another bullet slamming into the ground.

My breath whooshed out. Nick rolled me under his body even as he drew out his favorite Sig-Saur pistol. So much for being disoriented. I was a sitting duck inside a stone circle. I freed my hands in time to cover my ears, but the noise of his gun was like a string of firecrackers going off.

"Stay down!" He sprang to his feet and threaded his way around the stone columns, drawing a bead on the road. Like hell I would stay put, not with the adrenaline pumping and answers to be found. The shooter had to be connected to the canister. Scrambling up, I followed

Nick's weaving path. I'd reached his side at the circle's edge when an engine roar announced we were too late.

Nick swore but grabbed my hand. "Come on. If he didn't disable my car, we can follow him."

For someone with a bum leg, Nick could still move at quite a clip. We raced across the road to where he'd parked a black Land Rover. I opened the passenger door and flung myself inside. Nick inserted the key into the ignition and nodded with satisfaction as the motor roared to life. With a slide and a bounce, he backed the Rover onto the road and gunned the motor.

Hurriedly I fastened my seat belt and for good measure clung to the strap. I couldn't believe it. I was in an honest-to-God car chase. Somehow pursuing a monkey through an African jungle didn't quite compare.

"Did you see him? Was it van Velsen?"

"I didn't get a clear look, but definitely our shooter wasn't Willem. Too athletic. Van Velsen was a lab potato." The smile Nick flashed was downright wicked.

"That eliminates the possibility your scientist was acting alone on a Frankenstein motive."

"English, please," Nick muttered as he guided the car around a sharp curve.

"You know, a reaction to Janssen pulling the plug on his research. 'I'll show you. I created this monster bug so I shall set it free.'"

"So he's either sold the flu, in which case he's hiding out somewhere in luxury, or he's still involved in the development of the flu as a weapon," Nick mused aloud. "Either way, we don't know how many people we're up against."

"Then we better catch the shooter." Feeling more comfortable, I eased back in the seat. I was used to hashing out disease scenarios with my colleagues.

However, this was the first time Nick's and my jobs had crossed paths.

"What's he driving?" I squinted through the windshield, trying to spot another car.

"Dark, all-terrain vehicle. Probably a Rover like this one."

"I don't get it." We hit a rut in the road, and I abandoned the strap for the more solid door handle. "If the shooter and the courier are one and the same man, why return to the glider? He'd made a clean escape."

Nick accelerated down a straight section of road. "Could be van Velsen learned that he hadn't bothered to take the remains of the glider with him. Simply setting fire to the glider was sloppy, not Willem's style at all."

"Or the courier's arrogant," I added.

"That, too. There's another possibility though."

"What?"

"After dispensing his load over Damassine, he hung around to watch the aftereffects like an arsonist getting his jollies from a fire."

That gave me the chills. "That's horrible. A man who could bring such devastating misery to an unsuspecting village and still watch the effects like a lab experiment is a depraved murderer..." I thought of the little girl with so much promise who'd died so young. How far would such a man without conscience go with his instrument of death?

Nick continued, "Or he's simply a hired mercenary. With all the camera crews, he could have videoed everything for van Velsen without being noticed."

"I don't buy the mercenary idea."

At Nick's arching eyebrow, I hastened to explain. "Look, I'm not some wide-eyed innocent. I know there are animals out there who will do unthinkable things to a person all for the sake of money, but the sum of this man's actions suggest a deeper commitment."

"Like an assistant?"

"Yes."

"We interviewed several associates, who all claimed not to know where Willem was, but my team can take another look and check if anyone in his circle has been to Switzerland recently. Someone had to pick Damassine as the target. That means at least one scouting trip."

The road widened and the vegetation thinned out as we approached the suburb of Clendy, according to the sign we flew by. Had the courier turned off? Had we lost him?

Nick flexed his fingers around the wheel. "We're gaining on him. Once we get around this curve, you should be able to see his brake lights."

My pulse quickened. Sure enough, I saw the twinkle of red but I also saw the outline of buildings. Ruthlessly I pushed past my worry that we might lose the courier in traffic. Think of him as a virus and keep developing a profile to track him.

"The courier could be a fanatic."

"Great. Zealots. Unpredictable as hell."

"But loyal to whatever cause he believes in."

Nick shot me a dark glance. "What groups are you thinking of? What's the Centre's information on the ones with bioweapons?" I could see the wheels turning in his head as he mentally ran through terrorist organizations.

I bit my lip. Here we go. "I don't think the motive's political, at least not in the contemporary sense we've all become accustomed to since 9/11."

"Want to explain that cryptic statement?" Nick turned on to the main street of Yverdon-les-Bains. "Terrorism can be simply to instill fear."

"But ultimately the goal of fear is politically motivated," I argued.

"All right. What do you think this is about?"

I released a breath. "Some sick vendetta against women."

Ahead a light turned red, causing Nick to curse and hit the brakes. We had lost the courier. By the time the light changed, the man could be anywhere.

Nick turned slightly, resting his arm on the top of the seats. "Spit it out, Eve."

"First, an international women's sporting event was going on at Damassine."

"The athletes were the target?"

I shook my head. "If that was the case, then he would have sprayed them while they were in competition. He chose to contaminate the entire village."

"Then how do you jump to the conclusion women were the target? Last time I was at Damassine, there were men living there."

"Yes, but the population ran about fifty-five percent women to forty-five percent men." I licked my dry lips. "The death rate was eighty percent women to twenty percent men."

Nick whistled.

I balled my hands in my lap. "I don't know the 'why' yet, Nick. But so far the data points to a strain of Spanish flu specifically engineered to affect women. If van Velsen is behind the genetic alteration, I want him to pay."

"He will, Eve. We'll get him." For a moment I absorbed only the comfort of his quiet assurance before I realized he also believed me.

Stunned by his acceptance, I stared at my clenched fists. "Thank you, Nick."

He reached over and lightly placed his hand over

mine. Flesh to flesh. A vibrant pink glow formed around our hands, and warmth unfurled inside me. "We're in this together." At that moment the light changed and after withdrawing his hand, Nick drove through the intersection.

"We'll start with the airfield. It'll have both glider and car rental outfits."

A ripple of awareness passed through me as we drove by the Château d'Yverdon. Built by Peter II of Savoy in the thirteenth century, the massive castle was the town's focal point. I'd seen it a number of times but never taken the time to tour it.

The thirteenth century.

During my spell within the stone circle—and I didn't know what else to call that total sense of disembodiment—hadn't I "heard" the word *Cathars* in my head? Once during my teenage years, Maman had taken both Yvette and me on her personal "roots" tour of southern France, where she had grown up. While Yvette had been enthralled with the estates, I'd been haunted by Montsegur, where two hundred Cathar martyrs—men, women, children alike—had been burned at the stake.

Yvette had been left with dreams of living in a château while I'd been plagued with nightmares of people dying.

I studied my reflection in the side window. I was tired, walking the fine line of my grief over Yvette's death and doing my job. Had flying over the medieval structures of this town triggered a youthful bad dream?

*No,* the voice whispered.

Well, tough. This was my explanation, and for my peace of mind, I was sticking to it.

"Eve, are you coming?"

I blinked and realized Nick stood on the passenger side holding the door open. I needed a shot of coffee. Soon.

"Yes." I got out. Nick had parked in front of a shed advertising rental cars. We walked inside, and a young man in a colorful ski sweater rose from behind a counter.

"Can I help you?"

Nick sent me a warning glance. Oh, right, he was going to handle the interview. Do that macho security questioning where he angled to get as much possible information without disclosing one damn thing.

"Good afternoon," Nick said. "We were looking for an SUV that may have been rented within the past few days."

The man's brows drew together. "We rent many utility vehicles this time of the year. Is there a problem?" His gaze sharpened as he studied Nick. It wasn't hard to guess what he was thinking. Tall, fit man dressed in all black with observant eyes.

"Are you with the police?"

Bingo on his conclusion.

"No." Nick moved to drape his arm around me. Oh, no. He was going for the old couple routine. That wasn't going to work. "We're—"

"I'm with the European Centre for Disease Prevention and Control." I brushed past Nick and slapped my identification badge on the counter. "I'm sure you've heard about Damassine."

The clerk's face whitened. "Yes, it's all anyone's been talking about."

People might not fear law enforcement but they sure did microbes. However, I had to be careful. If he thought a disease was being transmitted, he could cause panic here, and our resources were already taxed to the limit with containing Damassine.

"We're trying to find a man who might have important information."

"Is he infected?" The clerk made a nervous movement toward his phone. He was ready to call his doctor.

"No," I hastened to reassure him. "This man we're seeking was not in town at the time of the outbreak."

The courier had been over it, yes, but the clerk didn't need to know that. I also assumed the courier had been vaccinated so that he wasn't a carrier.

The clerk relaxed slightly. "We've had a number of rentals this week."

Nick decided to regain control of the questioning. "It would have been a single man, no family. Returned within the past hour, if at all."

The clerk brightened. "Oh, you must mean Mr. Petter."

I blinked. "Who?"

"Mr. Nicholas Petter. He returned a black Land Rover only thirty minutes ago."

Okay, not only were we dealing with a madman spreading a lethal flu, but also one with a warped sense of humor. I kept a neutral expression as I looked at the stunned Nick. "I think we've established he's arrogant. Clearly, he's thumbing his nose at you."

"True, but it also means he knew I was in Damassine. Either there's a leak at Janssen, or van Velsen's new group of friends have good intel."

From the way Nick's eyes darkened, I knew his staff would shortly have a new assignment of rechecking the Janssen employees for a link to van Velsen.

I turned back to the clerk. "Do you know where he was headed?"

"No. He took the shuttle to the terminal. Many private planes fly in and out. I believe he was flying out immediately."

My gaze fell on the phone on the counter. "Did he use your phone?"

"He had a cell."

My pulse kicked up a notch. "Did he call anyone else?"

"Yes, but he moved away from me as he spoke. I didn't hear him greet the person."

The brief spurt of excitement died.

"However," said the clerk with a smile. "I did hear one name. He said something about the Piazza Cavour."

I wiped my palms against my legs. "Nick, there's a piazza with that name on the Italian side of Lake Como."

Nick already had his phone out. "On it. I'll check our man's flight plan and arrange for transport. It shouldn't be hard to confirm his plane and destination."

Italy, I thought. Here we come.

# *Chapter 5*

One thing was definite. The pockets of Nick's pharmaceutical client ran deep.

Within short order, we boarded a private jet for the brief flight to Italy. Somehow Nick had managed to have my bags delivered from Damassine along with his own. He'd also confirmed that only one other private plane, bound for the same destination, had left within our half-hour window.

In my line of work, you learn to catnap. You never knew when the next chance to close your eyes would come. Besides, I wasn't quite up to making polite conversation with Nick, who sat in the leather chair across from me. The moment I buckled my lap belt I shut my eyes.

However, my mind revved like the jet's engines as the plane roared down the abbreviated runway. Were we doing the right thing staying on the trail of the courier? We had only a vague physical description from the car rental clerk that he resembled Nick in height and build. Unless Nick's investigators came up with a possible van Velsen associate, we stood a better chance of winning the Powerball Lottery than finding the man in Como.

Would we be better off focusing all our energies on van Velsen? But he could be a dead end as far as recovering the flu. If his involvement extended only to selling the goods, for all I knew he could be enjoying the spoils of the sale, sipping a drink on some tropical island. However, if the scientist remained behind the scenes on the flu development, then he could be the person the courier had arranged to meet at the Piazza Cavour.

Wild-goose chase? Maybe, but until we had more solid intel, as Nick called it, this was the best lead we had.

But what if I caught up with either man? What then? Could I turn him in for the slow and uncertain workings of international justice? Some cultures I had come across still practiced the eye-for-an-eye form of justice and revenge. It wouldn't be hard for me to get my hands on a deadly virus strain and give whoever was behind this outbreak his own agonizing death.

I opened my eyes. Instead of my reflection in the plane's window, I saw my sister's face ravished by illness. Damassine hadn't been nature's slap at humanity; it had been murder on a massive scale. Death hadn't been quick and merciful; it had been terrifying and agonizing. Didn't van Velsen and the courier deserve the same?

*No, it's not the way.*

I sighed. My inner voice knew me too well. When you stripped my personality down to its core, I was a healer. Every time I found the cause of an outbreak, I felt soul-deep contentment. I saved lives.

Could I ever take a life? My hand clenched on the armrest.

"Eve."

I started and looked over at Nick. He shook his head. "Shut it down. We both need to rest. After we get him, there's going to be too much time to reflect. Trust me."

"After" we get him. Nick's certainty was absolute. A knot of tension in me unraveled. "Okay. Thanks."

"You're welcome." He relaxed against his seat and closed his eyes. While there remained an alert quality to him, I could tell by how his facial muscles eased that he was already in a light state of sleep.

Awareness jolted my nerve endings. My fingertips tingled as I remembered the raspy texture of his jawline. I knew that if I reached out, those electric blue eyes would flash open and… No. Don't go there. Best to let a sleeping Nick lie and catch some shut-eye myself.

I closed my eyes and didn't wake up from a surprisingly dreamless sleep until the pilot announced we would be landing shortly. We sat down in another postage-stamp-size field that contained several hangars housing other small planes and jets. As we exited, a man appeared at the base of the stairs and handed Nick a backpack and set of keys. With Nick taking the lead, we crossed to where yet another black Land Rover was parked.

Nick hefted our bags into the back while I climbed into my seat, and then we were off. Before long we were weaving along the narrow streets of Como. We passed the Duomo, a grand cathedral that was a fine mix of Gothic and Renaissance styles with carvings on its facade and topped with a huge dome. Nick found a parking spot and pulled into it.

We walked to the stone-paved Piazza Cavour. Shops, hotels and bistros lined the crescent-shaped plaza, which ran to the sparkling blue waters of Lake Como. I caught my breath.

Perched at the foot of low-lying mountains, majestic villas and gardens lined the lake as far as the eye could see. Although it was November, trees close to the water's edge burst with vibrant yellow color while green pines rose high along the mountain slopes until they petered out, revealing brown rock.

Moored everywhere were sailing boats. Jaunty blue-and-white poles marked piers. I smiled at the sight of two men who stood rowing a strange-looking boat. That must be one of the Lucia boats, named after the heroine in one of the writer Manzoni's books. This area of Italy was steeped in the arts. One famous opera singer used to stand on the balcony of her palace and sing across the lake to her lover who lived on the other side.

"Wow." I slid my hands into the pockets of my pants. "Any of your clients live here so we can drop in and say hi?"

Nick flashed me a grin. "Actually, yes. We're using his airfield, but he's not home. His house here is only his summer place."

"Your agency must be really moving up in the world, Nick. Clients with private jets, Italian villas. I remember when you had trouble collecting for work you did."

"Still do," Nick dryly commented. "I had a well-known celebrity stiff me after we provided security for his attendance at a film festival in Venice. That's why I prefer international corporations for clients. They're a little more regular in paying their bills and don't squabble over the cost of security."

"I certainly like Janssen's style of having a private jet at our disposal."

I scanned the piazza. It was a mild winter day, and people were out in full force, sitting at the many tables. Normal animated people, talking, eating and drinking.

What description the car rental clerk had given had been nondescript. Tall, lean, dressed in black, possibly shaved head, but the clerk had been uncertain even about that latter detail as the courier had worn a knit cap.

I watched a young couple stroll by, hand in hand. It was a perfect day to be in love. Great. Since when did I wear romance-colored glasses?

*Since the day in Rome when you first met Nick and everything seemed right just because he held your hand by the Trevi Fountain,* I answered myself.

Clearing my throat, I opted for a light tone. "Any idea of how to begin? I doubt if we're going to spot a man in black acting suspiciously."

I slapped my forehead. "Oh, silly me. You're right next to me."

"Ha, ha." Nick gripped my elbow. "I see you haven't lost your warped sense of humor."

"It's hereditary. You haven't lived until you've been held as a captive audience by my father on a boat. It's either develop an appreciation for the good, the bad and the ugly in humor or die from exasperation."

Poor Yvette. She had hated those leisurely outings. She had only perked up when Dad had let her take the helm. He had insisted that both his daughters learn how to handle a boat. Maman loved all the trappings of culture from the arts to fashion, while Dad preferred the outdoors after being cooped up in operating rooms for years. Their daughters had been a split decision in interests as well, with Yvette favoring Maman while I'd taken after Dad.

"You still do a lot of boating?" Nick flashed me a quick glance before he resumed scanning the plaza.

"Not much. Only when I go home for visits." Watching the skiffs and boats skimming across Lake

Como, I experienced a pang of regret. It'd been over a year since I had been home and now I would be seeing my parents at Yvette's funeral.

"There's the Weaver statue," Nick pointed. "Assuming the courier's meeting van Velsen, I'm going to look around for him."

"Makes sense." I knew the scientist from his interview photographs so I began studying faces to see if I could spot him. At a table set in front of a café, I saw the last person I'd expected to see.

"I'll be damned."

"What is it?"

"That's Scarlet over there." What the hell was she doing here? Como was off the beaten path from Milan. First London and now Como? Scarlet had said her project du jour was antiquities. There couldn't possibly be a link to the outbreak, could there?

Only one way to find out.

"Who's Scarlet?" Nick asked.

I'd forgotten Nick had never met her. My friendship with Scarlet had intensified after I had broken off our engagement.

"A photographer friend of mine."

"Photographer?" Nick sounded alarmed.

I shot him an amused look as I started across the piazza. "Not to worry. She's not newspaper or television. She does color pieces for magazines. She also maintains a Web site with a blog about astrological phenomenon and her search for her biological parents, as she was adopted. However..."

Hmm. As a matter of habit, I check Scarlet's blog to keep track of her locations, since she moves about so much in search of stories. But when I checked it last night in Damassine, she hadn't posted anything for over a week.

"What's wrong?"

I shrugged off the strange sense of misgiving. "The last time I looked she hadn't posted any recent entries. Must be her new love interest." Not that I'd ever known anyone or anything to interrupt Scarlet's search for her parents. Whatever assignment she was on, she used every opportunity and resource available to research their identities.

"I'm going to continue looking for our mysterious courier."

Right. Nick just didn't want any unnecessary complications, such as someone being able to identify him.

"I'll catch you in a few." We separated and I made my way through a group of children chasing a flock of pigeons to the tables.

"Hey, Scarlet! What a surprise! Of all the piazzas in the world, you stepped into mine." Okay, so epidemiologists' humor doesn't extend beyond microbes.

"Eve?" Scarlet looked up in shock.

The two men at the table stopped talking and stared, their eyes hidden by dark, stylish sunglasses.

The other woman sitting with them lowered her glass of wine, her lips forming a tight line of distaste as she scrutinized me from head to toe.

Granted, I wasn't part of the chi-chi set that these lovely people before me exemplified. They wore their obviously expensive casual clothes with the type of elegance that both my mother and sister had given up trying to teach me years ago.

When it came to being a clotheshorse, you either had it or you didn't. I didn't. Traipsing about an African village in search of the Ebola virus didn't lend itself to the Ferragamo loafers and Givenchy outfit the woman was wearing.

Go figure why I was taking an instant dislike to her without one word being spoken. I eyed the vacant chair and wondered if I should plop myself down and stretch out my feet, encased in my dainty, stained field boots.

"Everyone." Scarlet spoke in a strained voice, with a pleading look in her eyes. Okay, so I wouldn't embarrass my friend. "This is my friend, Dr. Eve St. Giles. She's with the European Centre for Disease Prevention and Control.

"Eve, this is Joshua and Pauline Adriano. And the man to my left is Caleb Adriano." Her voice warmed ever so slightly on the last introduction.

Ah, the love interest. Although his features were not as refined as Joshua's, he had those rough-hewn handsome looks that would appeal to women. With a gallant air he rose and extended his hand.

"Hello, Eve," he said with a sexy Italian accent. "I've heard so much about you and your work from Scarlet. Would you please join us?"

I shot a quick glance around the piazzà, but Nick the Invisible was nowhere to be seen. Probably skulking in the shadows, scoping out the scene. Well, I could do some investigating, too. Why was Scarlet's group sitting so casually on the same piazza where the courier had set up a meeting?

"I would love to." Unfortunately, the chair was next to Pauline's. For Scarlet's sake, I gave the woman my best company smile. Once I made sure that this was simply a "get to know the lover's family" scene, I would say a few pleasantries and then cut out.

Pauline shifted and sun flashed off the purple crystal pendant in her necklace. A shiver of recognition raced through me, followed by an urge to take the necklace.

*Okay, get a grip,* I warned myself. *You just met this poor woman. Don't wig out in front of an audience.*

Then it struck me. If Pauline was a Marian, as my internal barometer was indicating, was she the real reason Scarlet was here? Was part of my friend's attraction to Caleb because he had a Marian sister-in-law? In her search for a family, Scarlet would view a Marian connection as significant.

We needed to have a real heart-to-heart, soon.

I took a deep breath. "Pauline, that's a stunning necklace."

She flinched slightly and I felt her withdrawing even further behind her cool demeanor. Did she sense the link between us and was rejecting it?

However, with a graceful gesture she raised her hand and covered the stone. "Thank you, it's a family heirloom."

Again, Pauline gave no outward indication of any interest in me beyond civilized small talk. Maybe I was wrong about her being a Marian.

"How nice for you." I glanced at Scarlet to gauge her reaction. Sunglasses hid her eyes, but I could see the fine lines of tension in her face. Apparently, the family outing hadn't been going well.

In a possessive yet protective gesture, Caleb draped an arm around the back of Scarlet's chair, as if to reassure her. "I understand you investigate diseases, Eve, for the Centre."

I smiled at him. "That's right."

He gave Scarlet an indulgent look. "Scarlet tells me that you're called the Flu Hunter."

"A label created by the press, I'm afraid." I shot Scarlet a dark look. The first time she had featured me in her photographs, she had given me that title, which the Centre's director had all too willingly picked up.

Joshua asked, "Are you here in the lake region on official business?" Although he spoke with a casual air as if simply making conversation, he leaned toward me.

"In a manner of speaking. How about you all? Holiday or business?"

For some reason, my question seemed to stump the Adrianos. While they looked at each other, Scarlet made a slight gesture with her hand, curling her fingers into the palm and the thumb up: "Call me." I nodded.

Joshua, settling back in his chair, was the first to respond. "We have a silk farm outside Como, so it is pleasant to combine business with enjoying its beauty, yes?"

However, Joshua's gaze drifted toward Scarlet rather than Pauline. The state of his marriage was none of my business, and certainly Scarlet was a big girl who could handle a man's unwanted attention. I would have condemned Joshua for his wandering eye but for the wistful expression I saw on his face.

"The area is certainly gorgeous," I said with an appreciative smile.

Caleb cocked his head. "You are not traveling alone, are you? While our country is meant to be savored, it is not particularly safe at the moment for a lovely woman such as you."

Oh, he was good with the compliments. No wonder Scarlet was attracted. "Thanks, but I know how to handle myself," I assured him.

"Eve, this is serious," Scarlet urged. "Over the past few months a number of women have disappeared in Milan and the immediate area. The authorities believe there's a serial killer on the prowl and are working on a profile."

"Now, *bella,*" Caleb murmured. "We do not want to

alarm your friend so much that she leaves before she can enjoy my country's hospitality."

"I'll be careful, promise." Suddenly, alarm gripped me.

Something black, rotten and oily slithered around me. I'd experienced the same sensation only once before, in a small African village when I had come face-to-face with a chieftain who had been terrorizing the people.

*Evil.*

My heart hammering, I waved off the waiter, pouring only a glass of water from the bottle in the middle of the table. As I sipped, I studied the Adrianos. Was it from one of them that I was picking up the bad vibes? Was Scarlet in danger?

I knew she also possessed a certain degree of sensitivity, yet she didn't seem to be reacting the way I was. She was tense, yes, but not alarmed. Did I dare open myself to find the source? So far my empathic abilities and that more undefined, uncontrollable Marian sense had been in the driver's seat with me, fighting to steer their capricious appearances. If I unleashed my abilities, could I regain control? Or would I have another time-warp experience like the one in the stone circle in Damassine?

I lowered my glass. No, too risky.

I don't know which happened first…the sudden shadow falling across my shoulder or the Adriano brothers becoming alert, much like dogs sensing a new competitor in their pack. Either way I knew Nick had decided to become part of the scene.

"Everyone, this is my assistant Nick."

While Scarlet's eyebrows about arched off her face, Pauline lost her bored expression. She smiled, extending her hand. "Such a general introduction. I'm Pauline."

"A pleasure." Nick did his European thing, taking her hand and giving the back of it a light kiss. Now, Maman would have approved of his manners; on the other hand, Dad would have snarled at any man kissing his wife's knuckles. In this instance I favored the latter approach.

On the other hand, Joshua merely looked bored. Scarlet and Caleb acted more like a married couple than the actual wedded pair.

As Nick straightened I spotted a man in black pants and jacket giving the table a wide berth as he hurried toward the pier. With sun glinting off his shaved head, he was about Nick's build and height with a scar running the length of his left jawline. As if he sensed someone was watching him, he glanced over his shoulder.

A shiver of recognition raced through me as his face twisted with a mixture of surprise and…malice. Scorching hot waves of hatred rolled over me.

The courier. He broke into a sprint.

"Nick. We've got to go. Now." I was on my feet. "Nice meeting you all." I ignored the startled expressions on the Adrianos' faces and gave my friend a pointed look.

"Scarlet, I'll be in touch."

Then I ran toward the water's edge of the piazza. Nick was right by my side, maintaining an easy conversational pace. "Any reason why we're drawing attention like this?"

I stepped onto the pier and checked the first bobbing boat. No man in black.

"Since you were so busy slobbering over Pauline's hand, I rather thought I would strike up a conversation with your long-lost twin."

Nick grabbed my elbow. "You saw him?"

I jerked loose and ran to the next docked boat. "He ran here after spotting me."

Once more Nick gripped my arm, this time pulling me behind him. "I go first. He's got a gun, *capisce?*"

But it wasn't a crack of a bullet shot that got our attention this time; it was the roar of an engine. Five slots away a white boat with blue markings pulled away from the dock in a gush of spray. On its side were the words *Seta Bianco...White Silk.*

Men on nearby boats cursed as the waves jarred them, sending a few dangerously close to the pier's pilings. One old sailor, his hands gnarled with age, spat into the water and continued to coil a line.

Nick ran to him, with me close on his heels, and spoke in Italian. He pulled out a wad of euros and waved it. The old man grinned and grabbed the money. I took that as an assent and clambered aboard, heading straight to the wheel while Nick and the old man went from piling to piling to untie the boat. As I started the engine, Nick jumped on. The old man tossed us the last line and gave us a jaunty wave as I backed the boat out.

Nick stood beside me as I slowly guided the craft out of the slip and swung toward the lake. As soon as we cleared the no-wake zone, I revved the motor.

"Do you want me to take over the wheel?" Nick asked as he kept his gaze on the stolen boat.

I angled the boat across the wake from a hydrofoil. "I'd rather have you running shotgun detail. You're the better shot, *capisce?*"

That was an understatement. Nick had won sharpshooter medals, while I was lucky to hit the broad side of a barn despite Nick's best efforts to teach me.

Smiling, he nodded and maintained his lookout, which was difficult. Given the beautiful day, boats abounded on the lake. I could hear guides' voices over microphones giving tourists the lowdown on the stately villas. But my focus was only on one boat threading its way through the traffic.

We had the courier in our sights. Would we finally get some answers? Why Damassine? Why women? Would his capture lead us to van Velsen or someone else? How far did the ripples of this Spanish flu plot reach?

I gripped the wheel tighter and widened my stance as the boat bounced across wakes. I wanted to let the boat go full-out but knew we couldn't pose a danger to others.

We were about halfway across the lake when our target must have spotted us, for he throttled up the *White Silk,* sending spumes flying high into the air as he made a sharp turn. My heart sailed up into my throat as he narrowly missed a boat packed with tourists. The guide's voice rang across the water as he cursed the courier.

I powered up as well but steered a wide berth around other boats, costing us precious distance. The courier veered toward the rocky shoreline.

"Is he mad?" I yelled to Nick above the engine noise.

Nick only shook his head as he reached inside his parka and brought out a gun. He checked the clip before sticking it in my jacket pocket and then bringing out his Sig-Saur.

Of course the courier was a psycho. Possibly mad with a cause but mad nevertheless. Advantage to him, as he didn't care what risks he took while I still valued my life.

Then disaster struck as the courier approached the ragged shoreline. Two men rowing a Lucia shot out from behind a spit of land that stuck out like a long finger into the water. Intent on maintaining their strong, rapid pace, the rowers didn't see the other craft speeding far too close to land. The courier swerved but caught the edge of the boat. A horrible *crack* filled the air and the Lucia tipped up before flipping over.

Immediately I slowed, preparing to go to the men's rescue, but the two rowers bobbed to the surface. The sound of another motor came from our starboard, and a skiff raced toward the men. Relieved, I sped up again but in the few chaotic minutes, the blue-and-white boat had disappeared from sight.

"He went around that bend ahead, by that white villa." Nick indicated. "He hasn't cut across open water so he must be looking to dock at one of these house piers."

I steered closer to the shoreline and coasted along. Here the three- to four-story villas clung with determination to narrow bands of land separated from the water by stone walls. Tiers of stylish gardens covered the slopes. All the mansions either had their own pier or shared one, with various boats and skiffs tied up. On this lake water remained the main form of transportation.

"Eve, stay low." Nick ordered as he scanned the hillside. He was right. We were easy targets. Any one of those topiary gardens or stone walls provided ample ambush cover. I scrunched down as much as possible while continuing to steer the boat.

Ahead a skiff bobbed and shifted. Blue and white flashed. "Nick. There."

I pointed and then glided to a stop alongside the small wood dock. Only a single line secured the boat we'd been pursuing, an indication the driver had been in a hurry. Nick leaped onto the pier and then went into a crouch position as he checked for any movement. Satisfied that no one lurked above, he rose and made a gesture to secure the boat. As he stood on guard duty, I tied up the boat and joined him on the dock.

After a short rise the stone stairway veed at the top. On the left was a butter-yellow villa with green shutters while on the right was a shell-pink mansion with brown shutters. Both appeared to be deserted. Many of these houses functioned as holiday retreats for the rich and famous and had only nominal housekeeping staff to oversee them while the owners were away.

Nick motioned to go right first. I kept on his heels as the path wove back and forth until we reached a topiary garden filled with shaped shrubs and clipped trees. Gesturing, Nick sped up so fast that I lost sight of him around a line of shrubs. Had he gone left or right? I couldn't call out so I went right.

Suddenly, the path ended back at the stone stairway. From this vantage point, I could see across the grounds of the yellow mansion. The owner favored beds of vibrant flowers as opposed to trees and shrubs. Motion along the house's loggia caught my attention. Had someone just gone in through the window?

I looked around for Nick but saw no sign of him. Should I wait here or check out the other house? Had that been Nick going in after the courier? What if the man had set a trap? From what I could tell from our approach from the water, these two houses were the only accessible ones on this particular section of hillside.

Only one way to find out. I'd been in dangerous situations before, tracking down pathogens. Nothing different here.

Other than a man who'd already taken a shot at me.

Taking a deep breath to steady my nerves, I hurried across the open expanse. Reaching the side of the house, I immediately plastered myself against it. The windows were shut with curtains drawn. Everything was still.

I crept farther along until I reached the loggia opening onto yet another garden. Something thumped against my hip as I halted. Of course. Nick had given me a gun. Bringing it out, I took off the safety. I didn't like guns, in fact I hated them, but facing a madman called for exigency measures.

I needed him alive to get information, but…

*You need to stop him more,* my inner voice urged. *He's going to release the flu again.*

There you have it. From my woo-woo factor's lips straight to my ears.

Stepping onto the loggia's marble floor, I studied the windows and the French doors to the house. A movement caught my attention and I dropped to a crouch. There. The edge of a sheer white curtain fluttered in the slight breeze.

I ran in a bent-over position to the last low-lying window on the corner, which was open about an inch. Carefully I looked through the glass. No movement inside. I took another deep breath and released it slowly. One good thing about having my identification. Should I come upon very startled homeowners, I could explain my presence. Sort of.

I curled my fingers around the rim and raised the window higher, praying all the while that it wouldn't make a sound. When I had enough room, I crawled inside. Immediately I twisted from side to side but the room appeared empty.

It was a corner room. Mama would have called it the drawing room. Heavy red-and-gold-brocade curtains framed the window sheers and an ornate marble fireplace dominated the other outer wall. Wonderfully aged tapestries covered the other walls while massive pieces of furniture circled a faded Persian rug. The rest of the floor was warm, speckled terrazzo.

Straining to hear any sound, I stepped farther into the room. A glint of metal by the door caught my eye. My already racing pulse kicked up another notch. Was that a cylinder?

I was rushing forward when I became aware of

motion from the side. I whirled but caught a glancing blow to my head. Stars exploded and I fell forward, losing my grip on the gun. It skittered across the floor.

Legs clad in black pants stood before me. Scooting forward on my stomach, I reached out and gripped my attacker's ankle as I lowered my internal guard.

Contact.

Hatred seared through my body, overwhelming me with its painful intensity. Gasping, I released my grip and instinctively curled up into a protective fetal position.

Another set of legs appeared and through a haze of emotional and physical pain I heard the grunts of people fighting. The black-clad legs disappeared as my vision blurred and darkness claimed me.

# Chapter 6

"Can you hear me?"

A cultured man's voice drew me up from swirling blackness. Had I had another spell?

I opened my eyes and immediately shut them. Even the dim light sent a shaft of pain through my throbbing head. Man, it hurt like a bitch!

Not a spell. This was a "take two aspirin and observe for signs of concussion" situation. That I could handle.

I took a deep breath, exhaled and opened my eyes again. Hovering over me was an old man, tall, slim with piercing gray eyes. At the moment his hair and clothing was askew, but I suspected he normally carried off being dapper with ease. He also had that confident, arrogant air of the rich.

The villa's owner. Uh-oh.

Gingerly, I pushed up to a sitting position. I ran my

fingers through a snarl of curls and found a lump on the side of my head. "Ouch!"

"Let me help you up." The man extended his hand and I took the assistance all too willingly.

My knees buckled slightly but I braced them. As I gathered myself, I scanned the room but the man was the only other occupant. Where was Nick? Was he all right?

"Thank you. You must be the owner. I'm—"

"I know who you are. Dr. Eve St. Giles. Epidemiologist for the European Centre for Disease Prevention and Control."

I stumbled back a half step and my hand went toward my pocket where I kept my identification. Had he searched me while I was unconscious? A shiver went through me. I looked around for the gun but didn't see it. Where was it?

"When I saw you being interviewed on television in Damassine, I knew I had to find you." Although his English was perfect, the cadence of his speech indicated that he was Italian.

I wet my dry lips. "But you just saved me, didn't you? If you don't live here, how…?"

He lifted a shoulder in a purely European gesture. "I've been following you."

"How?" It wasn't as if Nick and I had been on a guided tour with a published itinerary.

"I have my—" the man paused as if searching for the right words "—sources. I also have my resources. I was watching you in the piazza when I saw you run toward the lake. Like your friend, a few euros allowed me the use of a boat. I arrived in the nick of time, as you Americans say."

He reached into the pocket of his very fine Italian-wool jacket and pulled out my gun. "You are all in danger."

"No joke." I jerked my chin at the gun. "I don't get it. You help me only to point that thing at me. I have no valuables." True enough. I only stashed my emergency cash and a credit card in a money belt I wore under my clothes.

His smile transformed him into being rakishly handsome. I couldn't put my finger on it, but there was something familiar about his features. With a smooth movement he reversed his hold on the gun and extended it, butt toward me.

"Be my guest. Ladies should always have the advantage over men."

If he'd been thirty years younger, his comment would have curled my toes. The man probably had cut a swath through countless women. However, I didn't miss the ease with which he handled the gun. I took it all too eagerly, its weight in my hand a strange comfort to one who lived by her wit.

"Who are you?"

With a negligent air the stranger leaned against the doorjamb. "Just call me Myrddin."

The man was as much Welsh as I was, but I would go along with him for now. "Interesting name for an Italian."

Amusement flickered across his face. "Let's just say my family's into legends."

"All right. Let's try this question. Why have you been looking for me?"

"Ah. The ever straight-to-the-point scientist. Tell me, Dr. St. Giles, do you use your directness to act as a shield for your being an empath, a Marian or both?"

*Marian.* Like a body blow the word slammed into me. I stumbled back a half step. "I don't know what you're talking about."

"Don't you, Eve? Hasn't your friend Scarlet told you

about the other women whose destinies are linked to yours?"

He knew Scarlet?

Myrddin straightened and advanced toward me, his eyes blazing with fervor or...madness? "Don't you know that you're a descendant of a once-powerful group of priestesses? Do you not feel it?"

Okay, not to panic. This guy's woo-woo factor was even worse than mine. I moved so that a settee stood between us. "Scarlet talks about a lot of things. The mercury retrograde, pomegranate juice, the coming Age of Aquarius…"

He made an impatient gesture. "I don't have time to explain everything. I saw your companion in the lower gardens so he will be at the house soon."

Relief flooded inside me. Nick was safe.

Gripping the top of the settee, Myrddin leaned toward me. "You must understand what is at stake. The countdown has begun. They are going to destroy all the descendants. *All,* I tell you."

"Who is going to destroy what descendants?" If there was a plot to kill someone, Nick could contact his Interpol buddies.

"An Italian family with more power than you can imagine. They are going to finish off the last of the Marians and leave nobody else who can stop them."

I fought off the headache in order to follow this increasingly bizarre conversation. The Marians, as I understood from Scarlet, had been some sort of religious order.

"What is this family after? Why is a group of women a threat to them?"

Wait a minute. Hadn't I sensed that the little girl in Damassine had been a Marian? The possible connection to the outbreak victims snicked into place. Maybe this guy wasn't so loony.

"Not just a group of women," Myrddin explained. "Very special women who can claim birthright to the priestesshood of the Black Madonna."

The Black Madonna? Hadn't Scarlet recently attended an exhibition of Black Madonnas in Paris? Were those the antiquities she was researching?

"Eve, you must be careful." Myrddin spread his hands in a beseeching gesture. "You are a target simply by being a Marian, but you represent an even greater danger to the family."

The painful throb of my growing headache intensified. "The outbreak. This family is behind the Spanish flu."

"Yes, and they will have heard about your reputation as I did." Myrddin lifted his head as if he heard a sound. "I must go."

"No!" I circled around the settee. "Tell me the family's name!"

For an older man, he moved swiftly toward the door. "Do not worry. I'm going to help you whenever it's safe for me to do so. What you're seeking from Damassine can be found at Baleno Nazionale in Milan."

"Eve!" Nick's voice came from behind me.

I glanced over my shoulder and saw him climbing through the open window. When I looked back, Myrddin was gone. I swore and ran out into the hallway. At the other end the front door was ajar. Frustrated, I kicked at the fringe on the area rug.

"Hey!" Nick rushed into the hall. "Why didn't you stay with me? Are you trying to get killed?"

I sighed and gingerly touched the knot on my head. "Fortunately, I have a thick skull."

Nick's face paled. "You caught up with him?" He

reached out and lifted my hair up. Cursing, he dragged out a handkerchief and dabbed at the lump with all the delicacy of a sledgehammer.

I winced and grabbed his wrist. "Please. It's not bleeding. It's nothing that an ice pack tonight won't cure."

A muscle twitched along his jaw, but he gave up jabbing at me. "Fine. Care to tell me what happened?"

"Set up. I found the same window you did and crawled inside. I spotted a similar canister on the floor and went for it. The courier jumped me. If it hadn't been for Myrddin…" I shrugged.

Nick cocked a hip and ran a hand over his head, the epitome of a man at the end of his patience. "Who's Myrddin?"

"Italian, older man. Probably close to his eighties. Educated. Saved my butt."

"The villa's owner? Where is he?"

"Not the owner. A trespasser, like us."

"How—"

"He's been following me."

"Why?"

That question I didn't know how to answer. *Because I'm a descendant of a priestess?* Nope, that one I would keep to myself. Didn't want Nick rolling with laughter on this lovely marble floor.

"He had a peculiar story about a crazed family plotting to murder women."

"What's the connection to Damassine?"

One of the many things I had loved about Nick was how fast he could connect the dots. "He gave me the name of a company in Milan, Baleno Nazionale."

"Lightning National?" Nick let out a low whistle. "The lightning bolt from the canister's logo."

"I thought so."

"I'll call the name in." He checked his watch. "By the time we can land in Milan, it'll be evening."

I moved back into the salon. I didn't know where the owners were, but I was sure they wouldn't appreciate the window being left open. "That doesn't mean we can't check the building out."

Nick snagged my arm. "Hold on. We first need to set some ground rules. I'm the security expert, remember? When I tell you to stay close, I mean it, Eve."

"Then don't go off in a cloud of dust on me, Nick." I pulled free and crossed to the window, slamming it shut. "I didn't intentionally go off on my own out there. I lost sight of you and took the wrong turn. When I saw someone outside this house, I thought you might be in trouble."

The tense lines around Nick's mouth softened. "Eve—"

"Let's get going." As much as a pissed-off woman could do in field boots, I swept by him. "The courier's going to strike again. I know it."

In my brief connection with the man, his heated dark excitement over a new attack had been practically frothing. Would the courier's next target be another group of Marians? How did he know where to find them? Had he selected Damassine because of Yvette and the little girl Marian I'd met? Only one person could possibly tell me.

I needed to speak with Scarlet. Soon.

Dusk had fallen by the time Nick unlocked the door to a small bedroom suite of a quaint hotel he had located off the historic quarter in Milan near the Piazza del Duomo. We were also within walking distance of our target, according to the directions Nick had secured. However, he had nixed any scouting of the Baleno Nazionale tonight, citing my concussion as the reason.

Both before and after the abbreviated flight from Lake Como, I had tried calling Scarlet several times to no avail. Frustrated, I tossed my phone on the bed. "She must really be in love."

Sitting in the hotel room's only chair, Nick looked up from checking his equipment bag. "Who?"

"My friend Scarlet. She's either turned off her cell phone or is out of reach of my signal. She hasn't checked in with her main editor, who knows only that Scarlet is somewhere working on a story."

I ran my fingers through my hair and paced the small area between the bed and door. Although Nick and I were practically tripping over each other in the cramped quarters, he hadn't been receptive to any argument concerning separate rooms. He wanted me where he could monitor me for any signs of concussion. Period.

I didn't have to be an empath to feel the tension. The small room acted like a laboratory flask, holding our volatile awareness of each other's closeness and needing only a spark to combust.

After being shot at, taking a blow to the head, and experiencing the emotions of my attacker, I had to admit that I really hadn't put up much of a debate over the room issue. How I was going to survive spending a night confined with him was beyond my limited social graces, so I focused on what I could control: the hunt.

"Which man was the object of Scarlet's affections?" Nick asked. "We never finished the introductions in Como."

"Caleb Adriano. The man to her left."

"Adriano?" He frowned in concentration as he brought out a sleek laptop computer. "The name's very familiar." His brow smoothed. "Ah, yes, of course.

Wealthy Italian family with roots and connections almost as old as Italy itself."

"Really?" I perched on the edge of the all-too-comfortable bed. Hmm, it wouldn't hurt to stretch out while we discussed our game plan. I sank backward onto the duvet. Much better than the cot in the lab trailer or the chair on the jet.

"Trust Scarlet to find a real catch." I closed my eyes. Nick's voice rumbled but I couldn't understand him. "Hmm?" Then I heard nothing at all.

Light struck my face, drawing me out of velvety darkness. I opened my eyes and blinked. It took me a moment to remember where I was. A hotel in Milan. I had been on the bed and must have fallen asleep. One thing with my profession, I could fall asleep anywhere, anytime. I started to stretch my arms when I felt the slide of the cotton sheets across my bare skin.

Didn't I have my clothes on? I didn't recall changing to a T-shirt, my usual nightgown. Then weight shifted on the bed.

Uh-oh. Cautiously I twisted my head and met Nick's sleepy but amused gaze. "Anything I should know?"

"We made mad passionate love all night and you've only just now fallen asleep…snoring no less."

I shot up, gripping the sheet to my chest. "I do not snore."

"Oh yes, you do, *chère*. Very charming, a series of breathing hitches before you release your breath, but a snore nevertheless." Nick folded his arms behind his head.

"If you can get past the insult, you'll notice you still have on your undies, items that never would have survived my lovemaking, if you would recall."

He was right. My camisole never would have stayed

on during sex with Nick. He was a breast man, another puzzlement as to why me as a girlfriend. On a good day I might be a B cup.

I also remembered how he liked to wake up and if the current tent in the sheet over his groin was any indication, his preferences hadn't changed one iota. My traitorous body began to hum in anticipation. If I stayed in bed one more minute, I might take matters into my own hands.

I spotted my pants draped across the chair. The moment my feet touched the ground, my mad dash across the room had nothing to do with modesty but everything to do with the fact the wood floor was like cold blocks of ice. I pulled on the pants and slipped my turtleneck over my head. Next up the bathroom down the hallway.

When I returned I was relieved to see Nick out of bed and pants on, although I would have preferred his chest covered as well. The urge to run my hands over the contours and trace the crisp hair down below his waistband raced through me and warmth flooded my cheeks. Desperate to look at anything else, I turned away and spied a laptop now on the chair.

"Wireless with Internet access?"

He smiled and gestured. "Knock yourself out. I need to check for messages from my team after you're finished."

After he gave me instructions on how to guest access, I sat on the edge of the bed with the computer. First I sent my niece and nephew an e-mail.

Then I typed in Scarlet's Web site and clicked onto her blog. "That's strange."

Nick placed his equipment bag on the chair. "What is?"

"Scarlet uses blogging like a diary. What she's interested in, what articles she's writing and..." I skimmed through past entries. "And people she knows. There it is, damn her."

"What?" Nick came over to sit beside me on the bed.

"The Myrddin character knew personal information about me that he intimated Scarlet had said. I assumed she'd talked to him, but, oh no, not just him. She's gone and blabbed it to the whole world."

Nick pressed closer so he could read the screen. His body radiated heat that sent a shiver through me. I inhaled carefully and caught his all-male, musky scent. The room seemed to condense even more.

Nick read aloud. "My scientist friend Eve fights to keep her analytical side in control while she ignores her amazing empathic and other psychic abilities. When I'm done with my current story, I plan to write about the paranormal in the hopes I can help her to open up to the full range of her capabilities and understand her past."

Nick's brilliant blue gaze fixed on me. "You have more than one power? You never told me. What else can you do? Are you clairvoyant?"

I squirmed. Big mistake. My butt brushed his thigh.

The sudden tension in the room was so palpable that I could have cut it with a scalpel. Nick's breath feathered my ear, sending all sorts of yummy tingles through me. A potent mix of anger, frustration and bewilderment brewed inside me with a temporary fix at hand.

I could forget everything for several hours of hot and heavy, as sex with Nick was never an abbreviated experience. The same patience that served him as a Swiss Guard made for a focused lover.

A very focused lover.

But opening the door to sex could lead to a Pandora's box. Old love doesn't die easy and I was in no shape to handle another personal screwup.

Nick nuzzled my hair. "God, I'd almost forgotten how much I love the smell of your hair."

My hormones decided my head shouldn't have the deciding vote and kicked into action. I eased into the solid feel of his body. The heat radiating from his skin filled me.

"Eve." Nick's fingers slid up the nape of my neck.

*Desire. Confusion. Hurt.*

The intensity of Nick's emotions seared me. Off balance, I whispered, "I'm sorry, I didn't mean to hurt you—"

Nick's head shot up, his expression furious. He released me and stepped away. "You aren't apologizing to me after all this time for the hell of it, are you, Eve? You got inside my head!"

"Not in the way you think." I stood to face him, wrapping my arms around my middle.

"What way was it, then?"

"I can't read your thoughts, Nick, but I can feel your emotions."

Especially now, I thought ruefully. It was like I had cornered a lion in its lair. To say Nick was feeling defensive would be putting it mildly. He was one angry male.

"Ever since Damassine, my empathic abilities have gone into overdrive. I don't even have to be in physical contact to experience a person's feelings."

"You don't think another person has a right to know what's going on, Eve?"

"Wait a minute. That's not fair." I lowered my arms and advanced on him. "You knew about my empathy, but you never bothered to ask me about the extent because it freaked you out."

Nick glowered. "I did not freak out."

"No? Remember that time I almost passed out in Vienna because a terminally ill person brushed against me? You changed, Nick. You watched me like I was a lab rat, wondering when it was going to happen again. Yet at the same time you treated me as if I was made of fragile glass."

"What did you expect?" Nick rubbed his face. "You never confided in me that you had paranormal abilities. One minute you were laughing and then the next you turned white and almost pitched forward on your face."

He dropped his hands. "You didn't appear to be able to protect yourself from these spells. It was…terrifying to watch you go through them."

If he only knew how petrifying it was to be the one going through them. Was I blessed or cursed? What good was having a gift if it only served to isolate me from the people I cared about? First my sister and now Nick.

"Well, where do we go from here?" I asked, steeling myself to have the "let's be friends" speech I had given him a year ago flung back in my face.

"How about breakfast?" As I gaped at him, he stepped forward and lightly touched my hair. "I need time to absorb this, Eve. So let's get something to eat. By the time we're finished, Baleno Nazionale should be open."

He turned and grabbed his sweater from the chair. "Let me just hit the head and we'll be on our way."

"Sure." After he was gone, I blew out a long stream of breath. Not precisely an olive branch extended by Nick, but it was a small step toward…

Toward nothing. *Get real. Nick wants kids and you don't. There's no future. All that you can hope for is his understanding.* I picked up my bag and looped it over my shoulder.

Now, if I could only get through the day without another psychic incident.

* * *

Inside the historic quarter we found a cozy café and pastry shop on the Piazza del Duomo. After grabbing an outside table where Nick sat with his back to the wall, we ordered. Nick idly read a local newspaper he had bought along the way. Typical male way of dealing with a problem…retreat behind a paper.

I downed the first cup of milky cappuccino but savored the next while I marveled at all the bristling spires topped with statues and flying buttresses of the Duomo. The majestic cathedral dominated the bustling square.

As I watched the passing pedestrians, I ate a warm puff pastry, licking my fingers to get the last bit of ricotta cheese. When I noticed Nick watching me lick with intense interest, I switched to a buttery croissant. He smiled, tossing aside the paper.

Looked as if he was ready for conversation. Go for the business spin.

"Anything noteworthy?" I asked. "Is Damassine still in the news, or has some other crisis pushed it aside for the inch of column space?"

He shrugged. "Pushed aside for Milan's version of the serial killer. They finally found a body of one of the missing women." He grimaced over his cup. "If you read between the lines, the body's in such bad shape that forensics will have a tough time coming up with any evidence."

"How many are missing?"

"Ten others over the past three months." He shook his head.

Ten? A fissure of unease quivered through me. I had women dying on the brain, that was all. "Let's just skip that headline for the moment. Pick a lighter topic."

"All right. How long do you think it will be before

the man to the left of us is going to hit on you? He hasn't taken his eyes off your butt since we sat down." Nick gave him a steely glare.

I rolled my eyes, but at last we slid into easy conversation. We talked about the area, the weather, but not about the case. Still I watched the people milling around the piazza. The tourists were easy to separate from the citizens as the former either wore cameras plastered to their faces or were in large groups led by a gesturing guide.

However, if I'd hoped to have the same luck in spotting the courier as I did at Lake Como, I was sadly disappointed. First, there was the tremendous difference in the population size, as Milan was Italy's second-largest city and arguably the most commercial with its strong industrial base. My chance of having the courier walk into view was nil to none.

In this piazza alone most of the local males on their way to work favored black with flashes of color in ties or wool scarves tossed casually around their necks. There were also more than a few shaved heads. One such man accompanied by a beautiful young woman, sat down at the table next to ours. For all I knew, he could be the courier watching us while he nibbled on his companion's hand. With his face half-hidden, I couldn't see if he had a scar.

I sighed. I needed more information. I needed a name, a close-up picture.

Wouldn't I sense him if he were near?

Staring unseeing over the plaza, I lowered my cup and cautiously opened myself to the possibility.

Time for honesty. For whatever reasons, I could feel illness in other people. Wouldn't I be able to sense madness? Going even further out on the woo-woo branch, wasn't evil a sickness of the soul?

*Yes,* my voice urged.

"Eve?"

I started and looked across the table. A slight frown puckered Nick's brow. "Are you all right?"

I forced a smile. "Yes."

"Ready to go?"

I nodded.

After Nick paid the tab, he startled me by reaching across the table and taking my hand. He rubbed his thumb across my palm. "Do you realize we've been engaged in light conversation for nearly an hour without worrying about sex or fighting or discussing our jobs?"

I swallowed but met his intense gaze. "Yes."

"Ever wonder why we couldn't do this when we were involved?"

Of course I did, but I wasn't going to own up to the wistfulness that now filled me. Safer to shake my head than trust my voice.

Nick smiled and brought my hand closer so he could kiss my fingertips. "Liar. You know why. Normalcy would have meant we were getting intimate on a level we weren't truly ready for."

Stunned, I stared at him as he rose and tugged me to my feet. "Come on, we have a bad guy to catch."

My sister's murderer. Reality splashed like a cold spray of water over what had been a pleasant interlude. Clouds passed across the morning sun, casting a pall over the square. Focus on the hunt, I reminded myself. This is neither the time nor the place for personal feelings.

I tugged my hand free from Nick's grasp and grabbed a map out of my pocket. Irritation flashed across his face, but without comment he guided me from the square. Since walking was easier than driving, we cut back and forth across winding side streets with their tapestry of contemporary and medieval buildings toward our ultimate destination.

When we turned onto the street on which Baleno Nazionale was located, Nick spotted a faded sign on the side of the corner building.

"Look. Maybe I should check this organization out."

I squinted as I translated Uomini per Uomini Da Comitiva and grimaced.

"Really, Nick. Society of Men for Men. A social club?"

"How do you know? It could be a men's support group. God knows we need one after stumbling through the minefield of women. Our egos are so fragile."

"You have that right. You need all the help you can get." We continued along the road. At a brownish pink marble structure near the next busy intersection, I caught the glint of sun on a sign.

"Nick, look!" I pointed at the bronze plaque with the words "Baleno Nazionale." Engraved below was the logo with two opposing crescents on horizontal planes but with the jagged slash across the middle and a star in the center. The other difference from the canister's markings was the larger size of the lightning bolt, overshadowing the other images.

My pulse quickened. Nick gripped the doorknob. "Ready?"

"More than." We had found the canister source.

# *Chapter 7*

Inside a small but elegant reception area, an exceptionally beautiful young woman glanced up from behind a desk. Her questioning look turned to interest when she drank up Nick. I got dismissed after she took in my clothes. I had to admit that my parka, worn khakis and boots didn't match her expensive, trim, black suit worn with eighteen-karat gold loop earrings and bracelet.

"*Buon giorno,*" she greeted Nick with a flashing smile.

"*Buona la mattina,*" he returned.

My Italian wasn't too shabby, but I wanted to assume control of this conversation, so it best suited my purpose to steer it into English.

"Good morning. I'd like to see the owner or manager."

I got only a polite smile. "Do you have an appointment?"

"No." I pulled out and displayed my identification. "I'm Dr. Eve St. Giles with the European Centre for

Disease Prevention and Control. I'm here on an official investigation."

A small frown marred her smooth forehead as she reached for the phone receiver. She spoke low and rapidly before replacing the phone. "*Signore* Martelli will be out shortly."

"*Grazie.*"

"Shortly" stretched into ten minutes before the inner door opened. I blinked. Martelli was one of those classically handsome Italian males. Tall with black, styled hair, liquid brown eyes, Roman nose and golden olive complexion, he wore with panache a tailored navy suit with a blue shirt and perfectly knotted red silk tie.

He also had charm and presence. He didn't bat an eye while approaching me, his gaze full of appreciation for a woman. "Dr. St. Giles." When he extended his hand, I did likewise. But instead of shaking it, he bent over and brushed a light kiss across the backs of my fingers. "What an honor."

"*Grazie,* Mr. Martelli."

"*Per favore,* call me Lorenzo."

"Lorenzo, may I present my assistant, Nicholas Petter?"

The men shook hands, silently taking each other's measure. Then Martelli turned on me the full blast of his charm. "Why don't we go back to my office and we'll see how I can assist you?"

He led us through a warren of hallways. During one stretch we walked past a glass wall through which we could see the manufacturing area. Shining metal canisters whirled along a conveyor belt.

Hundreds and hundreds. How many of those innocuous containers filled with Spanish flu were being carried about Europe? I wanted to linger but Lorenzo whisked us inside a spacious corner office.

He indicated the dark-green leather chairs before sitting behind his huge antique desk. "Sofia indicated that you're here about an investigation." He placed his elbows on the desk, steepling his fingers.

"Yes." I leaned back in my chair lest I appeared too anxious. "I'm tracking down the source of a canister."

Lorenzo gave me an indulgent smile. "As you saw when we walked past the manufacturing area, we make many types of containers. Our clientele and distribution is international." He spread his hands. "We do everything from custom ordered to mass production. What is it that you need?"

"Not need," I corrected. "Locate."

*"Mi scusi?"*

Nick opened up his phone and brought up the photo he'd taken at the crash scene. He handed over the phone to Lorenzo.

"Is that one of yours?" I asked.

Lorenzo frowned. "What is this about? Has there been an accident?"

By the way the man eyed his own phone, I could tell that he was considering whether he should call in help. I didn't want the company throwing up stone walls before I had a few answers so I hurried to reassure him. "No, *signore.* The canister is not the problem. But it could lead to the person involved."

Lorenzo's expression lightened. "What makes you think the container was made here?"

I rose to point a finger toward the phone's viewer. "See the marking."

"Ah, *si.*" He opened a drawer and removed a slender magnifying wand that he held up to the screen.

"Isn't that Baleno Nazionale's logo?"

"Ah, *si*." He held out the phone and Nick took it.

"Yet it differs from the sign outside." Out of the corner of my eye, I noticed Nick slip the phone into his pocket. Was that a plastic bag poking out? Then it struck me. Nick was going to run the man's fingerprints.

Lorenzo shrugged. "We have many variations. The owner gets bored with everything looking the same."

Since I had a cousin who was a graphic designer, I had a fair idea of the price tag on having variations on a logo. Either the owner was very wealthy or Lorenzo was lying to me. If the latter, why?

"I was hoping you'd be able to tell me the name of the client for whom the canister was made."

"*Scusa*, Dr. St. Giles, but that is...how do you say...privileged information."

"I need it for an official investigation."

"So you said, but you also said our product was not part of the problem." He adjusted a cuff. "Since you are from the Disease Centre, am I to presume some sort of agent was carried in that container?"

I nodded.

"I will look into the matter, but even if I can track that particular brand, it hardly means the customer is involved. If it is a mass-production item, then whomever you seek could have bought it anywhere."

Walls were definitely being erected. I stood and handed him a business card. "Thank you for your time, *signore*. Should you be able to track the client for that series of canisters, I can be reached at this number."

Crisis averted, Martelli was all charm again. "Please, Lorenzo." He caught my hand and kissed it. "I will be only too happy to help such a beautiful woman."

Really. Then all he had to do was turn on that sleek

computer on the corner of his desk and pull up inventory records. I smiled. "The Centre and I would deeply appreciate any assistance. Lives are at stake."

"Of course."

Martelli escorted us out of the building. The moment he shut the door he probably was rushing to call the owner.

"I almost drowned in the bullshit he was dishing," Nick commented.

"We were so close, Nick. All he had to do was tap one of those manicured nails on his computer keyboard to access the inventory records. I'm going to call Frederic to see if he can work some magic with the local authorities. Maybe they can do the Italian equivalent of a subpoena."

"I have a better idea if you're willing to ignore a few legal niceties."

I halted in the middle of the sidewalk. "Ignore what niceties?" I asked suspiciously.

"Accessing his computer tonight."

"You mean breaking into the building?"

"Yes. Are you game, Eve?"

I thought of all those canisters inside. "I'm in."

Nick's eyes flashed. "I didn't realize the Centre condoned illegal activities."

"The Centre isn't going to know about this, so let's hope you can get us in without detection. I don't fancy spending time in an Italian jail."

"Speaking of time." Nick consulted his watch. "How would you like to spend ours before tonight?"

I leaned close and ran my hand along his side. "Well, big boy, I think you ought to—" I pressed against him and whispered in his ear "—run the prints you're going to lift from that phone." I patted his pocket, turned and strolled down the sidewalk.

After our return to the hotel room, I first checked in with my team's progress. Testing had confirmed that the Spanish flu agent had been carried in the destroyed canister. The lab was also making progress testing the sample vaccine Nick's client had sent. Janssen Pharmaceutical was also speeding up its schedule to produce more antiviral serum. It would take a while before we had an ample supply, but the next time an outbreak happened, we would be able to save more lives.

Before I could ring him, the director called me. "Eve, where are you?"

I settled more comfortably on the bed. Nick had commandeered the chair so that he could do his computer thing. He'd already lifted prints off his phone and sent them to his staff.

"I'm still in Milan. The manager of the canister manufacturer wasn't particularly helpful. I'm exploring other approaches to get the information of who the buyer was."

"There's been a new incident."

"What? Where?"

"Milan."

*Here?* "Say again."

"We had a call a few minutes ago from a local medical examiner. The police brought in the body of a woman who is a suspected victim of a serial killer."

Nick must have read something in my expression for he rose, walked across the room and sat close to me.

"I read about the serial killer. Ten missing women."

"Well, this victim's internal organs were liquefied and her lungs filled with blood."

"Spanish flu." Possibilities whirled in my head. "Was she in Damassine within the past week?"

"No. She's been missing for several weeks. The

examiner is sending us tissue samples, but I want you also to speak with him and the investigating officer." He gave me their directions.

"On my way." I disconnected. Nick grabbed my bag and his and we were out the door.

An hour later I was positive that I was looking through a microscope at the lung tissue of a Spanish flu victim. I raised my head at the three men silently watching me: Nick, Deputy Police Chief Gianni Lupo and the local medical examiner, Dr. Silvio Guaglione.

"The lab at the Centre will of course run the tests to confirm, but I don't think there's any question the victim had Spanish flu." Possible scenarios raced through my head as I stood up.

"You are positive?" asked Dr. Guaglione.

"Yes. No." Frustrated, I ran fingers through my hair. "Yes. A hemorrhagic agent could also have liquefied the internal organs like that, but we haven't had reports of any Ebola cases in Western Europe. You're certain the victim hadn't been to Switzerland in the past month?"

Deputy Chief Lupo, a stocky middle-aged man, shook his head. "She was a stock model in the fashion district. She had been working day and night for a fashion event until she disappeared."

So did we have a new hot zone that needed to be mobilized?

"She wasn't killed immediately," said the examiner, another young, classically good-looking man, who managed to wear the proverbial white coat with panache. "Although she's been missing for nearly a month, she was kept alive for at least two weeks."

I suppressed a shudder. The poor thing. What had been done to her in those weeks?

The examiner continued. "Her body was remarkably

well preserved, as if she had been kept in refrigeration for a period of time."

"What? Why?" I asked.

The officer paced. "Those are precisely the questions we would like to have answered. I still have nine missing women as well as..."

"As?" I prompted.

Lupo hesitated before answering. "This is not for public information, but several boys and men have been reported missing."

Dr. Guaglione said, "This victim had a puncture wound on her upper arm."

"Was she a drug user?"

"No. No other marks."

One injection. I gazed around at the police lab with its shining equipment. Like any other medical laboratory except...no cages of animals for testing. I inhaled sharply.

Nick, who had blended into the background, stepped forward. "Eve, what's wrong?"

"The victim was a lab rat."

*"Mi scusi?"* Looking baffled, Lupo spread his hands. "My English fails me."

"Sorry. The woman was an experiment, a test case to make sure the Spanish flu worked. Nick, did van Velsen do any testing at your client's lab?"

"No, the project was halted before testing on animals."

"Then he would have wanted to test it before dispersing the viral agent to test its efficacy."

Lupo's expression hardened. "But if some sick experiment is going on, why are the victims mainly females? The youngest missing is age seven and the oldest is age seventy-seven."

Mentally I said a small prayer, for there was no doubt in my mind that all the victims were dead.

"We suspect that the Spanish flu DNA segment that's been recreated has been genetically altered to affect women more." I glanced between the Italian officials. "This information has to be kept confidential, but the majority of the Damassine victims were female, from babies to the elderly."

"If it's the missing scientist, he would have to have a place that's secure where he could watch the victim's reaction to the virus over a period of at least forty-eight hours," I mused aloud. "Although he's been vaccinated, he wouldn't want to play Russian roulette himself. He's having too many jollies getting off watching the effects of his work."

"We have a monster on the loose," said Lupo. "We must stop him."

"Monsters, plural," I corrected. "Nick?"

He nodded in agreement. "Van Velsen's definitely not acting alone. He's not the type to do his own dirty work, picking people off the street."

"At least one of his helpers has been coming and going from Milan," I said. "He's been to Switzerland and Lake Como in the past week."

"We will check all the major transportation centers." Lupo removed his radio unit from his belt.

As the officer sprang into action shooting off orders into the radio, Nick offered the services of his security company to help expedite the search and handed his card to the chief.

"*Grazie, signore,* but we can handle..." Lupo glanced at the card. "Nicholas Petter. I know that name. You were the Swiss Guard who took a bullet for our Pope, yes?"

Nick hunched his shoulders. "Yes."

The chief flashed a smile. "We would be most honored if you want to work with us."

Within short order Nick was set up with a phone and computer. I told him I would meet him at the hotel later and he grunted his response. I took the unintelligible word for agreement and left.

The police station was situated on the edge of central Milan's northeast quadrant. I wandered along the boulevard that looped around Parco Sempione. Although I admired the soaring tower of the Castello Sforzesco as I passed the ducal palace, I wasn't in the mood to sightsee at a place with such a dark and turbulent history.

I fended off a few gypsies and dodged traffic to cross the street away from the park. As I walked, I smiled at the sight of a tree and red flowers growing on the roof of one building. Along this street, most of the buildings featured Baroque detailing and window balconies.

I followed a side street and then halted in amazement. For a moment I could have sworn the area before me was awash with soft glowing lines whose power lured me closer. Was this the same energy I had seen inside the stone circle?

A blaring horn jerked me out of my trance. A taxi screeched to a stop to drop off a load of tourists who wore the usual camera accessories. I blinked.

The illumination was gone, replaced by a short line of people curled along a brick building with circular windows. A guide led a few through a porch supported by Corinthian columns with a lunette above them. I walked closer and saw an image of the Madonna with an unknown man and woman. A discreet sign indicated that I was at the Santa Maria delle Grazie, home of Leonardo da Vinci's *Last Supper.*

I hesitated only a second before joining the line. As it was off season I only had to wait a short period before

I was admitted to the refectory. I stood before the restored tempera painting and simply soaked up the facial expressions and body language depicted.

"The moments of betrayal and sacrifice captured in one place for all eternity," a man said from behind me. I spun around to find Myrddin studying the da Vinci masterpiece.

"Where did you come from?" I demanded.

He shrugged. "Like you, I was in need of inner reflection."

"You've been following me again!"

His mouth curved. "That, too. So how does da Vinci's painting speak to you?"

I recalled his words. "You mentioned sacrifice." I frowned. "This captures only Jesus's announcement that one of the apostles will betray him."

Myrddin turned and indicated the opposite wall where another painting dominated the chamber. "That's the *Crucifixion* painted by Montorfano on the opposite wall. Action—" he nodded at the *Last Supper* "—and consequence."

"You're right." I studied the lesser-known painting, which was a dense composition and not nearly as realistic as the da Vinci work.

"You see the despair of Magdalene as she hugs Christ's cross?"

"Yes, it's in stark contrast to those Roman soldiers playing dice in the right corner." Curious, I glanced up at Myrddin. In the chamber's dim light the man appeared frailer than when I had seen him at Lake Como. His expression was somber, with sadness filling his eyes.

"Do you believe, Dr. St. Giles, that all betrayal is wrong?" he asked softly.

I shifted uneasily. Philosophical discussions were never my forte. Give me microbes to analyze any day rather than the workings of the human soul.

"I suppose it would depend on the motive and what is being betrayed."

"Ah, the scientist's world view. Is there a quantum merit to deceit? A sliding scale to sin? Certainly your namesake, the first Eve, must have thought so to bite into the apple."

"She also paid the consequences."

"That she did, for her betrayal of her oath to God." Myrddin continued to stare at the *Crucifixion*. "Tell me, Doctor, what if Eve knew that Adam was up to no good and took the bite in order to save him? Would she still deserve to be expelled from the Garden of Eden?"

"No, but now you're speaking about sacrifice with its own set of consequences."

Myrddin smiled. "So I am. Do you think the person who betrays should ever be forgiven? Do you believe in redemption?"

I'd better or else I was going to be damned. I had forever lost the opportunity to reforge the bond of sisterhood with Yvette. I had failed her and so many others.

"I think forgiveness is a quality of a person's heart while redemption has to be earned."

"Interesting, Doctor. And hope?"

I looked at the image of the woman clinging to the base of the cross. "I think there is always hope."

"Then I hope you are right about forgiveness and redemption for both of us."

I reached out and gripped his arm. "Why are you following me? How did you know about Baleno Nazionale?"

"Because we can help each other. Those I seek to help don't understand the consequences of their latest actions."

"The release of Spanish flu?"

"Yes." Grief etched Myrddin's face. "I cannot believe that they comprehend the evil of the men in whose hands they have placed the virus. Those men are insane and must be stopped."

"Who are 'they'? That family you spoke of before?"

"Yes."

"Tell me their name. The authorities can stop them before more die."

"I cannot," Myrddin replied hoarsely, his voice tight with tension. "Neither the authorities nor the public can possibly understand the family's world. Even betrayal has its limits."

"Then tell me why they want to hurt women." If I knew the motive, then maybe I could follow the connection to van Velsen.

"Not all women."

I counted to ten to rein in my impatience. He was going to go off the deep end again. "The descendants of the priestesses. The ones called 'Marians.'"

"Strong women like Magdalene. Warriors."

Oh God, not back to biblical history. I tightened my grasp on his arm. "Please. I need names. I think there are going to be more strikes."

"Check out the holdings of Uomini per Uomini Da Comitiva."

"The Men for Men Society?" That was the club Nick and I had noticed this morning. "What is it?"

"A group of men dedicated to turning back women's rights. Your scientist and courier are members."

Myrddin's gaze sharpened. "I must go."

"No, please." But a new group of tourists converged in front of the painting and I had to let go. Myrddin slipped through the crowd. I pushed through the milling bodies but bumped into a human granite slate: Nick.

He slipped his arm around my waist to steady me. "Whoa! Why did you leave the station? I told you to wait for me."

"You did not." Frustrated, I stood on my tiptoes but couldn't spot Myrddin anywhere in the chamber. "You grunted when I said I would meet you at the hotel later."

A guard motioned that it was time for us to go. We joined the line filing out. Still no sign of Myrddin. He really knew how to pull off a vanishing act.

"That wasn't a 'yes' grunt. That was a 'wait' grunt."

I rolled my eyes as we emerged into the sunshine. "I think you need to work on your grunts, then, because they all sound alike."

"It's all in the context that they are made."

I looked up at him as a question struck me. "How'd you find me in there?"

"Your cell phone is on. I tracked your location."

"What! You couldn't just call and ask where I was?" The line moved and I stepped forward.

Wooziness hit me as the very ground felt like it was vibrating. Whoa. It wasn't warm enough for me to be experiencing a heat stroke. I took a deep breath and the light-headedness dissipated. Stress and not enough sleep, I decided.

"Who was that man you were speaking with so intently?" Nick asked.

Nick's eagle eyes certainly never missed a trick. "Myrddin's been following me."

"What?" He swung me around to face him. *Fear. For me.* "Did he try to hurt you?"

The waves of Nick's anxiety continued to ripple through me. Panicking, I yanked free of his grip. Immediately his emotions receded from inside me, leaving only a slight aching residue. I rubbed my arm where my flesh still tingled from the contact.

Must tamp down. Must observe not receive his emotions, I almost chanted to myself. My self-control ground over and over again like the ignition on a car with a dead battery.

"What's wrong, Eve?" Nick demanded. "Did he hurt you?"

Myrddin, he was asking me about Myrddin. "No, I don't think he means me any harm."

Yet. If it came to a choice between this "family" and me, I was certain that I would end up on the short end of the stick.

"What did he want then?" Nick scanned the group walking away from the church.

"Don't bother looking for him, he's long gone. However, he gave me another lead."

"How do you know he's not behind the outbreak?"

I shrugged as we reached the sidewalk along the street. "I don't, but I truly believe he's trying to stop another one. He won't tell me who he is, but I suspect a member of his family is involved. He talked about betrayal and sacrifices like he was in pain."

Nick held out his digital phone. "Well, we'll know soon enough who this Myrddin character is." He pressed a button and an image of the two of us appeared on the screen.

"How long were you watching us?" Stunned, I halted in the middle of the sidewalk.

"Long enough to get a few clear shots. I've already sent them to my team to run his identification."

"While you were skulking about, did you even look at the paintings?"

"Of course." Nick placed his hand in the small of my back and pressed me to move again.

*Hurt.*

I practically bolted away from his touch. Nick frowned but let his hand drop. Why was he experiencing pain over my mention of the paintings?

"I particularly appreciated the deniability factor in da Vinci's painting," he continued.

"Deniability?"

Nick shot me a dark look. "Yes. All the apostles denied they would betray Jesus and their reward was the Last Supper. If Judas had owned up, do you think he still would have been rewarded with a meal or kicked in the teeth?"

"Forgiven. Why?"

"It seems to me that you deny to yourself and others that you have paranormal abilities and yet those talents continually betray you. Instead of beating yourself up, isn't it about time you accept your capabilities and open up to others?"

I opened and shut my mouth. Forgiveness might be a quality of the heart, but mine wasn't ready yet to let me off the hook. I had lost too much already.

# Chapter 8

Someone bumped into me from behind. "Sorry, luv." A rosy-cheeked woman wearing a tweed jacket and a plaid muffler gave me an apologetic smile as a tour group milled about us.

*Joy.* Seeing the *Last Supper* had filled her with happiness. A man carrying a camera paused to take a picture.

*Irritation.* Someone had moved into his shot.

With growing horror, I realized that I was a walking antenna, receiving emotions from everyone around me. I had to get out of here and regroup.

Blindly I turned down a street in the general direction of the historic district.

"Eve." Nick kept an easy pace beside me. "Someday we need to talk about what happened between us."

"Why rehash ancient history? We both know what happened. I broke it off." I continued stalking along the eighteenth-century pavers.

"Without giving me a reason."

"I thought men preferred clean, nonemotional endings."

"Something scared you off, so it has to be an issue with your abilities."

"Getting empathic, Nick? Or did you analyze me?"

"Neither. I had quite a lengthy conversation with your mother about you and the family dynamics."

I stopped where the street intersected with another paved road. "You talked to Maman about us?"

"I wanted to understand why you ran like a scared rabbit when I said I wanted a family *with you.*"

Despite all the time we had been separated, my panic at the idea of having children welled up. What if they were born with some of my unusual traits? How could I burden them like that? As before with this discussion, I took the easy way out.

"I couldn't then and I can't now. Not with my career."

"Why? There are at least five epidemiologists at the Centre who have families."

"Not field investigators."

"No, but they still do important work."

I wasn't about to tell him about a written request for transfer from the field sitting in my locked desk drawer. What had Nick said? The deniability factor? By going through with a transfer, would I once more be avoiding who I was?

"Psychic abilities are not necessarily inherited." With his easy tone, Nick could have been commenting on the weather.

So much for using the job as an excuse for not having children. I poked a finger in the middle of his chest.

"Oh, really? My mother's talent runs to clairvoyance with a dash of being able to detect place memories.

Maman can't visit a place of great tragedy like a battlefield without freaking out. Suppose we had stayed together—every one of our children could have been born with paranormal abilities."

His eyes blazing, he wrapped his hands around mine. "I admit, the gift you have does rattle me at times. Sometimes it terrifies me. But you have to trust me to love and protect you. I have to trust you to do the same."

Tears burned my eyes, running down my cheeks. I pulled loose and stumbled back. "Damn it, Nick! Don't you get it yet? I can't always control myself!"

I ran. But how could I ever run from myself? Even now I felt compelled to follow a side street that wound between a block lined with older buildings.

*Danger.*

I stumbled and slowed. Where? Whose emotions was I plugging in to now? My heart sped up; adrenaline surged in conjunction with the other person's.

Midway down the street I saw Myrddin arguing with a man with a shaved head and dressed in black. The courier?

I broke into a run when the man put his hand into his pocket and withdrew something. Sun glinted off glass.

"Myrddin, watch out. He's got a needle!"

He also had a gun—in his other hand—which I saw the moment he turned and fired at me. But I wasn't where I'd been standing: Nick had shoved me between two cars parked on the street. With a quick move he had his own gun out and fired a single shot.

I poked my head over the car's hood and watched the courier climb onto a motorcycle and gun the motor, speeding away. I looked for Myrddin but like the great mage for whom he had named himself, he had vanished into thin air.

"Come on," Nick urged. We ran to where another cycle was parked. I didn't know motorcycles could be hot-wired, but Nick had the engine running by the time I'd clambered on behind him. He peeled away from the curb and raced to the main street.

Problem. Motorcycles and scooters are a way of life in most cities in Italy and the street was filled with them, all filling the air with loud raucous noise. However, Nick turned right, shouting over his shoulder, "I saw him go this way."

As we passed side streets, I looked for the courier. At the fifth one I saw a blur of a bike turn left at the other end. I thumped Nick's shoulder. "He went down that one."

Nick nodded, gunning the motor. As one we leaned into the abrupt turn. We emerged at the other end in time to see the bike ahead veering onto another road.

I don't know how long we played the cat-and-mouse game up and down the narrow streets of the historic quarter. Vrrumm. A hairpin turn. Vrrumm. A race down a stretch of a main artery.

At times we gained ground and at others we lost ground. My eyes watered from the stinging wind and the constant squinting. My thigh muscles ached from clamping so tight as I clung to Nick for dear life as we rounded yet another twist in the road.

Suddenly, less than one hundred yards directly ahead of us was the courier. He looked over his shoulder and then reared back, riding his bike onto a crowded sidewalk. People yelled and screamed as they scrambled to get out of the way. A woman with a little boy in her arms dashed into the street.

Nick hit the brakes, but our bike's tires didn't grip the surface. We skidded out of control and began to tilt. Fighting the machine like a beast, Nick shifted his body and I followed suit. We came to a stop against the curb without crashing.

I propped my forehead against Nick's sweat-drenched back and released a long, shuddering breath. Then I straightened and looked around at the pandemonium. "Nick, he's gone." He swore, started up the bike and motored slowly along.

"Nick, over there!" I pointed over his shoulder at a cycle lying on its side on the sidewalk. Nick pulled over and kicked down the stand. We both dismounted and he crouched beside the abandoned bike.

"Engine's burning. It's his." He rose, running his hand over his head. "Damn. No telling which way he went. The streets are a warren in this section. I'll call this in to Chief Lupo."

While Nick spoke on his phone, I walked until I reached the next side street, more an alley, really, because it contained pavers and the buildings appeared to be one shade shy of ancient. Despite its narrowness, cars lined one side. I spotted an awning over what looked to be the entrance to a shop. Maybe someone had noticed the courier. I started down the road.

Everything blurred. The entire block was awash with a grid of pulsating light. Where there had been cars parked, suddenly I saw stands piled high with rags where men in tunics and women in long gowns haggled. My knees buckled and I was falling…

*The healer lifted the edge of the poultice and smiled with pleasure at the wound's appearance. The angry red flesh and puss had dissipated, and the edges of the jagged skin were knitting together nicely.*

*She glanced at the knight's face and with a start saw that he was awake, watching. A shiver coursed through her. His remote, veiled expression was like a man studying a bug before he crushed it.*

*Then the warrior flashed a smile and her strange sensation fled. He asked, "Will I live?"*

*"Yes, the wound is better." She replaced the dressing, tucked the blanket around him and rose. Although she realized her reaction to him was silly, the healer never liked being close to the man. She wished that she could say the same for her apprentice, but the girl had relieved her of much of the nursing burden. A forfeit she must be willing to pay.*

*"Soon you will be strong enough to leave."*

*His laugh was low and rough. "Have I been that poor a patient?"*

*"No, but I am certain you want to return to your own kind."*

*"My own kind." He mulled over the words. "What if I wish to remain and become one of your kind?"*

*Her heart racing, the healer picked up the bundle of herbs and the pail of precious water. "What do you mean?"*

*"The girl has told me about your group of special women. Women with extraordinary power. I would think, though, in such treacherous times that you would need a warrior's protection. I could help your friends to pay back the debt I owe you."*

*She grasped at the latter remark to temporize. "There is no debt. What I did was from the charity of the heart."*

*"But what about the others?" he persisted. "The girl claimed she was a priestess in training. With the crusade raging you could use protection."*

*Fear gripped the healer. What had the apprentice done? How much had she said?*

*"No one will hurt us. We are not Catharis. We are merely women of charity."*

*"All the people were killed and a village destroyed because the crusaders could not be bothered to tell the difference between Catholics and Catharis."*

*The healer had heard of the slaughter at the start of the crusade, and her heart still grieved for such indiscriminate killing. Did man not know how precious life was?*

*"We will be all right, but thank you." She had to find the apprentice and find how much the warrior knew. Then she must warn the others. They must work quicker to hide the evidence that they had ever existed. "If you would excuse me." She hurried away through the narrow passage of the grotto.*

*The warrior waited a minute. "She is gone."*

*The healer's apprentice stepped from the shadows. "Why did you tell her I have been talking? She will be very angry."*

*"Come here, girl." He extended his hand. "We should have plenty of time."*

*Hesitating only briefly, the girl sank to her knees. He ran his hand over her shoulder until her rough tunic slid off, revealing her tanned skin. He steeled himself to nuzzle her. When her head fell to the side, he took her earlobe and bit lightly. She moaned and slid to the ground. He did not need to test her to know that she was ready. A whore never needed to be prepared.*

*If only the older woman realized exactly how healed he was. He loosened his clothing and rolled on top of the girl. Without preliminaries, he plunged into her. As she arched and bucked, he whispered into her ear. "Tell me, my pretty. Tell me about the other women."*

*He would sacrifice himself to gain her loyalty for the inevitable betrayal.*

"Eve!"

My bed was hard and cold as an ice-covered rock. I opened my eyes and saw concrete. I planted my hands on the surface and, wincing at the raw pain in my palms, pressed myself high enough so I was no longer eating ground. Someone slipped an arm around my midsection.

"Eve, can you stand?" Nick demanded.

"Working on it."

He grunted, his arm tightened around me and I was airborne. Nick set me on my feet, my knees protesting as vehemently as my hands. He maintained his steadying hold on me.

I looked around and saw a circle of curious onlookers. "What happened? Did I slip and fall?"

"More like pitch and fall." Nick shook his head. "One moment you're dashing off on your own, *again*, and then the next you're doing the American version of a headfirst slide."

"I was not running off, I was..." I stared at the building we were in front of.

"You had another experience, didn't you?"

"Nick." I grabbed his arm. "Check this out."

He frowned. "It looks like a vacant business space. That sign says it's for rent."

Excitement raced through me as I crossed to the window. "But it once was a restaurant. There are still tables and chairs inside."

"If you need to sit down—"

"Not that," I said impatiently. "What do most restaurants have? Walk-in freezers."

"A perfect place to store a body."

"Exactly." I rubbed at the dirt film on the glass and spotted a tattered sign on the floor. I could only make out the first few words.

"Call Chief Lupo. He needs whatever their equivalent to a search warrant is."

Nick's eyebrow arched but he pulled out his phone. "By the way, what did you see?"

He was referring to my psychic experience. I glanced over my shoulder. "I saw evil in another time, another place." Like the evil I was sensing even now, emanating through the glass. Maman said objects and places could retain emotions. Was that happening now or was someone inside?

"But what I'm seeing at the moment is a flyer with the word *Uomini.*"

*Check out the holdings of Uomini per Uomini Da Comitiva,* Myrddin's voice echoed in my head.

"Tell them to hurry, Nick, with a decontamination unit and equipment."

Chief Lupo arrived with a well-equipped antiterrorist unit. Comprehensive quick field detection remained a practical problem with local first response to the threat of a biological agent, but they did have a mass spectrometer. Within short order his unit evacuated the entire block and set up a controlled perimeter.

When I was geared up and had briefed the responders about the flu agent, I entered after his advance team had determined no one was in the building and it was cleared of any booby traps. We moved rapidly. In the kitchen area we found signs that someone had recently been there. I spotted a metal door with glass window. The freezer.

A tech moved to open the door and I called out, "Stop!" I ran over and checked the thermometer. Forty-five degrees. Warmer than freezing, but a person would eventually die from hypothermia.

*It is also the average winter temperature this time of the year at Damassine,* my voice whispered.

Had there been concern about the potency of the flu in colder temperatures? Had that been the purpose of the hideous experiments on the model?

Through the small window I saw that the freezer's sole content was an Army-style cot with straps at the corners. I pressed my hands against the door. Time for my own experiment. Was I developing place cognition like Maman? I closed my eyes and tried to sense what was in the freezer.

At first I heard only my shallow breathing within the suit and the rapid beat of my heart. Then something dark and virulent slithered around my neck, choking me. Seething, it tried to burrow through my chest to get at my lungs. A red haze blurred my vision while weakness swept through me. I needed to succumb to its demands.

*No!*

With all the strength I could muster, I pushed hard against the door, breaking away. The swirling darkness disappeared in an instant. Fighting for breath, I bent over.

"Eve! What's wrong?" Nick materialized beside me.

"Fine." I sucked in another breath and ordered my pulse to settle down. "Tried an experiment. Worked."

"What type of experiment? Do I need to get you decontaminated?"

I shook my head. "No. I wasn't exposed in the usual manner." Through his mask I saw his puzzlement, but I didn't want to explain, not with other people milling around. I straightened and signaled one of the Italian techs. When he approached, I pointed to the freezer.

"It's a hot zone. Don't open the door. I'll call the Centre. We'll need to control the influenza before it's released."

He nodded and moved away to instruct the others.

"Eve?" I looked at Nick. "I came to tell you we found a room upstairs where it looks like our man may have stayed."

"I'll be there in a second." After I contacted the Centre and filled Frederic in on the latest development, I crossed the kitchen to the stairway Nick had indicated. Going up the narrow wooden steps, I emerged into a small room. Here again was a cot but outfitted with a blanket and pillow rather than straps. The room also boasted a lamp and a plain wooden desk.

I caught a flash of white and, turning, saw Nick and another white-suited man in the water closet going through a tiny medicine cabinet. As the drawers were open on the desk, I wandered over. Obviously nothing of interest to the officers, but they were looking for a killer and victims. I was looking for a flu bug.

But the drawers were empty of anything other than the usual Bible. Idly I picked it up with my gloved hands and flipped through the pages. Toward the front I found a small piece of folded paper, marking the passage. I glanced at the text. While it was in Italian, it didn't take a linguist to make out the words *Eve* and *Adam.* The courier had been reading about the expulsion of man from paradise.

I opened the folded paper to find what appeared to be a printout from a Web site. Although it was in Italian, I could make out enough words to gather it was a calendar of international events. I swallowed hard. *Women's* events. Festivals, craft shows, tributes, religious ceremonies, you name it, it was on the calendar. I scanned and found the entries for the beginning of November. Yes, there it was. The international biathlon, Damassine.

"Eve? You're paler than a ghost behind that mask. What did you find?"

I held out the list. "The potential target list for a group bent on the destruction of women, and no telling which one they'll strike next."

Nick whistled. "Lupo will have to call Interpol in on this. An alert will have to go out to all the countries."

"Even if we call in all the resources of every major international health organization, we can't even begin to cover the outbreaks if the virus is released at all these places. We need the antiserum."

"Eve, I'll call my client as soon as we get out of here," Nick reassured me. "They have teams working nonstop on the vaccine."

"But can they produce enough?"

"Janssen has agreements with other pharmaceutical companies whose facilities can be called into play."

"If Frederic works with the other international health organizations, hopefully the approval process can be shortened on an exigency basis."

All the agencies and authorities would have to unite and work together. If we failed, then God helped us. In my hands I held a death list of unbelievable magnitude.

Because of the contamination potential of the room, I left the note in the Bible. After going outside and through decontamination, we located the police chief and advised him of the note. He issued several directives. As his team sprang into action, I touched his arm. "Chief Lupo. A moment."

"Yes, Doctor?"

"This area. Does it ever have medieval reenactments?"

He looked bemused. "Not that I'm aware of."

One logical possibility for my earlier vision down and one more to go. "Is there a street where they sell rags or squares of cloth?"

He shook his head and turned to address an officer. Then he faced me again. "Do you speak of the historic rag street?"

My heart skipped a beat. "Yes. Where is it?"

He spread his hands. "Lost to time. My wife, who is into Milanian history, could tell you more. All I know is a non-Catholic religious group called the Cathars used to sell rags to make into paper before they were run out of existence. *Me scusi.* I have calls to make."

"Certainly. *Grazie.*"

I stared at the block as he moved away. I could tell him the rag street was not lost. It had been here, where even now I sensed the energy flowing beneath the pavers, connecting the past to the present and future.

Why was I experiencing these flashes of the past? Had something happened all those centuries ago that could not rest and reached out to me for resolution?

"Eve, are you ready to go? I want to check in with my staff and get them working on this 'man for man' society angle."

"Yes, let's go. We need to figure out where they're going to strike next." As the police were returning our "borrowed" motorcycle, we struck off for the hotel.

Myrddin had talked with anguish about betraying his family. Guilt. Such a strong emotion—one that could survive through the mists of time.

How was I linked to the people in my visions? Had I been the one betrayed…or the betrayer?

# Chapter 9

Hours later Nick worked his security magic and got us into the Baleno Nazionale. We stole down the hallway past the now empty factory area and into the executive office. Wearing gloves, we rifled through the few sleek black filing cabinets, but we found no sales records. That left us with trying to hack into Martelli's computer.

Nick sat in the leather chair and switched on the computer. As the computer monitor flickered to life, he checked the desk surface, even lifting up a calendar and looking under it. When he caught me staring, he smiled.

"People tend to forget their passwords so they write them down and hide them near their computer."

I grimaced. "I do that myself."

Shaking his head, Nick turned his attention back to the monitor. I moved behind him as a dialogue box requiring a password popped up.

"Right," Nick said as he reached into his black

knapsack, bringing out a compact disk case. He flipped it open and then slid the gleaming gold disk into the hard drive.

"What's that?"

"Oh, a little password-cracker program my company devised. It comes in handy every now and then."

"Works for me."

"Here we go. I'm in."

Nick rapidly tapped in the password, and the main screen popped up. He next opened the directory. While the sales folder was massive, we had done our homework on Nick's laptop. Baleno Nazionale had embraced modern times, and its Web site contained not only photographs of their products but also inventory numbers and descriptions. We had narrowed the aerosol cylinder down to three possibilities, those with industrial-strength O-rings. If you're carrying a container of a deadly agent, the last thing you would want to risk is it leaking.

"Try sales for the past month to out-of-country clients," I suggested.

"Right." Nick entered one of the cylinder numbers and ran a search. "Shipments to Canada and California." He plugged in another canister number. "This one sold to companies in Ohio and Leeds." He ran the third cylinder style. "Germany and Spain."

"What kind of quantities are we looking at?"

"Let's see." Nick tapped on the keys and gave a long, low whistle.

"What is it?"

"Distribución de Estrella Gas in Ponferrada, Spain ordered a thousand canisters last month."

"Star Gas Distribution? Hmm, what better place to create aerosol weapons than a gas distributor." I tried to place the city but couldn't. "Ponferrada. I've never heard of it."

Nick pushed back in the chair. "It's a small town along the pilgrim's trail with a Knights Templar castle as its main claim to historical importance. Its principal industries have been iron and tourism."

The Spain connection nagged at me. "Is Ponferrada near Barcelona?"

"As a jet flies. They're almost on opposite coasts, but Ponferrada is near a few ports."

"Nick, there's an international women's musical festival scheduled to begin this week in Barcelona."

After taking out another CD case, he slipped the disk into the hard drive, sent a print command and began to close out the program. "How big?"

"The Web site indicated at least a hundred performers and thousands of attendees."

Rising, he shut off the computer. "Come on. So far the courier we've been tracking has had the same unlimited access to transportation as we've had. The jet can be ready to go by the time we reach the airport."

As we ran down the hallway, all I could think about was how many of those canister orders might be for the Spanish flu and whether all of them were destined for Barcelona or other cities.

Once more Nick was a man of his words. The jet was in the last stages of fueling when we arrived at the Milan airport. I used the opportunity to call the Centre.

"Eve." Frederic came on the line. "You were right."

I swallowed. "How right?"

"Additional testing has substantiated that women are far more susceptible to this virus."

I should have experienced the thrilling hum of

victory. By understanding its DNA makeup, we should be able to expedite the vaccine. This was a significant breakthrough. Instead, I felt only emptiness. I updated the director on today's events and switched off the phone. Sitting opposite me, Nick remained on his phone as he spoke with his team.

I had nothing to do. No analysis to run, no data to access, no one to chase. All I could do was sit and wait.

I hated these silent moments of inactivity, for that's when emotions could come stealing in like a thief in the night. Even as I stared out the jet's window, all I could see was my reflection and the weight of responsibility on my shoulders.

Was I as guilty for my sister's death as a murderer whose knife drips blood?

After all, Yvette in desperation had reached out to the sister she viewed as a freak, and I had failed her. I leaned forward and buried my face in my hands.

These…abilities that I had… If I could experience the virulence of a disease or like a spectator watch events of the past, why hadn't I been able to save my own sister?

"Hey." Nick slid his hands under mine to frame my face, gently forcing me to look up at him. "What gives?"

"Quiet."

Understanding lit his eyes. "Ah, that time when all our skeletons come out of the closet, yes?"

"Yes."

"What you need is sleep."

"Can't. The body may be willing but the mind isn't."

"Yes, you can." He rose, scooped me up and settled in my chair. I squirmed to get loose but he circled my waist with an arm of iron. "Be still. Let me fasten the safety belt."

Since there wasn't any point in waging a battle at the moment, I stopped.

"There. Rest your head on my chest."

"Nick—"

"Hush." He placed a finger over my lips. "I'm not going to ravish you, though the idea certainly has merits. But you're going to be worrying so much about what I'm up to that those other ghosts haunting your eyes won't stand a chance."

I snorted but my heart remembered what it felt like to press my face against Nick's chest. Surely it wouldn't hurt to relax until takeoff. Then we could talk about our strategy for Ponferrada. Gingerly I lowered my head.

His chest was as solid as I recalled. The sense of being safe enveloped me as his arms tightened around me. Without trying to be obvious, I burrowed closer, seeking his body heat. He grunted, adjusting his hold without speaking. His chest rose and fell in a steady rhythm, lulling me to close my eyes.

For this moment I was safe, secure and…loved? The power of the emotion flowed from him, deep and unquenchable but tinged with hurt. Due to me.

I drew in a long breath and released it. As connected as we were, I could open myself and let my emotions touch his, and learn how he really felt about me, about us. But to do so again without his consent would be the betrayal of trust he had spoken of earlier today?

*Yes. The power's not yours to abuse.*

Let's hear it for the voice of reason. I rubbed my cheek against his chest, seeking the sound of his heart. Could a heart that beat so steadily still be mine? I sighed and slid into sleep.

I woke with sleeper's mouth and my ears hurting. I swallowed several times until they popped. We must be losing altitude. I struggled to straighten up but was caught up in a snare of a blanket, arms and seat belt.

"Hold on before you make me a eunuch!" Nick grumbled in my ear, his warm breath feathering the sensitive skin. As my bottom hit his rather too alert male anatomy, I stopped squirming.

He tossed aside the blanket and unfastened the belt. I couldn't get up fast enough. On the other hand, Nick continued to sprawl in the seat. In a rumpled state with an overnight shadow of beard and mussed hair, he looked sexy as hell. Then he gave me a slow smile and patted his lap.

"Why don't you sit down again? I rather enjoyed the way you wiggled."

I gestured toward the lavatory, ready to escape, but then I saw the smug expression in Nick's eyes. He expected me to run. Right.

Although sex with Nick had been…mind-blowing…he had been the one who usually initiated it. And toward the end of the relationship, he'd accused me of running from intimacy.

Was he right? Had my growing connection to him scared me away from even seeking out physical intimacy? One way to find out.

I placed a knee on one side of the seat, appreciating his stunned expression. I then shifted my weight and swung the other knee up to the other side of Nick. I ran my hands along his shoulders, down his arms and then across his chest.

Tension filled the cabin, sexual tension with all its tingling expectation. "Ever have a mile-high, Nick?" I whispered as I pressed my chest against his.

He swallowed. "Not that I can recall."

I sank one inch. "Oh, then would I be your first?"

"First and last." He raised his hands and covered my breasts, sending a shock wave straight to my core.

Damn, I was getting hot.

I sank an inch lower. My thighs might have been screaming, but Nick's glazed expression was worth every agonized muscle. He bucked beneath me and I immediately sat up and slapped his shoulder. "Uh-uh. That's not how this dance is played."

"Dance is it? I would call it torture." He rubbed his thumbs over my nipples, sending another heated rush through me. "But two can play the same game."

I sank lower. "Any bets on who will be the victor?"

He rolled my nipple between his thumb and forefinger. "In this type of game, *chère*, there are no losers."

Maybe not in sex, but in love, yes. However, the sensual haze we had generated wrapped me in its power. One more inch and the anticipation would become reality.

The jet's intercom came on. "Mr. Petter. We'll be landing in Leon in fifteen minutes."

We froze, looking at each other, and then I sighed and raised myself away from temptation. I placed one foot and then the other on the floor, effectively grounding myself.

Nick snagged my wrist. "We're going to finish this soon. Very soon."

"We'll see." I flashed him what I hoped was a devastating, sultry smile over my shoulder and swayed my hips as I headed into the lavatory. Angelina Jolie, eat your heart out. I slid the bolt closed and the light flickered on.

I went to splash water over my face and froze, catching my mirrored reflection. "Ack!"

My hair resembled a Brillo pad, my eyes were ringed like a raccoon's from the mascara that in a moment of vanity I had dabbed on at the Milan hotel, and a splotch at the corner of my mouth resembled...oh my God...dried drool.

I sank back against the wall. Oh, terrific. I, in my first production as the great siren, had been seducing Nick looking like a victim from a horror movie?

"Arrgh!" I grabbed a paper towel and dabbed at the mascara rings.

Where could one hide on a Lear jet about to land?

Somehow I managed to return to my seat and calmly buckle myself in. Nick didn't comment on the change in my appearance, but amusement had replaced the heat in his gaze. Shortly after the smooth landing, Nick, after much grousing about the limited selection in rental cars, procured us an ancient—or classic, according to the rental agent—lime-colored Citroën 2CV, and we headed out west to Ponferrada.

The landscape of the Castilla y León was certainly breathtaking and yet ethereal at the same time: spectacular expanses of ocher plains enclosed by hills crowned with castles. Vineyards punctuated waving grain fields that crisscrossed the fertile land.

"Resources," I said.

"What?" Nick shot me a glance.

"You said in Milan that the courier's access to transportation is as good as ours. That means money. Was van Velsen rich?"

Nick shrugged. "Well paid but not necessarily in the wealthy bracket, unless he was richly rewarded for stealing the virus."

"So who's financing van Velsen and this entire operation?"

"We now have two candidates—the society and your buddy Myrddin's family."

I thought about the Italian society and wondered how

much hating women cost for members to belong. On the other hand, Myrddin seemed to have money to burn. Did we have two players in this scheme to release the virus or only one?

Shut it off, Eve, I told myself, and enjoy the scenery.

We reached Ponferrada and first checked into a hotel that, with its decor and stone walls, mirrored the medieval roots of the town. The helpful clerk gave us directions to Distribución de Estrella Gas along with a handful of tour brochures. Although we were off-season, he assured us that there was plenty to see.

Oh, we had sights to see but not during normal working hours. I wouldn't waste time by first approaching the company's management as I couldn't imagine them owning up to filling canisters with a deadly virus. In fact, if such an operation was going on, most likely it was done after hours when the locals had gone home.

However, Nick and I used the time to conduct "reconnaissance"—his wording—of the town. Although situated by the river Sil, the Knights Templar castle with its standing towers and working drawbridge dominated the town, the Clock Tower and Town Hall indicated the legacy and former prosperity of this town on the sacred Camino pilgrims' route to Santiago de Compostela.

After checking out the area, we settled at a café and chowed down on hearty local dishes of Castilian soup and a pie of sausage, beets and potatoes called empanada Berciana as we watched modern-day pilgrims with their backpacks, sturdy hiking boots, cameras and reverent expressions wander through the piazza.

Nick indicated a young couple. "You know, I envy them. I've always wanted to make the walk but never found the time."

I lowered my spoon. “The Camino de Santiago pilgrimage?”

“Yes.”

“Isn’t that about—”

“A five-hundred mile journey, yes. It begins in the Pyrenees and ends at the cathedral in Santiago.”

I digested this startling piece of information. While Nick wore his Catholicism close to the vest, I knew his religious convictions ran deep. The years as a Swiss Guard in Rome had made him the man he was: steady, calm, dependable and…

*Understanding,* my voice whispered.

I shied away from exploring the disturbing thought at this precise moment and tucked it away for later self-examination.

Nick’s lips quirked as he drank coffee. “Don’t look so astounded. The churches here form the heart of every village and town along the Camino. I thought it would be a good way to enjoy the history and culture of the land.”

But those weren’t the real reasons this man would make the journey, I realized. He would journey for faith.

I leaned across the table and tapped my cup against his. “Here’s to dreams and walking the Camino.”

He acknowledged the toast and polished off his coffee. His phone rang, and as he listened he rose and moved away from the tables. I signaled the waiter for the check. After Nick returned, he tossed a few bills on the table and we crossed the small plaza, heading in the general direction of the gas facility. To make sure we weren’t followed, we silently wound back and forth along side streets.

As the darkness of night enveloped the town, we crouched behind one of the more urban buildings, studying the rear of the gas distribution center. “What was the call about?" I whispered as we watched the last group of workers call out "adiós" as they left. "You were gone so long."

"Hmm, why don't you read my mind?"

Indignation filled me. "I'm not a telepath..." My voice trailed off as I saw the flash of his white teeth in the dark. "You were pulling my leg."

"Yes, I—hey!"

I punched him in the arm, and he bit back an oath.

"Take it easy."

"Don't do that to me."

"Do what? Were you really worried about me when I was on the phone so long?" His voice was low, coaxing.

"Of course I was." I faced the gas plant and wrapped my arms around my middle. "I need you physically fit to break inside."

His warm breath tickled my ear. "Is that the only reason why you were concerned about me?"

I hunched my shoulder against my ear. "Stop. The call."

"That's my Eve. Always focused on the task at hand. My staff traced the logo on the Damassine canister. It's the trademark of the Stelle Consortium."

"*Stelle's* Italian for *star.*" Excitement hummed through me.

"You got it."

"And this place is Star Gas Distribution. And Baleno Nazionale's logo has a star in it."

"Right again. The Consortium's a holding company with the owners hidden behind a mountain of paper trails. My expert's trying to trace them. I gave her the names of this place and the Milan one, and she was able to verify that both list Stelle Consortium as their parent company."

I sat back on my heels. "We have a money connection."

"Possibly, Eve. This could lead us to another blind

trail of corporations. If there are any criminal dealings going on, the owners would have hidden their identities very well, running monies through Swiss and Caribbean banks."

But we were on the right track. I knew it. Dig beneath Stelle Consortium's corporate veil and we would find the person or persons funding the courier. "Nick, look!"

A battered, dark-colored van rattled into the yard and backed up into the delivery area of the plant. The driver exited the van, climbed up the stairs and opened a door, leaving it ajar as he entered the plant. Nick and I took one look at each other and dashed, bent over, across the yard. Quietly we climbed the steps, and Nick held up a hand as he listened by the door. He then gestured that he would enter first. The thin light from the doorway glinted on his gun.

Nick slipped through the opening, and after a deep breath I followed. We were in a dim narrow hallway with several closed doors. We stole along the hall, with Nick testing each door, but all were locked. The passage came to a dead end at a larger hall that ran vertically to the smaller one. Faint sounds came from the left of us. Spotting white suits hanging from pegs on the wall, I placed a hand on Nick's arm and gestured for us to go that direction.

As we crept closer, I saw that a series of laboratories with large observation windows and sealed entrances comprised this wing. At the corner of the first lab, I halted and cautiously peeked inside. Three people clad in white suits worked on a line of canisters. One operated a mechanical arm to inject a substance into each container while the other checked the seals, placed the filled ones on a specially designed cart and replaced them with empty ones.

Craning my neck, I counted the grooves on the cart: twenty-four. But what were the contents? For all we knew it could be a gas used in an industrial process. There was only one way I could know for sure.

I reached out and pressed my palm against the cool glass. Closing my eyes, I unlocked the internal gate on my abilities. At first I felt nothing. Then the glass began to burn my skin and then something insidious began to invade my body. I jerked my hand away clear and opened my eyes.

I gave a thumbs-up to Nick, signaling that I thought the contents were the Spanish flu. He motioned for me to follow him so that he could summon the authorities. I turned, but a flash of movement in the lab caught my eye. I paused and saw a fourth man in a white suit in the corner by the cart. As he bent to check the canisters, I sensed something familiar about his build. The courier.

Although I didn't make any noise, he suddenly looked up and spotted me. He shouted and then ran to the glass door. I leaped up and raced toward Nick.

"Down!" he shouted as he spun and raised his gun. I hit the floor and shots rang out in the hall. "Up!" As I clambered to my feet, Nick grabbed my hand and half dragged me around the corner. Alarms wailed to life and a wooden door exploded into pieces as I passed it. Nick half turned and fired again. "Keep going!"

Even as we raced across the yard, I could hear Nick yelling out orders into his headset. Spotlights lit up the gas plant like the Fourth of July. Men and women in dark uniforms and holding weapons that I couldn't even begin to identify swarmed the yard.

# *Chapter 10*

As soon as we reached the safety of a perimeter of cars and vans, I shook off Nick's arm and planted my fists on my hips.

"Did you forget to tell me something?"

At least Nick had the grace to appear sheepish. "Ah, like I spoke to a few friends at Interpol, who interceded with the Spanish authorities?"

"Yep. That part."

"Oops."

"Oops? That's all you have to say?"

An officer approached us. "Señor Petter? If I could have a word with you. I have a few questions."

Dust wouldn't collect on that man's shoes as fast as Nick moved away from me. In frustration I kicked at a pebble and then moved away from all the milling authorities. It would take some time to sort out everything before we would be allowed back in the building. I

wanted a look at the shipping records to see where those canisters were intended to go.

I found a small, smooth boulder and sat down. From my vantage point I could see the lit face of the Templar castle. Sighing, I rolled the kinks out of my neck and froze. On the road leading to the castle, shadows stirred on the barrel-tiled roof of a house. A figure dangled from the roof's edge and then jumped to the ground.

Evil slithered across my skin. I was only too familiar with this person's vibes.

The courier. How could that be possible? We'd had him trapped!

With disbelief I studied the row of buildings and how low-lying and close together they were. I wouldn't be able to do it without sliding off, but someone who was athletic could possibly travel along the roofs without detection.

Frantically, I searched for Nick but couldn't spot him in the milieu. I took my phone and punched in a text message to him before rising and heading down the road. Passing St. Andrews Church, I ran across the street and up the steps to the broad path that curved along an incline to the Templar castle. I crossed under the double semicircular arch to find myself confronted by a vast courtyard. While the facade had been bathed in colored spotlights, here the only light was cast by the half-moon.

A sound startled me but when I glanced up, I only saw the turret flags flapping in the wind. I stood close to the wall, hugging the shadows, as my eyes grew accustomed to the dim light. While I had a flashlight, the last thing I wanted to be was a moving target. I also didn't want to break my neck over some medieval ruins.

But the courier was here. He had wanted me to follow. I knew that with as much certainty as I knew I had to stop him.

I heard the scuff of a sole on stone and then the rattle of pebbles. Was I the hunter or the hunted? It didn't matter. Pressing against the stone wall for guidance, I moved around the corner and stubbed my toe on a step. Before me was the stairway up the tower. I felt pressure pushing at me to go up the stairs, as if someone was willing me.

Oh, no, you don't, I thought. Not that way. I wasn't about to be trapped like a rabbit in a hole. I continued along the walkway. Had Nick received my message? Was he on his way? Coming to a lookout slot that many of the Knights Templar must have used, I peeked through it. No pedestrian traffic stirred on the street below.

In its heyday centuries ago, the castle had served to protect the Camino de Santiago pilgrims and those fleeing the bloody battlefields of southern France during the Crusades. Now it stood only as an empty sentinel to the past. Would the evil that now prowled inside it awaken any spirits who still lingered here?

If so, I could only hope they would see me as a pilgrim needing safe harbor.

When the hair on my nape lifted, I hurried along the path. The courier was near. Now that we were engaged in a cat-and-mouse game, how exactly did I think I was going to catch this guy?

My fingers hit a dip in the wall. I traced out what felt like a flattened *M* carved into the stone. Cautiously, I peered into the darkness and saw that it was an alcove with a stone bench, most likely put there for tourists to rest.

Dizziness seized me. No, not now. Not with a killer on the prowl. I fought the spell, digging my fingers into my palm, willing the pain to keep me in the present.

The alcove began to glow with light and I watched two women in medieval dress huddle together, glancing over their shoulders as if they did not want to be overheard. A third woman emerged from behind a stone pillar that I hadn't realized was there, it blended so well with the wall. From beneath her gown she removed a jagged tile. When she rubbed her hand across it, the tile began to pulse with energy, its low hum resonating with me.

A sound drew their attention, and the three women vanished....

A snap drew me out of my reverie. Without thinking, I slipped inside the alcove and hid behind the ruins of the pillar. On the ground I spotted a rock and picked it up. I didn't relish being close enough to the courier to use it, but the rock would have to do as a weapon. I also scooped up a few pebbles.

"Ee-eeve."

I hadn't expected the courier's voice to be rich and cultured, but then again if the devil had an unpleasant voice, he wouldn't get any takers, would he? From the accent, I placed him as Italian. I pressed closer to the pillar.

"Dr. Eve St. Giles." My name was a soft hiss on the night air. "Important name for such a bitch. Your curiosity is going to be the death of you. I will see to that, but your death will be slow. A study in agony. Since you are so anxious to find the source of the virus, I shall be happy to introduce you to it."

Polite bastard, but I wouldn't take him up on the invite.

"Eve. What an appropriate name. Tell me, how many have you caused to fall from paradise?" From the way his tone grew edgier, I could tell that his excitement was growing to a fever pitch. "Have you played your siren's song of seduction on a violin and lured that Swiss hero to sin? You must be punished for your transgressions."

Out of the corner of my eye I saw mist coalesce, and the third woman I had seen in my vision reappeared. She placed a finger across her lips. Oh, sure, I'd planned on yelling out "I'm here" but I nodded. After all, the old gal was only trying to help.

A crunch of loose gravel sounded right outside the alcove. The mist grew denser, darker like a shroud. I held my breath. When I next heard the courier speak, he was farther away. I released a sigh and the mist dissipated. Although I was sure they didn't have the two-finger salute of thanks in the thirteenth century, I gave it anyway.

As I stole outside I could have sworn I heard a woman's voice whisper, "Marians always help Marians."

In the dim moonlight I saw the courier searching among the foundation ruins. I crept closer. Fortunately, the jerk was yakking so loudly the noise covered my approach.

"We're going to purify the world, you know. Rid it of women and start anew."

With what? Had the women-hating society found a new way to reproduce?

"Before the end of the week thousands more will join you in death. Within months there will be a pandemic of biblical proportions."

The courier broke off his taunt to curse in Italian. The situational dynamics had changed, but why I didn't know. I gripped the stone tighter.

"Eve, are you here?" *Nick.*

In a crouch the man moved past my hiding place. As he raised his gun, I leaped up and swung. His hunting instincts must have sensed my presence for he threw himself sideways. My blow glanced off his shoulder, but he dropped his gun as he fought for his balance. He swore and righted himself.

The sound of someone running along the walkway told me Nick was on the way. The courier heard his approach, as well, and lashed out sideways with his foot. Although I avoided the kick, the rocky surface I was standing on crumbled, sending me falling backward into a shallow pit.

"Oomph!" Although dawn was breaking, I saw my share of stars.

"Eve!" Nick's face loomed over mine. "Are you hurt?"

"No." I braced my hands on the ground and pushed up with an assist by Nick. "Just got the wind knocked out of me." I blew a dangling curl out of my eyes. "Where is he?"

"He took off the moment you fell."

"Gotta get him." I twisted onto my knees. Nick cupped my elbow and I scrambled to my feet.

"We'll get him. I got a good look at his face. We'll get his description out to all the authorities."

Bees buzzed in my ears but I shook off the sensation. "How many cylinders did they recover in that room?"

Nick frowned. "They were just securing the room when I realized you were gone. Let's get you out of here and I'll call the officer in charge." Nick's way of helping me was a hand on my butt as I climbed the slight incline.

When we were at the top he seized my shoulders and lowered his head so he was face-to-face with me. His steel-blue eyes blazed.

"Don't you ever, ever pull that stunt again!"

I didn't feign ignorance. Never had I seen him so mad. "I had to act." I folded my arms and adopted an injured attitude. "You were busy playing security and were nowhere to be found. What was I supposed to do? Let the bad guy get away?"

"Next time, yes!" Then Nick seized and held me close. "God, Eve, yes. You added a hundred years to my life when I got your message."

I allowed myself a moment to press my cheek against his chest and inhale his all-male scent. I took in his relief that I was safe and that he'd used anger to work off his anxiety, and I smiled.

Pulling away, I stroked his face. "I'm fine, Nick. Really. But I need to know how many canisters were recovered. The courier spoke of other attacks."

Releasing me, Nick dug out his phone and made the call. He told the officer to hold on. "They recovered twenty-one."

The buzzing increased in my ears. "Nick, there were twenty-four canisters in that room. I counted them. Three are missing."

Nick relayed the information to the officer and switched off. "They're doing a street-by-street sweep. They only captured one worker in bio gear and a janitor who walked into the fray, so at least one man other than our courier got away. The building not only had a ladder leading to the roof but also a basement with access to a side yard."

I shuddered. How many canisters filled with Spanish flu were out there? "Is the captured worker talking?"

"No, but apparently the janitor, a local, is. He was told not to report to work tonight, but he had left a pouch of his favorite tobacco in his locker. This shutdown of the facility to the local workers has only happened once before. The workers complained about the down time and lost wages. Each time, a team of outsiders would come in for the night, mess up the work areas and equipment, and then everything would have to be decontaminated. Made everyone here nervous."

"Assuming the plant was closed to fill the canisters with Spanish flu, hopefully we're not facing hundreds of them unaccounted for."

"Unless this facility is only one of many owned by the Stelle Consortium," Nick grimly said.

"I can't deal with the forest right now, Nick, I need to deal with what trees I can see." I needed the finite, which I could break down into manageable steps of action to take.

"Come on. You're exhausted. Let's go back to the hotel and get packed up."

I ran my fingers through my hair in frustration. "I had the courier."

"And you'll have him again. The authorities have set up roadblocks and a perimeter around this town. We're not going to be doing anyone any good if we break our necks stumbling about in the dark. Dawn's in a few hours and we can resume the hunt then. In the meantime we can get a little shut-eye."

It made sense, so we went back to the hotel. "Go ahead and stretch out on the bed," Nick suggested. "I'll wake you if there's any problem."

Promising myself only a catnap, I lay down on the bed and closed my eyes. The courier's words whirled in my head along with the sound of a woman's voice until an image formed....

*Pain filled the healer's heart: pain for what they must do and pain for the end of a way of life. The fates had decreed it wasn't enough that the priestesses had been driven underground to do their work. Now they must destroy all traces of their existence and scatter to the winds.*

*For countless generations the mosaic of the Lady had been the center of their order. Now, to save her, they must dismantle her. Deep inside the temple, no one talked as they used knives, sticks and even spoons to break apart the tiles.*

*Once a priestess secured her share of the sacred tiles, she went her way. The healer had already bade farewell and safe journey to several friends who bore their precious cargo along the Camino de Santiago.*

*Her hands, normally used for healing, now were cut and scraped from the arduous work of tearing up the mosaic. Wiping sweating from her forehead, she frowned. The circle was only half destroyed. They had so much to do yet.*

*When someone touched her shoulder, she glanced around. Alinor. Her friend was to carry the greatest burden of them all. Rising, the healer hugged her, wishing with all her heart and power that Alinor reached safety in her journey north. After the other woman left, the healer resumed her task, for tonight she had to send off her own precious cargo.*

*The end was near. Evil was all around them. She could not fail.*

*With sadness and regret, she studied the mosaic. Even though only the half profile of the Lady remained, the sword on her hip glittered in the lamplight, a reminder of the power the mosaic once had. With a last effort, the healer tore loose her assigned tiles.*

*Turning, she left the chamber without a last look. They all must do what had to be done.*

"Eve!"

I jerked upright. I was in the hotel room, not the…where had my vision taken me? Some underground chamber?

Nick snapped his fingers in front of my face. "Wake up, *chère*. The courier just ran a blockade."

"Where?" I bounded off the bed and went for my bag.

"At a highway access that goes to León."

"They have a description of his car?"

"Even better." Nick already had his gear in hand. "They got a few shots off and believe they hit a tire. He disappeared off the highway, probably to change the tire. That will slow him down."

León. Why go west rather than north or east toward all the port cities?

Although we were out the door and the hotel in the space of a few minutes, Nick's phone rang as we reached where the Citroën was parked. He answered and from the way his mouth tightened, I could tell it wasn't good news.

He tucked away his phone. "They found the courier's car abandoned. He apparently carjacked another, so he could be heading anywhere now."

"East, back to the León airport."

"How can you be positive the courier's going to head there now that he's been spotted?"

"I don't know, but I do know what his ultimate destination is. Barcelona. He's got at least one cylinder of virus he's just dying to release, no pun intended."

"Why Barcelona, Eve?" Nick asked quietly. "That list we found in Milan had any number of events on it. Did you connect with him in the castle?"

"Yes, but not in the sense you mean. During his ranting about how he was going to kill me, he gave me a clue. He asked me if I had lured you to sin by playing my siren's song of seduction on a violin."

"Music. Barcelona's hosting a women's musical festival this week according to that schedule."

"Exactly."

"I'll call the information in and order the jet to be ready."

Nick opened the passenger door to the Citroën, but as I moved past him, he pressed a kiss to my cheek. I shot him a startled look. "What was that for?"

"Next time we run into our elusive courier, I'm going to tell him that you have indeed played your siren's song for me."

I swallowed. "Oh?"

"And if heaven on earth exists, then it existed every time I was in your arms."

He gave me a nudge and I slid, boneless, inside the car. As my whirling thoughts tried to assimilate what had happened, on automatic I fastened my seat belt.

Nick turned the key and the Citroën's engine roared to life. He flashed me a wicked smile before he guided the car into the narrow lane.

"By the way, anytime you want to sing that particular song, I'm more than willing to listen to it."

"And anytime you want to follow the Camino de Santiago pilgrimage, I would love to do it with you," I said quietly.

Reaching over to grip my hand, he brought my hand up to kiss the back of it. "I'd like that, Eve."

As we passed the Templar castle, I tried to ignore the flutter in my stomach his tender gesture had produced. Last night the past and present had melded together in the shadows of the castle.

What I hadn't explained to Nick was my growing conviction that I would be able to sense the courier's presence even in a crowd. It was as if his emotions had left their brand deep inside me.

How about that for woo-woo?

# *Chapter 11*

Van Velsen and the courier weren't the only ones who knew how to pull a vanishing act.

Also on the missing-in-action list was my friend Scarlet. After we landed in Barcelona and checked into a hotel, I tried to reach her but without success, so I left an urgent message on her answering machine.

I really, really needed to speak with her. No one knew more about the arcane and paranormal than Scarlet. She probably would have a ready explanation of why I was having visions and would know the precise name for those energy lines I kept seeing. The dots were there, just waiting to be connected.

But even more than discussing all the strange things that had been occurring, I really wanted to curl up and have a cozy chat with Scarlet about Nick. Sometimes a woman just needed her girlfriend to listen to her heart's uncertainties.

Putting aside my worry about Scarlet's whereabouts, I next checked in with my niece and nephew followed by a call to my parents. Even speaking with Maman didn't soothe me, leaving me with too much to think about.

My personal calls finished, I contacted the Centre. After getting an update, I rose from where I sat on the bed and went to the window. Feeling exhausted, I studied the bustling streets around the hotel.

"What's wrong?" Nick asked, looking up from his equipment bag. "You look troubled." Given the events of the past few days, I hadn't even tried to protest our sharing a room. If truth be known, I was happy to have his solid presence near me.

I rubbed my temples, trying to ease the throbbing tension. "We've been monitoring local health reports across Europe. Barcelona's reporting a spike in colds and other ailments."

"Any signs of the flu?"

"No, but…" I shrugged. "In the days leading up to the outbreak at Damassine, we've discovered that there had been a sharp increase in people being sick."

"What's the connection?"

"I don't know. But it's a variable that we can't afford to ignore at this point."

"You look tired, Eve. Why don't you get some sleep?"

"Can't. Give me a second and then we can go."

I slipped inside the bathroom and shut the door. Leaning against it, I closed my eyes and sucked in a deep breath. Nick's offer was so-o-o tempting. To hide away for a few hours. To sleep without dreams.

For as fatigued as I was, it would be difficult to maintain any emotional equilibrium in crowds. Yet what alternative did I have?

While Nick's team investigated the elusive owners of Stelle Consortium, the authorities were tracking down anyone connected with the gas facility, but…

The courier was here in Barcelona, whether walking along the tree-lined La Rambla or driving the Port Olímpic coastal road. He was ready to release another canister. Catch him and he could lead us to the others involved.

I flung open the door and strode into the bedroom. "Ready?"

However, minutes later, as we strolled along the La Rambla in the general direction of the harbor, I kept thinking about my conversation with Maman.

"Nick."

"Hmm?" Nick sounded distracted. There certainly was enough diversion for anyone. On this crisp winter day, a full array of buskers, from jugglers to living statues, were out to entertain. He stopped to watch a mime perform. Laughing at the performance, he tossed a euro note into the mime's hat. I waited until we moved along with the milling crowd.

I'd planned to talk about the case, to ask if he'd heard anything more about Stelle Consortium. But I saw a group of children laughing and shrieking at the antics of a puppeteer. One young girl chasing pigeons had bouncing dark curls exactly like my niece, Laurel's. Longing gripped me.

"Do you think I could be a good mother?"

Nick reached for my hand and lifting it, kissed my fingers. "I think you would be a wonderful mother."

He tucked my hand into the curve of his arm and continued walking. If only I could accept myself in such a role as easily as apparently those close to me could.

I blew out a breath to steady myself. "I spoke to my

parents. They'll be flying to France as soon as Yvette's body is released."

"When is your sister's service?"

"Next week. The children are at the château."

"Who's going to be their guardian?"

Hearing the question my parents had voiced didn't help my uncertainty any.

"Yvette's solicitor will be at the funeral to discuss the terms of her will with the family afterward."

"Did Yvette's husband, Jean-Pierre, have any brothers or sisters?"

"No."

"Then she's probably named you."

"How do you know that? Have you been talking to Maman again?"

"No, but you are the obvious choice and you did ask me about motherhood."

Of course I had. I couldn't seem to focus.

"Would you do it? The kids love you."

I frowned at the scene before me. People laughing, talking. Couples, like us, walking hand in hand and kissing. Children playing. By tonight this could all change. Tonight all could be sick with the flu. For all the Phillipes and Laurels, I needed to catch a monster.

"Eve?"

"Every day I work with dangerous substances."

"So do a lot of women at the Centre and they manage to have families."

"I'm in the field all the time, they're not."

"Granted, that part of your job certainly would have to change. Now more than ever the children are going to need you. Frederic would have to find a new flu hunter."

"But—"

"You love the chase. Yes, I'm all too familiar with

that side of your personality." With his free hand, he reached up and tucked a wayward curl behind my ear.

"And you're saying you don't?"

Nick shrugged. "Actually, that's about to change. I'm going to scale back to the management end."

Incredulous, I halted. "You, a desk jockey? I don't believe it."

A dull flush spread across Nick's cheeks. "It's not the years, it's all the hard knocks."

His leg. I'd noticed how more pronounced his limp was since Ponferrada. "I'm sorry."

"Don't be. I find I like being the general, marshaling all the resources. The good part is that I can operate from anywhere, whether it be Vienna, Stockholm—" he shot me a look "—or the States. Today's technology allows me mobility. I'm even looking to buy a house."

A major step for a man. Obviously, Nick was starting to set down roots. Next up, the little wife and family, but would he want a ready-made one, or his own?

"Enough about me. We were discussing your situation. Your giving up the field work doesn't mean you won't make a difference."

I stared at the busy street. "There are so many lives to save."

"And you will continue to save them, Eve. In addition you'll be enriching your own with two very special children."

I let the idea settle, take root. After glancing at my watch, I gestured at a bench. "Do you mind if I make a call?"

"Not at all." He meandered over to listen to a woman cellist.

When I called my parents' number again, I wasn't sure that it was good fortune that my mother answered.

"*Chère*. How are you doing? You sounded so shaken an hour ago when I asked if you would consider taking on Laurel and Phillipe."

"Well, Maman, that was quite a bombshell you dropped on me."

"Two small children are not a bombshell, Eve. If they were, I would have expired years ago."

My lips twitched. "Yvette and I were quite a handful, huh?"

"It is always a challenge to watch two different personalities emerge and then help them to find their own path."

"We were night and day."

"Oh, I wouldn't say that. You were more alike than either of you ever realized. But your fabric was stronger than Yvette's."

I didn't buy that. "Right. Yvette had it really rough with her looks."

"Beauty doesn't buy happiness, *bébé*. As I pointed out to you before, you have always been beautiful in your own unique way."

"You're my mother. Of course you think I'm gorgeous."

"Gorgeous, *non*. Beautiful, *oui*. As you will discover on your new journey, a mother's eyes, while filled with love, also see with clarity."

I sucked air.

"You have decided to be a mother to Phillipe and Laurel, yes? They need you, Eve. Both sets of grandparents are too old for such exuberant spirits."

"You think I can do this?"

"But of course. For someone who has seen such horrors, you have remained a warm, caring woman.

Being their mother will mean sacrifice, yes, but the rewards are endless."

"That's what Nick said."

"Wise man, your Nick."

"He's not mine, Maman."

"Then why are you talking to me, *bébé?* Go get him and bring to justice that bastard who murdered my Yvette and all those other people."

Click.

I tucked away my phone and Nick came to sit next to me on the bench. "How's your mother?"

"Direct and to the point as always. In fact she shared your sentiments about sacrifice…"

I straightened.

"Eve, what's wrong?"

"Sacrifice. That Myrddin character spoke of sacrifice and forgiveness. When he spoke of his family, he said 'they' didn't understand the consequences."

"And we concluded from your conversation that Myrddin's family might be linked to the development of this particular strain of flu but may not be behind the actual outbreak."

"What if Myrddin is wrong? What if someone in his family *is* linked to the Society of Men for Men? What if the family is Stelle Consortium?"

"We've run that photograph I took through Interpol's data banks, but he doesn't have a criminal record."

I shook my head. "I don't think the photo's going to help. I'm positive that he was wearing contact lenses, and he could have changed his appearance in other ways."

"I thought of that. My team has used the computer to alter the photo and run the versions through other sources, but those searches take longer."

Nick gave me a lopsided smile. "Next time you meet the mysterious Myrddin, try to get his fingerprints." He rose and extended his hand.

I accepted his assist up. "My secret-agent training is sadly lacking. How do you suggest I get his prints?"

"Give him your phone to call his family?"

"Right. What makes you so sure that he'll contact me again?"

"If he wants to stop the outbreaks as much as he professes, he'll make another appearance. After all, we're breathing down the courier's neck."

"We're hardly breathing at the moment."

"The first concert at the Palua doesn't begin until ten tonight. That hall is the most logical target."

The Palua de la Música Catalana was Barcelona's stunning music palace where many of the women's festival performances were scheduled. With its glorious inverted stained-glass skylight depicting angelic choristers…female angels…and the stage's backdrop of the *Muses of the Semicircle,* the authorities felt that the hall jammed to capacity with concertgoers would be the perfect target for a madman. Logical deduction but…

"I'm not as sure as everyone else is that the hall is the target." I glanced at my watch. "How are we going to kill time until then?"

Nick grinned. "Do what the locals do and engage in a little siesta? You could try singing that siren's song for me."

That was more than a little tempting. To lose myself in a few heated moments with Nick to keep at bay those dreams of another place and time. However…

To trap a mysterious man who spoke of ancient women, one must go to ancient places.

"I've a better idea. To pass the time, how about visiting Montserrat?"

"*Chère.*" Nick drew me close and kissed me. "You really know the way to a former Swiss Guard's heart, but given the hour, I'll settle for a visit to the cathedral. However, at the first opportune moment we need to finish that little lap dance you performed on the jet."

My cheeks heated at recalling my impromptu lap dance. "You're such a romantic, Nick." I turned to head toward the hotel where the rental car was parked.

"Eve."

Nick's serious tone stopped me. I looked up and he framed my face with his hands. "Romance, is that what you're needing? I realized I never gave you much of the tender moments. Mainly fire."

I lifted on my tiptoes to press a kiss against the dimple in his chin. "I never had complaints."

"But still you ran." His voice was raw.

"You wanted what I couldn't give you. And I was giving more than you needed."

"That's not true, Eve." He wrapped an arm around my waist and swept me close. I glanced around, but no one appeared to be taking any notice. Lovers making out or quarreling apparently was a common occurrence along this boulevard.

"We both have a job to do, Eve. But when this is over, I will show you precisely what I wanted between us." His kiss was hot, all encompassing, as if I was being absorbed alive. It demanded a response beyond physical; it demanded my heart.

Desire ripened in me, letting me match the heat of his kiss. Oh, yes. I could gobble him up, no question about it, but could I open more than my heart to him?

Through the sensuous haze Nick was creating with

his very clever mouth, I felt my skin prickle at the nape of my neck.

"Nick."

"Hmm." His tongue flicked the corner of my mouth.

"Someone's watching us."

Nick stiffened. Breaking contact and lifting his head only slightly, he surveyed the crowd over my head. "I don't see the courier."

"Not him. I think it's the elusive Myrddin."

"Okay." Nick stepped away and linked fingers with mine. "Let's continue strolling and see if he steps out into the open."

I walked beside him, but with all the pedestrian traffic, kiosks and cafés, anyone tailing us would have had ample cover. After all, La Rambla was like an open-air theater where everyone was the actor, meant to see and be seen.

My sense of the watcher was fuzzy, like poor television reception. Too many people, the confluence of their emotions acting as white noise. As we continued down the center walkway, I couldn't even swear the watcher was Myrddin.

Reaching an intersection, we turned down a street leading to the cathedral. We reached the large square dominated by the somber gothic church and its central spire. The imposing buildings cast a deep pall across the piazza.

No, not shade. More like a black light emanating from the ground. Stunned, I halted, reluctant to take one more step. Pedestrian barriers stood ready for an evening concert by an all-female string quartet. A worker on a ladder strung lights on poles.

However, I didn't see any slashing lines like the ones I had experienced when I had landed in Damassine. It was more like the swirling haze in a nightclub, except there was no smoke. Was this a prelude to another psychic experience?

"Eve, are you all right?"

I shook off the wisps of dizziness that were beginning to grip me. "I'm fine. Let's go inside."

Avoiding the flock of geese that considered the front of the church their rightful domain, we entered the nave.

In the hushed silence, Nick indicated that he was going up to the main altar. Respecting his privacy, I lingered at the back of the immense chamber. Not wanting to intrude on those locals there to pray, I took a seat and studied the vaulted ceilings and handcrafted woodwork.

"You do not light a candle or pray?" A man whispered from behind me. "Your spirit does not require healing?"

"I've never found reflection to be helpful, Myrddin," I said, twisting around. "I much prefer action."

He smiled. Other than his drawn, frail appearance, he looked the same with dark, understated yet expensive clothes. The guy might be on the lam but he did it with style. Once more the sense of recognition tugged at me.

"So, tell me, what connection does your *family* have to Stelle Consortium?"

"Ah, Mr. Petter has been busy."

"Why all the subterfuge, Myrddin? If you want to stop this, why didn't you tell me about Stelle Consortium from the start? Why have you doled out one company at a time when you knew that all were owned by your family?"

"It is true, the consortium is one of our holdings." He shook his head. "It is…a complex situation. As not all the family members are involved, I can not risk bringing down the entire empire."

"What if you're wrong? What if several of your relatives belong to this society that calls itself 'Men for Men' and are deliberately exterminating women?"

His mouth tightened. "I do not think that's possible. My son fears only a certain group of women, one grandson is married and the other has found a woman who appears to be redeeming him."

"What group does your son fear?" I pounced on the first concrete information that Myrddin had yielded about his family.

"The same group I, as generations before me, feared and hated."

I slipped my hand into my pocket. "You?"

"Yes, before I saw—" he tilted his face toward a stained glass window "—the light, I sought out these women to eliminate their threat to the family."

"How are they a threat?"

"The family is a slave to their legacy of fear. It is afraid of being returned to the state it once held. The priestesses and their descendants hold a key that must be found."

"What key?"

"A key to great power, beyond our comprehension."

The mosaic I saw being destroyed in my dream? Was that the connection? How could a mosaic of tiles be a threat to anyone? Then I remembered the vision I'd had at the castle in Ponferrada. The three women pilgrims had held tiles—tiles that seemed to be energized. If all the tiles were joined, would they have the power Myrddin spoke of?

"What does this ancient history have to do with recreating the Spanish flu?"

"Ever heard of the Black Death, Dr. St. Giles?"

"Please. The bubonic plague is Epidemiology 101."

"Yes, of course. But did your course include the impact of ley lines on the plague?"

I shook my head, trying to make sense of this turn in the conversation. "Ley lines? Energy pulses that run below the earth surfaces, what do they have to do with the plague?"

"Ancient wisdom advises us that the ley lines can impact negatively on people's health. Imagine what sustained levels of heightened activity can do to a person's immunity system."

My mind reeled. Those light grids I'd been seeing. Were those ley lines? Were they also magnifying my psychic powers? But if so, why now?

"You're saying the ley lines can lower it, making people more susceptible to viruses?"

"Tell me, Dr. St. Giles. How have you been feeling since your arrival in the lovely city of Barcelona?"

I had been feeling ragged, but what else was new? "I've been going twenty-four/seven."

"Of course you have. But I doubt if all the citizens and visitors have."

"Do you mean that the ley lines are being manipulated to affect people's immune systems?"

"Yes. Damassine was subjected to bursts of negative energy before the flu was released."

"That's…an incredible story."

"Eve, the family has known how to use the lines for centuries. Why do you think the bubonic plague was so widespread?"

A powerful family had controlled the health of countries for centuries? How could that be possible?

"If you're so convinced that your grandsons don't know what's going on with Stelle Consortium, why don't you call them?"

I tossed him my phone and in an automatic reflex gesture he caught it. "It is not so easy," he said as he held out the phone to me. Carefully, I took it by the edges and returned it to my pocket.

"Why isn't it simple?"

"As you know all too well, Eve, family matters are always complicated. The innocent can be hurt."

A tourist snapping a picture bumped into me, and I had to reach out to keep the woman from stumbling. "Beg your pardon," she stammered.

"That's all right. No damage done."

But I knew before even turning around that Myrddin was gone. I rose and rushed to the front where Nick knelt. "Myrddin was here."

He stood, looking around. "Where?"

"At the back. He's long gone now."

Nick opened his mouth, then realizing where he was, snapped it shut.

"Do you have a plastic bag?" I asked.

"Why?"

"I did what you suggested. I gave him my phone and asked him to call home."

He grinned. "Have I told you recently how crazy I am about you?"

"No."

He put his hand in the small of my back and guided me through the crowded aisle. "No? Then for starters let me say I love your devious mind."

We emerged outside, and a wave of faintness struck me. I stumbled against Nick. "*Chère*, are you ill?"

"I feel light-headed." I stared at the square with twilight descending and…something else.

*Here.*

I studied the square but saw only tourists snapping

their cameras, children chasing pigeons while parents talked and lovers walked arm in arm.

*Here,* my inner voice insisted.

"Nick." I gripped his arm. "The virus is going to be released here, tonight."

He frowned. "Are you sure? Inside the music hall would be more effective."

"Being sprayed from above *and* outdoors didn't make it any less effective in Damassine."

"Point taken. I guess you and I will be listening to a string quartet tonight."

He believed me without questioning my rationale. Shaken, I kissed him. "Thanks, Nick."

He wrapped his arm around my shoulders. "I know the real reason why you would rather be here tonight rather than the fancy event at the Palua."

"Why?" I continued to study the plaza's layout, wondering where the cylinder could be hidden.

"You were looking for an excuse not to wear a dress."

Caught off guard, I burst into laughter. "You got me, Nick Petter."

"Not yet, but I will."

I stopped laughing.

# Chapter 12

That night by the time we returned to the square, people filled the chairs. Teenagers hung out together, flirting. Fascinated, I watched one girl blow a large bubble with her chewing gum before popping it.

"There're a lot of hiding places," Nick commented, his gaze hard as he scanned the area.

I watched a canopy ripple in the evening breeze. "Near-perfect weather conditions for him. Not a strong wind. All the buildings will act as a container for the virus. This phase of the experimental outbreak could be used to test how far the flu will spread from a small infected group."

"If he's here, will he want to spray the contents or simply release them?"

"He sprayed before so he could opt to release, again as another testing phase."

"Then he may have the cylinder rigged with a timer."

"Terrific," I muttered as I noted all the adjacent

kiosks with vendors pitching their products. Where would the courier position the container? "Nick, this plaza's too large. We need to split up."

"No."

"Nick, be rational. The courier's going to strike here tonight. We have to stop him. We can cover more ground separately."

He rubbed his head. "I was afraid you'd be stubborn." He drew me to the side and, after rummaging in his bag, brought out a discreet communication headset. He fitted the ear hook on me and handed me the miniature radio with a push-to-talk switch and palm microphone combination.

"I want you to be in contact with me at all times," he ordered as he adjusted his own set.

I rolled my eyes. "Yes, sir!"

He gripped my upper arms. "Eve, attitude can get you killed. We're dealing with a madman."

Instantly I sobered. "No one knows that better than me, Nick."

"Just don't take foolish risks, *chère*." he drew me close and brushed a kiss against my forehead. "I'll be only a few steps away."

"See you around the plaza."

We moved apart and I headed in the direction of the cathedral. At this time of night the ornate front offered many shadowy crevices. Strings of lights ran between several poles, giving the performance area a festive air. Tables at a sidewalk café offered further cover.

I almost collided with two well-dressed men arguing as they exited a building followed at a short distance by another group of men.

"Excuse me," I apologized. Astonishment filled me as I recognized the younger man. "It's Caleb Adriano, isn't it?"

Something flickered across his face before he gave me a polite smile. "Dr. St. Giles. What are you doing in Barcelona?"

"I could ask the same thing, but I'm here on business." I glanced with curiosity at the man beside Caleb, who remembered his manners.

"Doctor, may I present my father, Simon Adriano." Although he was a striking-looking man in his own right, there was something familiar about him.

Wanting to connect with him, I held out my hand, but the older man followed the European way and barely took my fingers to air kiss the back of my hand. "A pleasure." He immediately released his hold.

"Likewise." I wasn't eager to linger over social conventions, either. I wanted to connect with my friend. "Is Scarlet with you? I've been trying to reach her."

Simon's mouth tightened, and Caleb cast a veiled glance at his father as if he was leery of the man's reaction. Uh-oh. Didn't Dad approve of Scarlet? Didn't matter if I'd stepped into a family can of worms. I needed to find Scarlet.

"Caleb?"

"I haven't heard from her." He gave a casual shrug. "You know how she is when she's on an assignment."

Something didn't ring true, but Caleb was clearly uncomfortable speaking about Scarlet in front of his father. Unease was rolling like storm waves off him. Simon made a pointed move of looking at his watch.

"*Scusi,* Doctor. My father and I have an appointment."

"Of course."

The two men walked away and then Caleb turned. "Eve? If you speak with Scarlet, please tell her that I miss her."

The request sounded off balance, stilted. I stuck my

hands in the pockets of my pants and gave him a bright smile. “Sure.”

Only after I had a heart-to-heart with her about his family. This was the second time I’d gotten strange vibrations from the lot.

Caleb’s request didn’t sit well with his father. I could tell from the heated conversation, that Simon was chewing him out over that *donna,* or woman. Since our only contact had been a kiss to the fingertips, presumably Dad was venting about Scarlet, not me.

Kind of surprising. Normally Scarlet could charm the socks off any man. Maybe Caleb was getting serious about her, and his father had different marriage plans for his son. Made sense.

A chill raced along my spine, warning me evil was near. I spun, scanning the crowd.

Four women dressed in black and carrying instruments walked out to the chairs in the performance area. The audience applauded as the women sat and played a few warm-up notes.

I didn’t have much time. If the courier or one of his cohorts was going to release the flu, it would be during the early phases to ensure contamination. Although Nick believed the canister would be rigged with a timer, I knew the courier well enough now. He would want to be present for the great event that had been orchestrated.

Then one of the teenagers started jumping and spinning to an internal hip-hop rhythm in stark contrast to the classic music that began to soar over the plaza. Several of the teenagers laughed, despite an old man reprimanding them. As the group shifted, I saw the man in black standing behind them. The glow of the streetlight gleamed on his shaved skull. He looked up as if admiring the heavens.

"Nick, nine o'clock to the stage. He's here."

"Stay put. I'm on my way."

Like hell.

Weaving through the crowd of pedestrians who lingered to listen, I made my way toward the teenagers. A tourist with a video camera stepped in my path, blocking my view. "Excuse me." I almost bowled him over as I pushed past.

He cursed loudly in German before being shushed by others. However, the disturbance was enough. The courier spotted me. His teeth flashed as he lifted his arm and tapped the watch on his wrist.

*Too late.*

Then he simply melted from sight into the crowd.

"No!" I broke into a run until I reached the spot where he had been standing. Frantically, I looked up as I had seen him doing. No, not toward the church's steeple. His neck hadn't been craned that much. Lower, more toward the stage.

My gaze grazed the top of the light poles and then snapped back to the one to my left. Earlier today a man on a ladder had been stringing the lights. As the pole swayed slightly light glinted off metal. The cylinder.

*Too late.*

I heard a girl giggle next to me and I spun around. It was the pretty teenager who had blown the amazing bubble gum bubble earlier. From the way her jaw worked, she was working on another grand production.

I held out my hand. "Spit!"

I must have sounded like her mother. Too startled to check her reaction, she spat the soggy pink wad into my palm. Nick materialized beside me. "Where is it?"

"There." I raced to the pole with Nick beside me. "Lift me!"

He formed a bridge with his hands, and I placed my foot on them. He lifted and I reached out for the cylinder but was six inches short.

"Higher!"

A uniformed police officer came running up, shooting off questions in Spanish with Nick grunting out answers.

"Nick, higher!"

Apparently the officer grasped the gravity of the situation and joined Nick in the lifting effort. I shot up and grabbed the top of the pole. The canister was secured so that the nozzle pointed toward the stage. Attached to the head was a timer. Despite the noise of the crowd that was switching its attention from the quartet to us, I could hear the faint ticking.

Then a click.

I reached out and jammed the gum over the nozzle. The can shuddered, whether from a breeze or from the activation, I couldn't say. I reached out with my senses, physical and otherwise.

Silence.

I could feel the pressure inside the canister but no hissing. The gum had worked as a sealant. I dissolved in relief.

Nick never stood a chance. An hour later the moment he closed the hotel door, I was on him, fusing my mouth to his. All the adrenaline and tension from the past few days that had been bottled up in me like the propellant gas in the cylinders had to go somewhere. Sex was the preferred method of release.

An escape from the mind, from the emotions. The pure thrill of the physical connection with a man.

*This* man. Whatever craziness was going outside our

hotel room, here in my arms was a man who was solid, steady. Tonight I needed Nick.

The force of throwing myself at him drove us against the wall. Reality disconnected as my tongue tangled with his and I rediscovered how good Nick tasted. I wanted to devour him like a candy bar. I rubbed my body against his, drawing a loud groan from him. With a slow, powerful rhythm he moved the bulge of his erection against my stomach. Pleasure speared through me.

I couldn't wait. To hell with extended foreplay. I needed him in me. Now.

With the warm male scent of his body filling my nostrils, I unzipped his pants and then tugged them over his hips. His expression savage with barely contained lust, Nick tore his mouth free from mine. "Eve, slow down!"

"Can't." Ahh, there he was, all hard, hot and throbbing. Mine. I cupped him.

"Shit." Nick fumbled with the button on my pants and then jerked down the zipper. He ran his hands under the material, shucking off my slacks and panties in one motion. Cool air fanned my heated flesh. My clothing pooled into a tangle at my feet.

Uh-oh. Technical problem. No way could I wrap my legs around him. I broke off the kiss long enough to toe off my shoes and step free of the clothes. Nick used the reprieve to do the same but not before fumbling in his pocket for a foil package.

"You had protection on you?"

He flashed a sheepish grin. "I was hoping to get lucky."

I considered for one microsecond as to whether I should be offended. But, hey, as a scientist I appreciated forecasting. I wrapped a leg around him and he put a hand on my bottom, lifting me up so I could coil the other leg around his hips. "I guess this is your lucky day."

I reached down, guiding the smooth head of his penis to my body, and sank down at the same moment as he thrust up.

Mission achieved. The combined movements sent his entire length deep inside me. I closed my eyes, relishing the delicious pressure. But it wasn't nearly enough. I ground my pelvis against him.

Groaning, Nick whirled, pinning me against the wall. So much the better for traction. Everything in me began to tighten as need roared through me. My inner muscles clenched around him, drawing him in deeper. Time spun away. The world receded to only the sensation of his thick shaft thrusting back and forth into me. Without warning, I climaxed, shuddering and crying out.

Nick came a second later, driving even deeper into me. He rested against me, his skin damp with sweat. Our chests heaved as we both sucked in air. Closing my eyes, I rested my head against his shoulder as I waited for my heart to calm.

Muttering something about a bed, Nick pushed away from the wall and, still inside me, carried me across the room. He lowered us both to the bed, settling his weight on top. Stripping my top off and then my bra, he nuzzled the sides of my breasts before licking one nipple and then another.

Then incredibly, he began to move again with a gentle rhythm like the calm after the storm. Still the tension spiraled through me, and when Nick made a guttural sound and climaxed again, I followed him over.

I awoke to find myself lying spoon fashion with Nick on the bed. Dimly I recalled our shedding any remaining clothes before collapsing into a deep sleep. I glanced at the glowing face on my watch. Five o'clock in the morning. Give me five hours of sleep and I was a new woman.

Nick's breathing indicated he still slept, so I enjoyed the sensation of simply being in his arms. I floated in a sea of contentment, my mind drifting. Images swirled like a kaleidoscope, coming in and out of focus.

I saw my sister and myself when we had been young and Maman had taken us to the beach during a trip to visit her family in southern France. Yvette had been the more daring, dashing out into the waves immediately. I had lingered, pretending to help our mother straighten the blanket.

"*Chère,* why don't you play in the water?"

"I will, Maman, when we're done here." I wasn't about to own up that I was afraid. Those waves made a lot of noise, like they were hungry and wanted to swallow me up.

"Eve!" Yvette skidded to a stop, sending a spray of sand onto the blanket. Maman only rolled her eyes and brushed away the grains. My sister grinned and, reaching out, tugged my hair.

I really hated when she did that, and pushed her hand away. "Stop!"

"How come you're not in the water?"

"'Cause I'm helping Maman."

Yvette rubbed her nose. "Naw. You're a scaredy cat."

"Am not!" I emphasized my point with another shove.

Not to be outdone, Yvette shoved back. "Are too!"

"Girls." Our mother stood between us, hands on her hips. "I'm ashamed of you. You are sisters and sisters take care of each other."

I scuffed my toe in the sand. "She started it."

"Did not. You pushed first."

"You called me a name."

"Scaredy cat, scaredy cat!" Yvette danced about but Maman's reach could be really long when she was mad.

"Yvette St. Giles! You are the oldest. It is your duty to look after your little sister."

"Yes, Maman." Yvette stared at her feet.

"If Eve is afraid of the water, you should be holding her hand, not teasing her."

"Yes, Maman." Yvette held out her hand. "Come on, Eve. I'll look after you." Taking a deep breath, I linked my fingers with hers. She led me over the beach into the water, stopping when it was only knee deep.

"Watch, Eve. When you see a wave, jump like this!" She hopped.

I nodded and when I saw the sea begin to rise jumped up. Water splashed in my face and I bopped for a minute before my feet touched the sand again. I howled with pleasure. "Yvette, again. I want to do it again!"

A sunshine memory to warm myself by. I would find others…

"Others!" I shot up.

"What is it?" Nick woke up, immediately alert.

"I've been so engaged in the chase that I'm overlooking the hunt portion." I sprung out of the bed and began to pace.

"What do we know so far, Nick? First, a DNA segment is stolen from your client's lab by a missing scientist. He has to have a lab and funding to further develop the virus so that it impacts women more. Next, a network is set up to manufacture not only the virus and cylinders but also fill them. Then there's at least one courier finding test cases and targets."

I glanced at him. "This takes tremendous resources and money."

Nick propped himself on his elbow. "We're running

the Stelle Consortium and its shell upon shell of holdings and corporations."

"But we're ignoring the courier's organization."

"The women-hating male society?"

"Yes." Something bothered me. Something I saw?

I snapped my fingers. "Damn it! I missed it last night. I was so focused on finding the cylinder that I didn't see the forest." I found my panties and stepped into them.

"Where's my bra? Never mind." The lacy lingerie, my one weakness to a life of wearing practical field clothes, dangled from the corner of a chair.

"Missed what?" Nick was up and dressing. I paused, startled by the punch of desire, as I admired his trim, muscled buttocks. Damn, I had it bad. Shaking my head, I slipped into my pants.

"Eve?"

"Last night I bumped into Scarlet's boyfriend or—" I tucked in my shirt as I considered the encounter "—former boyfriend courtesy of family interference."

"Please?" Nick headed into the bathroom. I leaned outside, ready to take my turn.

"Caleb Adriano. Last night he and his father were with a large group of men leaving a building on the plaza. When I asked Caleb whether Scarlet was with him, the father was irritated."

"Really? That's interesting. When you're talking about resources, the Adriano family has all that and more. Our initial query came up against a lot of stone walls. They've been a part of the fabric of Italy forever, as long as the Roman Catholic Church."

"Nick, you're talking over a thousand years." A shiver of fear raced through me. My God, what had Scarlet gotten herself into? Wealth and power accumulated over centuries? My bright, funky friend bumping against those types of traditions? It would be like setting her with her camera and New Age mentality loose in the inner sanctum of the Vatican.

Although I knew it was useless, I crossed to the hotel phone and placed a call. Once more I received Scarlet's breezy message on her answering machine. "Scarlet. It's Eve. Please, if you're there, pick up."

"'Allo?" A woman's cool voice answered.

Not Scarlet but I would take having a real person any day. "Hi, I'm Eve St. Giles. Is Scarlet there?"

"No, I am afraid she is away on an assignment." Definitely a French accent.

I wound the phone cord around my finger. "Any chance of getting a message to her? This is important."

"Eve." The woman sounded like she was rolling my name around her mouth. "Ah, yes. Her psychic friend. The doctor with the European Centre for Disease Prevention and Control in Stockholm."

I heard a low murmur in the background. "We are saddened by the loss of your sister."

"Thank you. But I need to speak with—"

"I am Catrina Dauvergne."

Catrina. The name clicked. This was one of the women Scarlet had been trying to get me to meet. "Catrina, it's really urgent that Scarlet contacts me."

"My friend Rhys and I only dropped by her flat to water her plants. Poor things. They nearly expired. Good thing Rhys remembered. He's good that way."

"Catrina—"

"But of course, you are not interested in plants. I will leave a message for Scarlet. Do you have her cell phone number?"

"Yes, but I can't reach her."

"Mm. This is strange. I will try, as well. May I have

your number just in case?" I rattled it off. "I shall call you if I get hold of her. If what Scarlet has said of you is true, we must all get together. Please come visit. In Paris or at my farmhouse in Lys, either is convenient. Just call ahead so we know where to meet you."

As she went on, with a start I realized the locale Catrina mentioned for the farmhouse was not far from where my sister had lived in southern France. Nick stood by the door, tapping his watch. I smiled and interrupted Catrina. "I'm sorry, but I have to go. I'll be in contact."

"Good luck and remember, come visit me soon."

"Will do." Hanging up, I grabbed my bag and crossed the room.

"Back to the piazza?" he asked.

"Yes. I want to take a closer look at the building Caleb and his father came out of. They obviously had been in a meeting. But what kind of meeting?"

# Chapter 13

The rising sun barely lit the narrow streets of the Gothic Quarter of Barcelona. Except for the occasional local hurrying to work or going into the church, the area was deserted. The hoards of tourists hadn't yet descended with guides and cameras.

Gone from the piazza, however, was the gray, draining pall. Today iridescence softly bathed the entire square. After a good night's sleep lying wrapped in Nick's arms, I felt energized, alive. But was rest the only explanation?

Ley lines, earth's circuitry.

According to the Internet research I'd done after my little chat with Myrddin yesterday, ancient monuments around the world had been constructed in the presence of this electromagnetic energy. That would explain what I'd seen at the stone circle outside Damassine. Some articles spoke of sacred places located at ley-line power centers. The cathedral and the Santa Maria delle Grazie would certainly qualify as venerated.

However, while the descriptions varied, most people who could feel or see the ley lines described them as glowing or white fuzziness. So what was the deal with the black lines I had seen at Damassine and the gray of yesterday?

"Eve, what's wrong?" Nick tucked a strand of hair behind my ear.

"Thinking about one of Myrddin's comments."

"I was rather hoping you were thinking about last night."

Warmth spread across my face. "Ah…it was…"

"Fantastic? Mind-blowing?"

Mutely I nodded. He smiled, taking pity on me. "Me, too." He wrapped his arm around my shoulders and together we moved across the square.

*Contentment.* Oh, yeah, Nick, I quite agree, I thought, as I felt his relaxed mood.

Halting in front of the building where I had bumped into Caleb Adriano, I studied the stone facade while Nick tried the door from which the group of men had emerged. Locked.

He glanced around and brought out a black pouch. I cleared my throat. "Have you ever considered becoming a cat burglar?"

His lips twitched. "Security calls for all types of talents."

My cell phone vibrated and I answered.

"Eve, it's Frederic."

"Morning, sir." I watched Nick place a pick in the antique lock.

"I was briefed on the events of last night. Congratulations!"

"Thank you, sir." Nick gave me a thumbs-up as the lock clicked.

"Eve, you do not sound happy about finding the cylinder."

"The courier escaped, Frederic. Crisis was averted, yes, but we still don't know how many canisters filled with the influenza are out there. We haven't tracked down the people behind him who are funding his movements."

"Ever since you told me about van Velsen's disappearance, I've been making a few discreet inquiries since our professional acquaintances often overlapped. I had a report that Willem was seen in Vienna as of yesterday."

"Really?" Interesting. If van Velsen had made a clean getaway, why would he return to the city where Janssen Pharmaceutical was located?

"I called to let you know that I am on my way to Vienna now for the congress."

"Congress?" I drew a blank. Obviously, the days and events since Damassine had played havoc with my memory more than I realized.

"Oh, that's right. With the outbreak, I forgot to tell you. The Centre has been requested to take part at the international conclave to draft a treaty on cost control regulations and distribution of global costs in drug research and development. Dr. Helene Danhauser specifically requested my presence." Pride and pleasure resonated in his voice.

"Frederic, that's fabulous. Better you than me having to listen to countries squabbling about pharmaceutical cost controls."

"Thank you, I think."

"Hey, is world availability of vaccines on Dr. Danhauser's agenda?"

"Don't worry, Eve. I've already discussed with Helene the urgent need for vaccines. She's going to make a real difference at this meeting. We might actually manage to get a viable treaty."

World community health leaders, Vienna, van Velsen. Dots formed and linked together.

My God. Were van Velsen and his backers planning an attack there?

"Frederic, are there any reports of increased illness cropping up in Vienna?"

"Nothing that has been brought to my attention yet."

"Do me a favor and have someone monitor Vienna. And you be careful."

"Of course."

After ending the call, I advised Nick, "Frederic says van Velsen was seen as recently as yesterday in Vienna."

"That's not my information, but I'll call it in."

"There's one other thing. Frederic is heading to Vienna for an international congress on health."

Nick glanced around, frowning. "I don't like the sound of that. Van Velsen returning to Vienna just as there's an international meeting."

"That's what I thought."

"I'll alert my office that Willem may have returned."

After he made an abbreviated call to his staff, I followed Nick into the building. The dim, empty hallway had several doorways with signs. At the third one on the left, I stopped, my heart pounding.

"Nick!" I pointed at the small sign: Sociedad Ante Hombre Para Hombre. Society of Men for Men.

He nodded and picked the lock before drawing his gun. He held up a finger and went inside first. A few moments later he reappeared and gave me an all-clear sign.

Disappointment filled me as I stepped inside the sparsely furnished suite. The first room functioned as a reception area with a desk, chair and phone. The next room contained a large conference table and leather chairs. A carved wood sideboard contained a silver pitcher and carafe along with glasses and cups. I checked one of the ashtrays that were scattered about. Clean as a whistle, as everything else was, although the smell of cigarette smoke lingered in the air.

"If someone met here last night, there's nothing left now," I said, moving to the sideboard. I pulled open the drawer, finding only napkins and silverware. "This can't be the society's headquarters—no computers, no literature, and only one phone."

"It's a front," Nick said as he panned a flashlight across the floor.

"If so, how are Caleb and his father connected?" I asked as I shut the drawer. "Or are they? There are a number of offices in here. It could be coincidence."

"Eve, please." He clicked off the flashlight.

"All right. So I'm trying to cut Caleb a break because of Scarlet." In frustration, I ran my fingers through my hair. "Okay, so they met here last night. It doesn't mean it was for a nefarious purpose."

"There's nothing here. Let's go, Eve." Nick moved toward the door.

I gripped the back of a leather conference chair and…

*Tension filled the room as several men argued. A few shadowy figures stood while others sat around the table.* Try as I might, I couldn't bring them into focus. I was receiving their emotional imprints, I realized, still resonating in the room.

But whatever residue remained did not contain the power of those I'd experienced from centuries past. Either the emotions emitted here had not been strong enough or…the ley lines weren't amplifying my abilities. I let out a breath as I tried to open myself more.

The person sitting in the chair I gripped had disagreed with the others. Fear. Disgust. Reluctance to destroy…what?

I moved to the chair at the head of the table and cool arrogance and even colder control flooded into me. Failure was not an option. They must go forward with the plan. The solution was so simple.

*The men's voices raised as the argument escalated. French, they had spoken in the once-universal language. Words imbued with emotion hung in the air.*

Almost too eagerly I circled to the third chair. My knees buckled as the hatred burned my hand.

*Kill. Kill the woman…*or was it women?

"Eve!"

I started, and the room crystallized back into focus. No more forms, no more voices. Nick was gripping my arm. "Snap out of it!"

I mentally shook my mind free of the psychic event. "I'm okay."

Nick ran his hands soothingly across my shoulders. "You were in the trance so long that I got worried. What did you see?"

"The place recognition wasn't as strong as my other experiences. Most of the men I didn't recognize as I haven't met them before. But I'm pretty sure Caleb and his father were in here. Simon Adriano has this control issue that stamps him emotionally. Caleb's more conflicted."

Nick's gaze hardened. "Then they're involved with the Spanish flu."

"I'm afraid so." Unease gripped me. "And I'm even more afraid that Scarlet's smack-dab in the middle because of her relationship with Caleb."

"You said Caleb's in love with her?"

"Yes."

"Then she should be safe for now."

I knew Nick meant to be reassuring, but he didn't know Scarlet or her natural inquisitiveness. I returned to the head chair and trailed a hand once more over the leather. What solution had you radiating absolute confidence?

*Vaccine.*

"Oh my God, Nick. We missed a dot. Your client's lab is also in Vienna. Think about this. If you want to create a global pandemic, then the last thing you're going to want is a vaccine ready to go."

His face paled. "Come on!" Nick was on his phone even as he raced out of the room.

By the time we had reached our hotel room and grabbed our gear, Nick had rattled off orders to his staff and to his client, Janssen Pharmaceutical. Then we were in the rental car, peeling toward the airport.

As the landscape passed me in a blur, my inner voice yelled at me. This time I couldn't afford to miss the forest for the tree. All points were converging on Vienna, including an international health conference.

After we landed at the Schwechat International Airport, Nick guided me through the bustling terminal. In the parking lot I only lifted an eyebrow at the sight of his black Mercedes before he bundled me along with our gear inside. As he started the car, he switched on the radio to an English broadcast.

I half listened to the news as we sped along the A4 into Vienna. "How far is your client's lab?"

"It's in the historic center, so, roughly fifteen miles as the bird flies, longer for a car. In the inner section, there's no straight path anywhere and several of the main streets are for pedestrians only." He flashed me a glance. "Tired?"

"Hmm." To my surprise, I was. I had catnapped on the plane, but from the moment I'd disembarked, my energy had waned. I stared out the window but didn't see any pulsating grids. Was it possible to use ley lines to affect an entire city?

"Why don't you lean back and close your eyes?"

I nodded and did what he suggested. However, my racing thoughts wouldn't let me doze. I had only been able to speak briefly with Frederic before he headed into a session at the UNO-City across the Danube. We'd arranged to meet later.

Nick must have turned up the radio, for the announcer's voice now droned in my head. "Health authorities warn that this flu season may be the most active yet in recent years. Already hospitals and doctors have reported a sharp increase of patients with cold and flu symptoms almost overnight. Government officials have sent out a call for more vaccine."

*Lowers immunity systems,* I heard Myrddin's voice say in my head. It was happening here.

I straightened and gripped Nick's arm. "Nick, Myrddin talked about this family, presumably his, using ley lines to lower people's immunity systems."

A frown puckered his forehead. "How is that possible, to manipulate ley lines?"

"I don't know. I gather they have some technology that ramps up the energy."

"Perhaps we can speak with one of Janssen's scientists as to whether it would be possible."

"Myrddin also said Damassine had been exposed to the bursts of ley lines right before the courier struck. My team did gather reports from local doctors indicating a surge of illnesses right before the outbreak."

I inhaled a steadying breath. "That radio spot indicated the same thing is happening in Vienna. Increased illnesses, meaning lowered immunities."

"And greater susceptibility to the Spanish flu," Nick concluded.

"Exactly. I hope your client has large quantities of vaccine. We may need it." Regulation strings would have to be pulled for it to be used, but after all, all the world health leaders were right here to hammer out the details.

Nick pressed down on the accelerator and within short order we were exiting from the highway into the city. By the way he drove through winding streets and some roads that could barely be called lanes, I could tell that Nick was in his element and knew Vienna like the back of his hand.

"Parking's a bitch, so we'll have to grab the first spot along the street here." He neatly cut off another car and backed into an impossibly small spot. I got out and we walked along a sidewalk in front of a row of Baroque-style buildings. I saw a banner flapping from a structure ahead. Nick checked his watch.

"It's lunchtime so I don't know how many of the supervisors will be there," Nick said. "I did give the owner an approximate arrival time."

Suddenly a siren blared and people streamed from the front and side entrances. "That's the lab!" Nick shouted as he raced toward it. I was only one step behind him when the earth heaved. Twisting, Nick grabbed me and suddenly we were airborne. The street rushed up toward me.

Jarring pain. Merciful blackness.

* * *

"Eve?"

The first thing that disturbed the gray haze that I floated in was the sound of the worried voice. The next thing was the antiseptic odor so irritating that I had to wrinkle my nose. No matter the country, the state or town, hospitals all smelled alike and I hated them all.

"Eve? *Chère,* talk to me."

Given the fact that a sledgehammer was breaking my head in two and had done a fair number on the rest of my body, I wasn't in the mood for talking. But since the persistent voice didn't seem as if it was going to go away, I opened my eyes.

And immediately regretted the action. Light drilled like a laser straight to the center of my head. "Ow!"

I clamped my eyes shut.

"Eve, it's Nick."

"No joke." I cracked one eye open. Only half the pain.

"Thank God. You must be all right."

That remark caused my other eye to fly open. "Are you kidding?"

Though Nick's complexion was borderline ghost white, he smiled with relief. "No, if you were really hurt, you wouldn't be your usual charming self."

"Ha, ha!" I reached toward my face, wanting to check to see if everything was in place, but pain seared from my right shoulder up to my neck. Then there was the problem of the sling hindering any further movement.

"Hey, take it easy." Nick sat on the bed and caught my hand. "You had a dislocated shoulder."

I croaked, "I assume it's no longer dislocated?"

"The doctor popped it back in."

"Terrific." Now that my vision had stopped swimming, I got a good look at Nick. He wore a nice square bandage across his forehead. "Ooo, took a knock to your hard noggin, did you?"

He looked upward toward the ceiling. "And I missed this?" Bending over, he brushed his lips across mine. "You scared me, *chère.*"

"Likewise."

"Oh, how perfectly touching," a man said from the door.

Nick ran his finger along my nose before straightening. "Hello, Frederic."

The director, his arms filled with flowers, entered the room. Since he was my boss, I struggled to sit up. "Frederic, the flowers are lovely!" Nick slipped his arm and carefully helped me up. He propped pillows behind me.

Taking in my sling, the director deposited the bundle on the bedside tray. "How bad is the shoulder?" He stood on the other side of the bed.

"Nick tells me it was only a dislocation."

Frederic's brow shot up. "Only?"

Normally Frederic was cool and composed in any crisis, but his gray silk tie was askew and his white hair looked uncombed. I reached out with my good hand and patted his lower arm. "I'm fine."

"Right." Frederic didn't sound convinced, but a few lines around his mouth eased.

"I will be fine, too," Nick offered with a grin, earning a withering glance from the director. Why had I never realized that the two didn't like each other? The last thing I needed was testosterone sparks flying.

What I needed was a good night's sleep or…was it morning? I squinted, gauging the light slanting through the blinds.

"What time is it?"

Nick confirmed my suspicions. "Don't you mean what *day* is it?"

"I was out that long?"

"After the doctor gave you a shot to reset your shoulder, you slept like a baby. Good thing, as they wanted to keep you under observation overnight."

"Am I sporting a spiffy bandage like yours?"

"Yes." Nick brushed his fingers across my cheek. "Sorry, *chère*. I tried to spare you the brunt of the fall."

His apology shot past all the guards I had erected around my heart. "We're both in one piece."

Then my mind stumbled past the aches and pains. "Nick, the lab—"

His expression hardened. "Destroyed. Preliminary reports indicate an incendiary device. The explosion killed two of my men, and several technicians didn't make it."

I felt nauseous. I must have looked worse, for Nick twisted, poured a glass of water and held it to my lips. His hand was trembling so I placed mine over it to steady the cup. Grief and anger churned within him. I let my sympathy flow. Surprise flickered in his eyes, but he only said, "Take it easy."

I complied, drinking the cool liquid in small sips. When my mouth was moistened, I managed to ask in a steady voice, "And the vaccine? All gone?"

Nick shot a guarded glance across the bed at Frederic. "Okay, boys, what's going on?"

Frederic smiled. "Nick had his client send samples of the vaccine to one of their other labs as well as to the Centre. Although the bomb was a setback, the vaccine still exists. It will not be long before more is made."

"But, sir, these people are planning to release the flu here."

"Are you certain, Eve? Perhaps the sole target was the lab."

I shook my head and then rued the movement. "There are too many coincidences. Think about it. An international health conference. What better way to disrupt the world health community than to release the flu during the conference?"

Frederic pursed his lips. "You may be right. I shall have to speak with Dr. Danhauser, if she is feeling better."

"Why? What is wrong with her?"

"She had to end a meeting early yesterday. She had a slight cold."

"Damn." I threw back the sheet.

"What do you think you are doing?" Nick demanded as he tossed the cover back over my legs.

"Getting up." I tossed off the sheet again and glared a warning at Nick. "Don't you see? The international leader in charge of this conference is ill. Her immune system has been compromised. No telling how many others attending the conference have been affected."

Scowling, Nick helped me out of bed. It was a good thing he had his arm around me for the moment I stood, my legs turned to jelly. "You should stay in bed."

I braced my hands on his chest and willed my legs to behave. "Frederic, the conference schedule. Is everything over at the UNO?"

He pulled out his electronic agenda from the inside pocket of his jacket and consulted it. "In terms of group events, yes. Of course, the attendees have free time between meetings. Oh, wait."

"What is it?" I demanded.

"There is today what I believe you call a 'photo op' at the Schönbrunn Gardens before the reception tonight. I have to admit, I questioned the wisdom, given the expected dip in temperatures, but I was advised that's what a number of delegates requested."

I looked at Nick. "The perfect opportunity. But how is the canister to be released? By glider or timer?"

"Van Velsen could have experimented with any number of methods," Nick warned as he went to the wardrobe.

"Why don't you rain on my parade?" I groused as I grabbed the clothes he handed me and stalked toward the small bathroom. However, once I shut the door, I stared at the image of a battered and bruised woman in the mirror.

How would the contagion be spread next?

# Chapter 14

At Frederic's request, Dr. Helene Danhauser agreed to meet us at a coffeehouse in the Hofburg Quarter. I was inhaling my second cup of café au lait when an attractive woman in her forties approached our table. She wore an expensive designer navy suit and an ivory silk blouse, her carefully streaked blond hair swept back in a chignon. Frederic's face lit up, causing Nick and me to exchange knowing glances.

"Helene! I am delighted that you were able to make it." He rose with Nick and I following suit. She extended her hand and he kissed the back of her fingers.

"Frederic, so nice to see you outside of a conference room," she said with a German accent. I knew from Frederic that she was Austrian. She smiled politely at us.

"Helene, I would like you to meet Dr. Eve St. Giles and Nick Petter."

"Ah, Dr. St. Giles. Frederic speaks so highly of you."

"Please...Eve."

"And I'm Helene."

We sat but not before my boss made sure the other woman ended up in the chair next to him. Looked as if he was smitten. Good, maybe he wouldn't have as much time to interfere in others' personal lives, such as mine.

"How are you feeling, Helene?" The director gestured for the waiter.

"Better, thank you."

I studied her and noticed her pale complexion and the dark circles under her eyes. Whether due to the stress of being in charge of the conference or illness, I couldn't say. However, she clearly was not in tip-top health. She turned her intelligent gaze on me, and I felt it.

A zing of recognition.

That gut-deep sense of connection. She was a Marian like me. She hesitated a second. Was she also experiencing my sense of awareness?

The air crackled with electricity between us. Then she lowered her gaze for a second. When she looked at me again, the current was gone. She said in a sympathetic tone, "Frederic has briefed me about the Spanish flu outbreak in Damassine. A great tragedy. I am sorry for your loss."

I tamped down the sharp pang of grief that welled up. No, the time to mourn was not here yet. I shot the director a quick look before murmuring my thanks. If Helene wasn't going to acknowledge the weirdness, neither was I.

"I understand that you believe the health congress is in danger?"

"Yes, madam." I quickly outlined the trail that led here and my analysis. With a thoughtful expression Helene listened without interruption.

After sipping some water, she lowered the glass. "I see why you would arrive at your conclusions, but the question is why the congress would be targeted?" Her smile was faint. "In this age of diplomacy, we are an equal-opportunity conference. Many of the health leaders in attendance are male."

"The original Spanish flu hit young healthy adults the hardest. Just because one variant was used in Damassinc doesn't mean others haven't been created."

I leaned forward. "You've been ill lately?"

"A mild nagging cold, that's all."

"Have any of the other delegates fallen sick?"

"Yes, but there has been—"

"A recent rise of illnesses in Vienna?" I asked.

She nodded.

"Exactly like Damassine." I shot Nick a look but he only leaned back in his chair and laced his fingers over his stomach. "We have a far-fetched theory we're investigating that may explain why both locations had spikes in ailments so that people's immune responses would have been lowered."

Leery of her reaction, I quickly ran over the concept of earth's energy lines being manipulated. To my surprise and relief, she didn't break out in laughter.

"What would you have me do, Eve? This congress has been long in the making. We need to come to terms on a treaty that will spread the expense of research development among nations and control drug costs. Third-World access to life-saving drugs is at stake here."

"I would imagine that the pharmaceutical companies are less than thrilled with the notion," I dryly commented.

"To say the least. I cannot walk in the hallways without tripping over a company representative. Fortunately, my assistant, who is familiar with such companies, runs interference for me."

She glanced at Frederic, who nodded his approval. "I will not cave to their pressure tactics, which is another reason why I cannot suspend the conference due to a vague terrorist threat."

I understood and appreciated her resolve, but a nightmarish thought occurred to me. "Helene." I leaned toward her. "What would happen if *all* the health leaders at this conference perished in an outbreak? What if someone carried the flu virus back to their countries?"

She shuddered. "It would set back international health issues and be devastating to the individual nations affected."

"Then this is what I suggest you do." Once more she listened as I outlined a plan.

Twenty minutes later our group took the tram to Schönbrunn Gardens to check out the location where the conference photo op would occur. Helene led us along the central paved path to where it intersected with another. "Here is the arranged spot. The Schönbrunn Palace will be the background."

Slowly, I did a 360-degree turn. Nothing but low-lying flowerbeds on all sides. Trimmed hedges and trees that ran perpendicular to the palace were too far away to this spot for the courier to risk a timer on the cylinder. So why had he wanted to experiment with that method?

"Was this photo op originally on the itinerary?"

Helene shook her head. "Yes, but not here. My assistant, Ricardo, whom I have asked to join us here, had arranged for it to be done at the UNO-City, but more than a few delegates protested."

Her shoulders moved in an elegant European shrug. "Ricardo had to arrange the transportation and security for the delegates, but after the photograph is taken, they will have a special tour of the palace before going to the reception."

A smile flitted on her lips. "Of course, I might point out the maze to the left of here in the hopes that a few of the more-contrary delegates get lost."

I grinned. "Anyone ever been lost and not found?"

"Unfortunately, no. But Ricardo tells me he has planned a special surprise to delight the delegates and he will not tell even me what it is. Speaking of whom…"

She held out her hand to a tall, dark-haired man who approached us from the direction of the palace. "Ricardo."

"*Bonjour,* Madame Chair," the man murmured as he kissed her cheek.

Poor Frederic positively bristled, but he didn't have to worry. While both men had that European chic, Ricardo lacked the director's presence. Surprisingly, the assistant was understated, possibly a quality he had honed to let others take the spotlight. He was a perfect second banana.

"Ricardo Adriano, this is Director Frederic Lutz and Dr. Eve St. Giles with the European Centre for Disease Prevention and Control, and Nick Petter."

*Another* Adriano? Working at the health congress? I opened myself up but couldn't tell whether I had felt his emotional imprint in the Barcelona conference room.

"A pleasure." The assistant gave a polite bow.

"Any relation to Caleb Adriano?" I asked.

He gave a negligent shrug. "A distant cousin, I believe. I have never met him."

Hmm. I had to admit he didn't resemble the Adriano clan I'd met to date. While I didn't think the name "Adriano" was comparable to the American "Smith," I shelved my question for later when I could discuss with Nick this latest twist.

Ricardo turned his attention to the other woman. "Helene, how may I be of assistance?"

"Would you please go over the events? Mr. Petter, here, is going to be providing extra security."

Now it was the assistant's turn to look surprised. He raised an eyebrow. "Is there a problem?"

"The Centre has reason to believe there could be a bioterrorism attack today."

Color drained from Ricardo's face. "No, that is not possible."

"We are going to make sure of that."

"Of course. I will be happy to give Mr. Petter whatever help he requires."

"First, what is the schedule? When and how are you getting the delegates here?"

Almost as one, the men circled around to talk strategy. No longer the center of attention, Dr. Danhauser stepped to the side, pressing the back of her hand to her forehead. Concerned, I lightly touched her arm.

"Security's not my thing, either. Why don't we go sit over near the maze until they're finished?"

She gave me an appreciative smile. "That would be nice. I have to admit that I am not totally myself."

We walked to where a bench had been set off the path and sat down. I immediately regretted the move. Waves of weariness swept over me. A low-grade sound almost like a vibration began to hum in my ears. Even the toothache pain in my shoulder ratcheted up a notch, more like a hot drill boring into the joint.

Was I on a ley line? Was that why I was feeling more sensitive?

I shifted. Helene, whose eyes had drifted close, started. "Sorry," I murmured.

"Don't be. Your shoulder, it is hurting?"

"Yes, but it's to be expected."

"Perhaps we should both rest this afternoon before…how do you say…it's show time?"

I grinned. "Sounds like a good idea."

"One that neither of us will do."

"You are correct." I watched a bird scurry across the path in search on any food dropped by visitors. Pickings at this time of the year would be slim.

"Have you experienced this sense of connection before with other women?"

So Helene had felt the snap, crackle, pop in the café. "Yes," I admitted albeit reluctantly.

She studied the garden. "So have I. I never know when or with whom. I can be in a meeting with a hundred women and nothing. Yet if I brushed against a total stranger on the street…" She snapped her fingers.

"The same here."

"What do you do about it, Eve?"

I studied my boots. "Nothing. My friend Scarlet has been nagging me to meet other Marians, but I've resisted to date."

"Marians," Helene murmured. "I've heard the term from others, but have found it hard to believe that I am one. Women like us with scientific and analytical minds can have more trouble embracing our emotional sides."

"Do we need to?"

"Oh, yes," Helene said softly. "Yes, we do." She rose but held her hand up when I stirred. "Please, sit here a while longer. I think you may have something with respect to your ley line theory."

"What do you mean?"

"Open your inner eye, Eve." With that cryptic remark she returned to where the men stood.

Open my inner eye? She couldn't know about my psychic abilities, could she?

Of course she did.

I sighed and then drew in a deep breath, released it, and repeated the process. Tuning out the activity around me, I turned my focus inward, letting my senses well up. The gardens at first blurred before beginning to vibrate. The humming in my head crescendoed, growing so loud that I almost clapped my hands over my ears. However, since vertigo swept through me, I curled my fingers around the edge of the bench to hold tight.

I blinked, and when I looked at the scene before me, I barely noticed Ricardo Adriano rapidly walking away from the group. Stunned, I stared at the gray light that encircled my friends' heads. The aura about Helene was a darker charcoal color as she circled her arm through Frederic's, drawing him along the path toward the palace.

For good reason.

Cold black lines slashed through the earth around them, forming a harsh grid throughout the garden. This wasn't like the golden, energizing light I had experienced in Milan. I could see the soft incandescence of life that silhouetted the trees flowing toward the lines, turning ashen as the good energy was sucked in and absorbed by the negative energy.

I despaired, powerless to stop whatever was going on about me. Give me any virus, I knew how to break it down, analyze it and come up with a way to counter its effects.

But I didn't know how to hunt what was before me and stop its harmful effects.

*Give up,* the shadow lines whispered to me. *Give yourself up to us.*

Wooziness sapped all my energy, leaving in its wake draining weariness. I drifted sideways, needing to curl up on the bench and rest.

*"Chère!"* Nick scooped me up, holding me against his chest. That would do as a pillow for my head. I snuggled closer.

I heard a murmur of concerned voices but it was like fighting off the drugging effects of a nap that had lasted too long. Still, a breeze fanned my face, and darkness no longer tugged on me.

I lifted my head and blinked. I was no longer in the gardens proper. I shifted in Nick's grip so I could peer over his shoulder as he carried me through a gate. No more black lines. Energy began to surge through me again.

"Hey." I tapped Nick's chest. "I'm all right. Put me down."

He complied but kept his arm around me. "What the hell happened in there? Helene came over, urging us to get out and the next thing I know, you were lying on the bench."

"A successful experiment?" I suggested as I tested my strength. Good, no jelly knees.

"Eve." Nick's curt tone implied he was not a happy camper and was in no mood for jokes.

"Where are Helene and Frederic?" Perhaps a diversion would work.

"Frederic's bundling Helene off to the UNO-City. She looked like death warmed over as you did a few minutes ago." He placed a finger under my chin, forcing me to meet his concerned gaze. "What happened?"

"You know Myrddin's ley lines theory? I experienced the lines in action back there."

"How?" he demanded.

Remembering the gray aura that had encircled Nick,

I studied him, checking for signs of illness. Other than the pink flushing his cheeks from the chilled air and the impatient expression stamped on his face, he appeared…vital. His arm remained like a steel belt around my waist, keeping me close to the warmth radiating from his sleek, solid body.

Relaxing, I allowed myself to open again. As I looked at him with new eyes, I saw his aura. A very soft glow of plum an inch off his skin, topped with strong yellow.

*Spiritual, strong, protected,* my inner voice whispered.

Puzzled, I placed my hand on his chest and felt the steady beat of his heart. "When you were standing inside the garden, didn't you experience any sense of weakness?"

"Only when I saw you crumpling like a wet rag." Pulling me closer, he dropped his forehead to mine. "Don't scare me like that again."

"Oh." Warmth and light once more filled me. I drew in his strength and made it mine. "Okay. I can't say it won't happen again, but I'll try."

He heaved a sigh, kissed me and then pulled away. "I guess I can't ask for anything more in terms of a promise."

As he linked fingers with my good hand and walked toward the street, I pointed out the obvious. "Look. It's not as if I am some sort of a psychic dowser trying to find these suckers."

Hmm, a dowser. Boy, I could use one about now. But whoever was behind that nasty stuff in the gardens had one thing wrong. I had a job to do and I would see it to the end: stop the courier and find Willem van Velsen before he developed any more diseases.

Nick and I took the U-Bahn line to the Greban where Nick's office was located. As he gave me a hand to exit the tramcar, I reached out with the wrong arm and grimaced.

"How is the shoulder? Do you want to go up to my flat and rest awhile?" Nick asked as he steered me around a group of laughing teenagers. "I live near here."

"I'm fine, thanks." I'd taken a shower at the hospital, but the limbering effects of the hot water had long faded away. The dull, throbbing ache now felt like a jabbing ice pick, but activity would have to keep my mind off the pain.

Besides, this wasn't the first time I'd dislocated the shoulder and probably wouldn't be the last. The orthopedist friend of my father's I'd seen in Boston had said I needed arthroscopic repair. That had been five years ago and still counting.

Nick's phone rang and he answered. "Yes, I am on my way there. What? I can't hear you." He drifted toward the center of the street.

I halted and watched the ebb and flow of people. Although it hadn't been that long since Damassine, I felt like I'd spent a lifetime chasing after the Spanish flu. The courier or one of his cohorts was here, somewhere, about to launch the biggest strike yet at the gardens today. I had foiled the trial run with a timer. Given the garden layout, the group must be going with airborne release. But how? Would they try another glider? Nick's contacts with the authorities were already alerting the local shops.

Dressed in a fur coat worn open, a slender woman walked briskly on the other side. I couldn't help but notice the purple flash of a distinctive necklace. Pauline Adriano? Here, alone? Had Ricardo told us the truth about not knowing that branch of the family?

I went on high alert. Two Adrianos in Vienna at the same time could not be a coincidence. Moreover, I had more than a legitimate reason to approach Pauline. After all, the last time I'd seen Scarlet she had been with Pauline.

I motioned at Nick, who was nodding his head as he continued speaking. I brought out my own phone so I could send him a message if I had to go too far. I crossed the street, trying to keep track of her progress in the crowd.

One moment I thought I had her, the next I didn't. I caught up with a woman in a fur coat looking in a store window. "Pauline…" My voice trailed off as I saw in the reflection that the woman wasn't wearing a necklace. She glanced curiously at me. "Sorry, I thought you were someone else."

I moved away, intending to return to where Nick stood, but the monument a few feet away in the center of Graben drew my attention. Wow, that had to be the famous *Plague Column,* erected to commemorate the city's deliverance from the bubonic plague. There wasn't often a permanent tribute to health.

I walked closer, studying all the ecstatic saints covering the pillar. Then I saw the contorting figure at the base.

Oh, please. So typical of that era, using images of women to represent evil. The artist had portrayed the Black Plague as a hideous hag.

My vision grayed around the edges, and all I could see was the writhing woman….

*The azure waters of the Mediterranean sparkled under the dazzling sun. Enjoying the balmy breeze fanning her bikini-clad body, the woman stretched like a contented cat in the chaise lounge on the secluded balcony.*

*If only her mind could succumb to this perfect day, but she couldn't totally relax. So much was at stake.*

*It was time to sever her man's familial bonds, which were keeping him from being the man he should be. And if Scarlet Rubashka knew anything, it was…well, all sorts of stuff, really! But it included how to set a romantic scene. What lover could resist finding his lady sunbathing against the exotic backdrop of St. Tropez?*

*After they both were feeling the buzz of sensual satiation, she would nail him down with a serious discussion about their future.*

*Caleb* had *to care for her. He couldn't make love to her as if she was the last woman on earth and not feel something for her.*

*Hadn't he said to her,* "Voglio essere come per eternità?" *I want to be with you forever? If that wasn't a mind-blowing thing for a man to say, she didn't know what was.*

*She could save him from his family.*

*Scarlet only wished that he was here, but he had called earlier, saying he would be late. A family emergency.*

*She pouted. After they had their talk, hopefully there would be no more such emergencies. Scarlet shrugged away the dark thoughts. So she would have to enjoy a fantastic view alone for a few hours more.*

*Tapping her fingers on the lounge's armrest, she considered her options. Perhaps she should return to Matilda's Millinery and buy that black-and-bronze fedora. Treating herself to beautiful hats was a woman's right.*

*She heard the soft scuff of a footstep behind her and a thrill shot through her. Had her lover surprised her by coming early after all? She sat up.*

*"Caleb—"*

*Strong hands wrapped around her throat. Gasping, she tried to rip the gloved fingers away, but they only tightened. She thrashed on the lounge, but the soft cushion she had been enjoying only seconds before now trapped her.*

*Her vision grayed. Desperately, she dug her nails into her killer's hands but she couldn't score past the leather. Her lungs screamed for air, yet she couldn't drag any in. With no energy to fight anymore, her arms grew limp and fell away.*

*Mistake! Her mind cried out what her voice could not.*

*She had made a mistake and it had killed her. Scarlet slid into the dreamless black void.*

*A woman writhing…*

"Eve!"

The sound of my name was like a splash of cold water, jerking me from my dream. Images swirled and drained away where I couldn't reach them. Where was I?

Nick gave me another gentle shake. "Eve, snap out of it!"

Still feeling woozy, I reached out and gripped his arms to steady myself. As I took a deep breath, I noticed people milling about, staring at me with curiosity.

"What happened?" My voice came out in a croak.

"I don't know. You disappeared on me and I found you standing here, swaying and moaning."

Moaning? I now was making noises when I had a vision? My face heated as I spotted the *Plague Column.*

The hag. I had been staring at the figure frozen forever in a contorted position when I'd had the psychic episode. But I hadn't experienced the past, had I? Although the dream had faded, I sensed it had been of a recent event. But who? What? Why couldn't I remember the details?

Yet hadn't I seen a tropical beach with a turquoise sea? I was in Graben Square with a bone-chilling wind and winter-gray skies above. It couldn't have been place cognition.

What the hell was happening to me?

Hold me, Nick, please.

"Eve." His strong arms enveloped me, drawing me so

close that I couldn't breathe, which was fine by me. Or was it? Was our connection such that I was now conveying my emotions to him? I broke free from his embrace.

"Are you all right, *chère?*" Worry darkened his eyes.

I risked reaching up and stroking the side of his face. "I'm fine. Really."

"Come on." Nick guided me into the building and then into the elevator that took us up to the penthouse. When the doors opened silently, I gaped. From the sleek, modern furniture to the model-beautiful woman sitting behind a desk, the reception area spoke of money and success. Of course the chrome and leather waiting chairs and gray walls and carpeting were purely masculine taste.

I cocked an eyebrow. "Ever hear of color, Petter?"

He grinned and fingered my shirt. "Ever hear of a dress, St. Giles?"

I stumbled slightly. A dress? He wanted me to wear one? In all the time we'd been together, he had never mentioned my clothes…or lack thereof.

"In your fantasies," I managed to spit out.

"Every damn day," he agreed, leading me past the very curious receptionist into the inner sanctum of his operations.

There I received my second surprise. I was in the center of a technical geek's heaven. In darkened rooms, computer and television monitors glowed. Men and women in headsets worked, gestured and talked. One man in his twenties, noticing Nick, motioned to him.

"Eve, this is Kurt."

The young man beamed. "Dr. St. Giles, it is a pleasure to meet you. How very clever of you to get those fingerprints!"

"Have you found anything yet?"

He puffed his thin chest. "Yes. I have identified them." Looking at us expectantly as if he wanted us to guess, he waited.

Nick folded his arms across his chest, practically glowering. "Kurt, we've had a rough day. Spill it."

Apparently a cranky boss didn't faze any of Nick's employees, for Kurt didn't look particularly worried. In fact, he took his sweet time in adjusting his glasses first.

"Kurt!"

"Yes, sir. Ever hear of Maximilian Adriano?"

*Adriano?* Surprise slammed its fist into my midsection, stealing my breath away.

Nick let out a low whistle. "I thought he was dead."

"I've put together a portfolio on the family," Kurt said. "It's on your desk."

"What?" I fisted my hands. "You knew more about the Adriano family than you let on, didn't you?" Those employees in the immediate vicinity, including Kurt, faded away.

Nick had the grace to grimace. "Let's take this up in my office."

"Let's." I fumed as he led me into a spacious room outfitted with the latest technology and the same gray-and-chrome theme. The moment he shut the door, I exploded.

"What have you been hiding from me?"

# Chapter 15

"Nothing, *chère.*" Nick tried to capture my hands, but I jerked away.

"Don't *chère* me. Don't you think it might have been important all the way back at Lake Como to tell me you knew the family?"

Suddenly I found myself trapped against the door with a furious Nick nose to nose with me. "If you hadn't wandered off and scared fifty years off my life—" he planted his hands on either side of me, effectively imprisoning me "—I would have told you that I was running a check on the Adriano family. That the family gathering in Lake Como, the run-in with Caleb in Barcelona and now a cousin at the health congress was just too coincidental to believe. They're involved, and I want to know how."

I opened my mouth but closed it when he glared a warning. "But, no, you don't trust anyone but yourself to get the job done. You have to go haring off without a thought for backup or consequences."

The truth of Nick's accusations stung, but since he was in a fighting mood, I might as well take my own shots.

I angled my chin. "Trust? What about lack of communication? I thought I saw Pauline Adriano walk by. However, when I motioned to you, you were too wrapped up on the phone to notice, so I had to take matters into my own hands and follow her."

"Pauline Adriano, here? Are you positive?"

"No." I sighed. "I lost her in the crowd."

He rubbed his hands up and down my arms. "How many white hairs have I grown since this morning?"

My lips twitched. "Oh, I don't know. Let me see." I narrowed my eyes and ran my fingers through his thick, cropped hair. "Hmm, maybe ten."

"I think I've calmed down enough to hear what happened to you by the *Plague Column.*"

I gave his cheek a light pat. "Later." As in "never" if I could help it. "Tell me how you know about the Adriano family."

"Of them," Nick corrected as he let go of me and moved to his desk. Leaning against it, he crossed one ankle over the other. "As a Swiss Guard, it would have been difficult *not* to have heard of the Adrianos. Old-guard Italian family with even more ancient ties to the Roman Catholic Church. But I'd never met them and certainly they would never have taken notice of someone like me."

"Did you know Myrddin was Maximilian?"

"No," he shook his head. "My information was that he was either dead or institutionalized. He disappeared off the face of the earth a while back."

I took a deep breath and sat in one of the black

leather client chairs. "Let me have it all, whether fact, rumor or fiction."

Rubbing his chin, Nick stared off into the distance as if he was mentally organizing the data. "Maximilian was the patriarch. Because of the family's longtime support of the church, it was reported that one didn't look too closely at their activities because the family always donates handsomely."

"Are they Mafia?"

Amusement gleamed in Nick's eyes. "No, the Mafia would be beneath an Adriano, although I wouldn't put it past the family to use the crime organization if necessary."

"Anyway," he shrugged, "the family notably guards its bloodline like it was the Vatican treasure. For generations there's been an heir, a spare and one for the church."

"Sounds feudal."

"But the feudal system provided the bounds of control, discipline and power for the best part of several centuries. If it worked for the Middle Ages, why not continue it on a lesser scale?"

"Brr." I shuddered.

"You of all people have had contact with the workings of European aristocracy."

Nick was right. The formality of the family of Yvette's husband had been something to behold—and for me to experience as little as possible.

"So the Adriano family has a glamorous sheen with rotten underpinnings?"

"That's the rumor, along with another one, that over the generations cousin killed cousin in order to maintain the main family. Certainly, their propensity to die violently helps to fuel the gossip."

"Who is Myrddin—or Maximilian?"

From the corner of his desk Nick picked up and

opened a folder. "The former patriarch. His son Simon now controls the empire. Simon's oldest son, Aaron, died in a sporting accident. Joshua was to be the church sacrificial lamb, but Aaron's death catapulted him into contention for the top spot. Apparently, your Scarlet's Caleb falls in and out of favor with Simon."

A foreboding, dusky and cold, crept inside me. "I wish I could find her, warn her."

He tapped the folder against his open palm. "I've assigned one of my people to track her down."

His stunning announcement, delivered in such a casual tone, touched me beyond measure. Scarlet was my friend, my concern, but Nick had made her his, as well.

Silently I rose and, going to him, wrapped my arms around his waist. "Thank you," I whispered as I kissed his cheek.

"You're welcome." He ran his fingers through my hair. "You look exhausted. That shoulder must be hurting."

I tried to step away but he wouldn't let me. "We have some time before we are due back at the gardens. I had your bag brought up from the car. Why don't you take a hot shower here? You can lie down on the sofa and rest."

I could do with more than a surface cleansing. I needed a mental one. Wiggling my eyebrows, I said, "Care to join me?" Running my hands over his chest, past his waist, I paused when I came across his erection. "I guess you do."

After making a choking noise, Nick bent, swept me into his arms and strode across to the bathroom. "I guess I do."

Even as he fought to switch on the shower, I attacked his clothes, tugging at his belt. Cursing, he shucked his before turning to me. His stripping was no-nonsense, effective. I shimmied up him to wrap my legs around his hips. Staggering from my shifting weight, he clamped my bottom to hold me still as he carried me into the shower. Bracing me against the stall wall, he thrust deep into me.

As the hot spray stung my skin and Nick pounded into me, driving me to a shattering orgasm, one thought ran like a broken tape in my head.

*I'm alive, I'm alive, I'm alive.*

Late that afternoon the delegates assembled in the Schönbrunn Gardens. Grumbling, artfully expressed, could transcend any language. They took their places on the three-tiered stand that had been set up in the center of the path while the photographer fussed with his equipment.

I turned to Helene Danhauser and casually asked, "How did your assistant, Ricardo, take the change in plans?"

The chair grimaced. "Not well, I am afraid. He was quite upset, saying we had ruined his special surprise by moving the photograph up by an hour."

"I don't see him here."

"He said he may be late. I believe he was trying to rearrange the surprise." Helene patted a nonexistent stray hair. "And where is your friend?"

"Nick? He's getting set up." Actually he was already in place. Somewhere in the deepening shadows, he waited. Uniformed police officers provided a more visible presence, strolling up and down the paths.

Helene glanced at her watch. "A pity. We cannot delay any longer, not if you are right about this madman. I would have liked Ricardo to be in the picture. He has worked so hard on this conference, but he insisted we go ahead if he did not make it."

Frederic walked over. "We are all set. Come, madam chair." He extended his hand. "You have the place of honor."

Excusing herself, Helene moved away. Overhead a police helicopter droned as it circled around the area. I watched as the photographer lined up the delegates.

Was the courier here in Vienna? Would he be the one to release the canister? I felt certain that despite the time change in the delegates' schedule, an attack would be made. But how?

The photographer called out for the group to smile. With the palace in the background, the picture would be stunning. A great memento of an important occasion. According to Frederic, despite all the lobbying pressure by drug companies, the delegation was close to an agreement on cost controls. Equal access to life-saving medicines would have far reaching consequences.

One woman called out in French, "Look!" She pointed as a hot air balloon floated into view over the palace.

It was a photo op made in heaven. The photographer frantically begged the people not to move, but the members did anyway, twisting to watch. Helene raised her voice, asking everyone to resume his or her position.

The brightly striped balloon drifted toward us. A man in the delegation broke out singing the old Fifth Dimension classic. Others laughed and joined in.

"'Up, up and away.'"

No, not away, over. It was going to float right over us in a perfect aerosol attack. As realization of the danger sliced through me, I screamed, "Get them out of here!"

The song stuttered to an end. I ran forward, waving my arms. "Frederic, the balloon. Get them out of here!"

With a startled look at me, Frederic started guiding people off the risers with Helene rushing to the other end to do the same.

Closer and closer the balloon came, too low, too

damn low. The Vienna police officers aided the group, urging them to run to the palace.

Time. We needed more time. I sprinted in the opposite direction to where paths intersected. Standing in the clear, I waved at the balloon. "Here! Come and get me you bastard!"

Amid all the noise, I heard two cries, one in rage, the other in protest. Lower and lower the balloon sank until I could see the courier in the basket. The late-afternoon sun's rays cast him in an eerie glow. He pointed a gun at me.

From the shadows of the trees lining the path, Nick stepped forward, his assault rifle raised. Seeing the danger, the courier spun around to the burner. With steady precision, Nick fired several shots. One side of the balloon fluttered, but the burner gave a low growl as the courier opened it up. The basket jerked and began to rise. Nick pulled the trigger again.

*Kaboom!*

A fireball enveloped the basket and lower part of the balloon. Against the orange flames I saw the shadow of the courier lift a metal cylinder.

Another shot cracked. The courier fell backward. The flames further engulfed the basket, and the balloon collapsed, as if all the air had been sucked out. As it spiraled to the earth a few hundred feet away, along with it went all my hopes of tracking van Velsen.

I scrambled toward the ruined remains. Nick caught my arm. "Where the hell do you think you're going?"

"The canister. I need to check to see if it survived the explosion or if it was compromised."

Nick indicated a van speeding along the path. "The containment unit is already here. Let them handle it."

"Oh." The adrenaline drained from me, leaving me

with limbs of mush. I sank to the ground and buried my face in my hands.

After my sister's death, and all the others killed in Damassine, after all the fever pitch of hunting, there was suddenly nothing. Crisis averted, but the major threat remained. I felt as deflated as the ruined remains still smoldering.

Dropping into a crouch beside me, Nick planted the rifle's butt on the ground. "You aren't ever going to listen to me, are you?"

"You've got fair odds—at least fifty-fifty."

"At this rate I'll be gray before my time." He sighed. "I'm sorry, Eve. I had to shoot him."

"I know, Nick. I know." Wiping the wetness from my face on my sleeve first, I then looked at him. "But we're back to square one. We don't know how many people are behind this or even the extent of van Velsen's involvement or his whereabouts."

Pebbles crunched as Frederic stopped beside us. "That's not quite the case, Eve." The director appeared to be a little green around the gills. Field action was never his strong suit.

"Oh? What's not the case?"

"One of the French delegates mentioned something interesting this afternoon. Van Velsen has reportedly been spotted in southern France."

There were times when one simply couldn't ignore serendipity anymore. My sister's home was in the Languedoc-Roussillon province. My pulse jump-started to life, and with an assist from Nick, I stumbled to my feet.

Fear filled me. France. My niece and nephew were there staying at the château with their paternal grandparents. The Swiss authorities finally had released Yvette's body, and the services were to be in several days.

"Did the delegate have anything more specific?" I asked calmly, all the while convincing myself not to panic. After all, southern France was a big area with many cities and villages. The mastermind behind this bug was after bigger fish than a single house.

"No, but I figured it was a start," answered Frederic.

"I'll take it." A buzzing sound grew in my head. I had run the source to ground. Very soon I would have the creator of the Spanish flu.

"My assistant called. Guess what family has vast pharmaceutical holdings?" asked Nick with a grim expression.

"The Adrianos."

"Dead on."

With a puzzled expression Frederic looked at us. "Was Ricardo Adriano involved in this?"

I nodded. "I'm fairly certain that he was, Frederic. Ricardo told Helene that he had a surprise planned for this photography session and yet he was called out of town on emergency. He was also upset when we changed the schedule."

"According to our sources, his cousin Caleb Adriano heads research and development while Ricardo has his hand in the marketing," Nick added.

"When can we leave for France?"

"That's my girl." Nick slung his arm around my shoulders and gave me a wink. "Always in a rush." The double meaning didn't escape me. Warmth spread across my face.

"I suspect we have more than a few layers of authorities with questions to answer first," Nick added. "Then we can take off."

"Good." I stared at the balloon and the white-suited team that swarmed over it. The hunt wasn't over yet.

* * *

Nick's layers of authorities proved to be endless. As he spoke with the local police, I wandered to the bench by the maze and sat down.

"It is not over," said Myrddin from behind me. Since the seat was smack dab against the topiary, I knew he had to be in the actual maze.

"Are you going to tell me why, Signore Maximilian Adriano, aka Myrddin?"

"So the industrious Mr. Petter finally tracked down my identity."

"Why are you hiding from your own family, Myrddin?" He was inked indelibly as "Myrddin" in my mind. His other identity didn't fit the man I had grown to know in this Twilight Zone.

"There are those who do not want to save the family."

"How are they poisoning the ley lines?"

"You can see the actual lines?"

I curled my fingers around the edge of the bench and gripped hard. "Yes."

"And the effect of the device on them? Is the negative energy black?"

"Yes. What device, Myrddin?"

"The family refers to it as their 'God Device,' as it matches the power of God himself. Through this technology, they have been able to master all types of natural phenomena. In fact, they created another machine, which they were using to cause all the blackouts that recently struck in France and Italy. Two of your fellow Marians actually helped to destroy that one. But I know they'll develop more."

"Pretty damn arrogant to view oneself as God."

"Unfortunately, that is the Adriano legacy. However, perhaps you are the one to stop them before it is too late."

"Stop them from what?"

"Wiping the Marians off the face of the earth."

My vision blurred for a moment and I saw the blood-stained hands of a man reaching for a woman.

*No!* I had to control this. To let these visions come whenever they wanted left me too vulnerable.

*Focus.* I inhaled and released my breath. The mist cleared from my head, but with its dissipation came certainty.

"You've killed some of these Marians."

"Yes."

"How many?"

"I did not keep, how do you Americans say, notches on a belt."

I swallowed. "That many."

"Yes. Do you believe in the afterlife, Dr. St. Giles?"

Did I? I thought about Yvette. Did I hope she was in a better place where the winds of self-doubt and destructive behavior no longer raged? Did I believe in a place where people could be at rest, no matter what lives they had led?

"Yes," I whispered.

"So do I, Eve. Unfortunately, I do not think all the penitence in the world will save me from hell, but I must try. If only to save my son and grandsons from a similar fate. I am afraid that I have set a less than stellar example. I pray that I'm not too late."

"Do you pray, Maximilian?"

"Max, please. The more formal name belongs to my other life." The brush rustled as if he shifted uneasily. "Do I pray? Probably not in the same sense as an ordinary person would. However, I do reflect, and I find myself drawn to ancient cathedrals where so many sins have been confessed over centuries and been forgiven.

I keep hoping that the enormity of my transgressions will shrink in comparison."

"Have they?"

A long silence. I'd almost thought he had gone when I heard the rough edge of his voice. "No, they only multiply."

"Tell me, Myrddin, was the recreation of the Spanish flu to undermine the world health community?"

"Yes."

"Why? To secure control of the international pharmaceutical market?"

"That would be…how do you say…small potatoes to them."

I fought not to turn around, knowing if I did, Myrddin would vanish like a wisp of smoke. "I thought your family was one of the richest and most powerful in Italy."

"Yes, but why stop with Italy when you have the power and money to control western Europe and beyond?"

"What!" I forgot all restraint, surging to my feet and turning to face the maze. The brush was so dense I couldn't see him.

"This may be the last time we can speak directly. Remember, Eve. Machiavellian puzzles have many layers, and my family has been able to weave them for centuries."

"Wait, don't go!" I ran toward the maze entrance.

On the evening breeze I heard Myrddin's fading voice. "Goodbye, Eve. While you cannot save the whole world, you can save yourself and those you care about. May God be with you."

Inside the maze I cut to the right, thinking it would take me by the bench. I stopped short at the green wall of plants.

Frustrated, I kicked at a rock. Spinning on my heel, I retraced my steps to the entrance. Another dead end.

* * *

Frustration still fizzed in my veins when Nick opened the door to his flat. Dealing with the authorities had kept us tied up until late, so we had agreed to spend the night at his place and leave for France first thing in the morning.

Although weariness nearly overpowered me, I still eyed Nick's living room with curiosity as I entered it and smiled. "Your place looks about as lived-in as mine."

"I pride myself on its homey look," he agreed as he shrugged off his jacket. Actually, his furnishings echoed those of his office: chrome, glass, black leather furniture and gray walls. I had this sudden urge to grab a brush and slap on a coat of sunny-yellow paint. Maybe I should do the walls of my flat when I got home. I had this intense yearning to surround myself with color and light.

Nick picked up a familiar bag from the sleek sofa. "I had your bags brought up. The one with your clothes should be in the bedroom."

I took the backpack and rummaged inside for my cell. After removing it, I checked for messages. I listened to several updates from my team at the Centre and then I heard Scarlet's voice.

Relief swept through me. My God, she was all right! With death surrounding me, I had feared…

"Eve, darling. You sound so concerned. I'm all right, truly. We do need to talk so I will try to call you later. Why is love so complicated? Why do women always have to fall for the wrong men? It must be our primal urge to save them. Anyway, Nick looked hot and I do trust you are, how do you say, jumping his bones. Later."

I hit Redial but a tinny voice informed me that the phone number I was calling was out of the service area. "Damn!"

Nick glanced up from a stack of mail he was checking. "What's wrong?"

"Scarlet must have called me while we were at the gardens. I turned off my phone while we were waiting to trap Ricardo." I released a breath of frustration. "She said she was all right but wanted to talk to me. I need to warn her about the Adrianos. She's playing with fire and doesn't know it." I'd filled Nick in on my conversation with Myrddin during our long wait at the gardens.

"Let me have your phone." Nick called in the update to his agent he had searching for Scarlet. "He thinks she's in France so this phone call should help. He'll find her."

France, where we would be heading next. A frisson of fear raced through me. All the dots were now converging there. Scarlet, with her nose for a story, and van Velsen and who knows who else were possibly in the same locale. I had to find them both, fast.

Nick gripped my shoulders. "Hey, she'll be fine. Why don't you grab a hot shower? You'll feel better."

My lips twitched. "That dirty again?"

He ran a finger along my nose. "You are like a child with mud pies. I have a small washer and dryer so we can get you set up with clean clothes."

Still distracted by my concern for Scarlet, I nodded and wandered into the bedroom. Grabbing up my bag, I headed into the bathroom. For an eternity I stood in the shower, letting the hot spray wash away the day's events along with the newest layer of grime. When I stepped out, I dried off with a large fluffy black bath sheet and then, with one look at the dirty clothes in my bag, wrapped another around my chest. Nick should have a T-shirt I could borrow.

I opened the door and blinked. Flickering light filled the bedroom. No lamps were switched on but everywhere I looked I saw lit candles. From the deep shadows of the corner Nick moved toward me, setting a lighter on a table.

Striving for an amused tone, I asked, "What's this? Did you lose power?"

Not answering, Nick came to a stop in front of me and then leisurely scanned me from head to foot. His heated gaze could have burned the towel off me. I shifted under his intense scrutiny. "Nick?"

"You are so beautiful." He cupped my shoulders before running his hands down along my arms. "Such delicacy and yet such strength." He raised my hand and kissed each fingertip slowly. I shuddered at the gentle caresses.

"Every time I look at you, I am undone."

Undone? I was becoming an emotional puddle. When had I begun to crave this tenderness?

I opened my arms and myself to this man I loved. Sweeping me up, he carried me over to the bed and, sitting me beside it, removed my towel. His mouth settled on mine, and as our kiss slowly built in intensity, I removed his clothes with shaking hands. As one, laughing, we tumbled back onto the bed.

When I shifted my hips, anxious to join us, he threw a leg over, trapping mine. "Don't be so anxious," he teased. "I have all this lovely, flushed skin of yours to explore yet."

"But, Nick—"

His mouth cut off my protest. When he had kissed me senseless, he began the assault on my body. Using his lips and tongue, he began his deliberate journey, beginning at my earlobe. Until he nipped it, I had never realized what a sensual trigger point my ear was. I almost shot off the bed, only to meet the anchor of his body.

Next up was my collarbone where he explored the

hollow with his tongue. Desire spiraled in me, and I held my breath when his mouth moved away, down the valley between my breasts. My nipples hardened, waiting for the heat of his mouth.

However, Nick's head lowered, with only his unshaven cheek rasping against the side of my breast. His clever tongue flicked at my belly button.

"Oh, no, you don't," I muttered. "Come back here." I gripped the sides of his head, trying to bring his mouth back up.

He raised his head, his grin positively smug. "What's the matter, *chère?*" He placed his finger on the tip of my nipple, sending a blast of heat straight through me. "Did I miss something?"

Okay, two could play at this game. Slowly I placed my finger in my mouth to wet it and then, as Nick's gaze darkened, ran the wet finger in a circle around my nipple. He let his breath in a hiss. "You don't play fair."

"All's fair in love and—"

His hot mouth covered my breast, and I lost all train of thought. When he had thoroughly suckled one nipple, he moved to the other. The sexual tension coiled even tighter in me so I moved restlessly under him.

"Nick?"

"Yes, Eve?" He returned to nibbling the corner of my mouth. His erection pressed against my thigh.

"Do you have to cherish every inch of my skin right now? Couldn't you save a few for the next time?"

His breath feathered my face, and I closed my eyes in anticipation. "Your wish is my command." Nudging my legs open, he settled between them.

But when he stilled, my eyelids drifted open to find him intently studying my face. "What's wrong?"

"I want you to look at me."

"Your wish is my command," I whispered, mirroring his words.

"Smart aleck." He smiled and dropped a kiss on my forehead. Then he slid into me, and together we built up a rhythm. When I slipped over into a stunning climax, he groaned and followed me. In a shimmering cocoon of warmth and light as he cradled me against him, I listened to the steady beating of his heart. Then I heard the words that I had waited so long to hear.

*I love you, chère.*

My eyes flew open. No, not heard, not in the normal sense. Once again I was so deeply connected to Nick that his emotions seared my heart. Once more I had invaded his thoughts.

Carefully I turned in his arms. As I felt him fall into a deep sleep, I curled into a ball. I couldn't be with this man without connecting with him on every level.

How could I stop myself from intruding on his emotions like some damn voyeur?

# *Chapter 16*

The trail was cold. It seemed as if all leads had gone up in that explosion with the courier. After nearly two weeks since the Damassine outbreak, I was no closer to the madman who had created the flu.

Two days later the jet landed at the small airfield at Carcasonne in Languedoc-Roussillon. I stared wearily at the blur of countryside as Nick drove the Land Rover he'd rented in a southerly direction along D118. We had chased down every rumor and gone to countless pharmaceutical companies along the Mediterranean coastline, centering our search in the Provence region where the delegate finally had tracked down the sighting of van Velsen.

Nothing.

Now we were breaking off the search to attend Yvette's funeral. I was going to have to face my niece and nephew without having found and brought to justice their mother's killer.

I wasn't looking forward to the recrimination in their eyes. After all, I saw it in my own every time I looked in a mirror.

My brain registered dull pain and, glancing down, I saw I'd clenched my hands so tight that my nails were digging grooves in my flesh. With an effort I straightened my fingers.

"I hadn't realized this region had become such a tourist mecca," Nick commented as he slowed for a bus turning ahead of us. "Traffic's been heavy since we left the airport."

"The Land of Oc has become the Land of Da Vinci."

"Pardon?"

"This is the main road to the village Rennes-le-Château where the priest Berenger Saunière created his church dedicated to Mary Magdalene. Yvette complained that ever since the book *The Da Vinci Code* came out, every treasure hunter in the world has descended upon the area."

"I wouldn't mind seeing the church sometime," Nick remarked. "There are more legends per square mile in this region than almost any other part of Europe. Templar treasure, secret temples, hidden bloodlines. Everything near and dear to a history buff's heart."

I frowned, not sure I should believe what I was seeing through the car's window.

"Property values have gone sky-high because even outhouses have been snatched up. The vineyard next to the Fouquets' estate was the latest victim to fall prey to the land grab, much to the Fouquets' annoyance as apparently the new owners aren't French."

I wasn't dreaming. The passing landscape vibrated with glowing lines. My God, the ley lines crisscrossed as far as the eye could see. I'd known that this was

Cathar country, its mountains still dominated by the exterminated religion's castle strongholds. Had the Catharians been attracted to build their communities here because of the earth's energy? If the ley lines were powerful here, wouldn't the Adrianos seek them out to either experiment or destroy?

*No, don't go there.* I couldn't take any more questions right now. I turned away from the scenery only to be blindsided by an equally troubling view—Nick.

With the mild Mediterranean climate, he drove with the window down on his side. The late-afternoon sun cast a warm glow, softening his normally harsh features. Although fine fatigue lines fanned from the corners of his eyes, he looked relaxed. It was, after all, a beautiful day for a drive in the country. He'd traded in sweaters for form-fitting T-shirts that displayed his well-defined, muscular torso and arms. My heart did a little spin, whether from desire or something deeper I didn't want to explore.

"Earth to Eve."

I started. "Sorry, I was thinking."

He shot me a glance and then smiled. "From the looks of your blush, perhaps you were thinking about getting naked with me as soon as we get to the house?" He reached over, but I slapped his hand aside.

"Got quite an ego, don't you?"

He rolled his neck. "I don't know about you but I could do with some relaxation after the past few days."

"Phillipe and Laurel are going to be there as well as Jean-Pierre's parents," I primly reminded him. Would my niece and nephew be happy to see me or would they shun me?

After all, I'd been e-mailing them every night. Only Phillipe had answered with reserved responses.

He reached for my hand again and this time I let him take it. "Why are you so nervous about seeing your niece and nephew?"

I shrugged. "I really don't know them. With my job and them living here, I've been a name to them rather than a flesh-and-blood aunt."

"Was that your choice or Yvette's?"

"What do you mean?"

"Did your problems with your sister extend to her children?"

"You know how to cut to the chase of my relationship with her, don't you?"

"I just wish I could do the same with ours." He rubbed his thumb over my fingers.

*Comfort.* God knows I needed it.

"The last time our family spent together was two Christmases ago."

"What happened?"

Unbearable pain, I could have told him but didn't. "Not much. I never had any time alone with Phillipe or Laurel. Yvette kept telling them not to bother me. If she saw us together, she would call them away."

Each time Yvette had dragged them away, as if I had a disease, I'd felt a deep slash across my heart. Maman had said to give my sister time to adjust to motherhood. I'd figured that meant when Phillipe and Laurel were in college or married with children of their own.

"She was afraid, Eve."

"Of what?"

"That the children would love you. She was very needy, *chère.* She wouldn't have been able to bear her children developing any emotional attachment to you."

The truth of his remarks resonated deep inside. Had

I always known this? Was that why I'd stayed away, sending only presents and cards for birthdays?

Nick raised and kissed the back my hand. "Kids are resilient, but they'll need you, even if they don't know how to ask or show it."

"A new beginning."

"Yes." When he lowered our linked hands, I tugged free. "Sounds crass with Yvette dead, talking about forging a bond with them that she would have been against."

"Isn't it out of the ashes of death that the phoenix rises? Mourn her, forgive her. Then forgive yourself and move on, Eve."

"That's easier said than done."

"Only if you want to make it complicated."

I wrapped my arms around my midsection and returned to staring out the window. Past the village of Couiza, Nick made the turnoff for the manor house.

The road turned, twisted and climbed through the extensive vineyards that had been in the Fouquet family forever. Taking a label once known for table wines, Yvette's husband, Jean-Pierre, during his abbreviated life had striven to produce several international vintages. Even after his death, his parents and the wine master had continued his work. The family had been only too happy to allow Yvette to go off and play while they groomed Phillipe to run the vineyard someday.

Of course, Jean-Pierre's parents had it all wrong. Laurel was the one born with the love of earth in her soul, while Phillipe's interest in green only extended to mold he could view under a microscope. Yvette hadn't been willing to do battle for her children, but maybe I could.

The drive ended in a sweeping curve before the Château Fouquet. Built in the eighteenth century, the stone mansion oozed tradition. Nick shut off the engine and gave a low whistle.

I stuck my tongue in my cheek. "Do you still feel like getting naked in the shower?"

He gave me an irrepressible grin. "If it's a Roman tub, I will be happy to switch to a long soak, with you scrubbing my back." Exiting, he came around and opened my door. As I got out, the front door opened and Jean-Pierre's parents, both wearing polite smiles, stepped onto the front porch.

"*Bonjour!*" I called out and walked toward the steps. Two smaller figures emerged from the house, causing me to falter to a stop. While fair-haired Phillipe had his father's coloring, Laurel favored the Gallic side with her dark eyes and hair. Both stared solemnly at me.

Great. This meeting was going to be even harder than I'd imagined.

"Remember," Nick said quietly, "kids know love."

I swallowed. "Phillipe, Laurel. I'm so sorry about your mother." I opened my arms slightly and prayed that I wasn't being a fool.

With a stiff gait my nephew came down the stairs. Dressed in black chinos and sweater, he looked older than his eight years. "Aunt Eve, so good of you to come." He extended his hand.

With disappointment crushing my heart, I let my hands drop. Then his lower lip quivered. "Oh, honey." I reached out and wrapped him close. "She loved you so much." His thin shoulders shook as I stroked his hair.

On the porch Laurel watched us with dark solemn eyes. A tingle of awareness shivered through me. Two years ago when I'd last seen her, I would have denied the significance. However, the past few weeks had shown me

I could no longer ignore this awareness. Somehow I needed to get past Laurel's shield and help her.

I started awake. Nick's breath fanned my shoulder as he slept spoon fashion next to me. I lay quietly, not wanting to disturb him. Not hard to do, given the four-poster bed we were in. The suite we'd been given was paradise in comparison to the conditions we'd been in over the past few days. The goose-down mattress won handily over the leather chair in the jet.

The gauze curtains stirred on a gust of wind. The night had been so mild that we had left the balcony doors open. Then I heard a sound on the breeze, a muffled cry.

Lifting Nick's hand from my waist, I slid free. He murmured and I tucked his arm around my pillow. I padded across the oak floor to the door and opened it, wincing at the creaking hinges. I stole a glance at Nick, but he remained asleep. Walking down the hall to the next room, I opened the door and entered.

In the middle of another mahogany four-poster bed, my niece turned and whimpered. "Laurel, are you all right?" Crossing the room, I sat on the edge of the bed.

She sat upright, gasping. "Aunt Eve, is that you?"

I stroked her damp cheek. "Yes. Did you have a bad dream, sweetie?"

Stiffening, she drew up her legs, creating a physical barrier between us. "No."

"Well, now, you're lying, but I will respect your privacy. Call me if you need anything. I can always listen." Wishing I could do more, I rose.

"Aunt Eve?"

"Yes, Laurel?"

She hugged her knees even closer to her body. "Do you ever see strange things?"

Slowly, I sat down again. "What kind of strange things?"

"Like people in another time and place kind of strange?" she whispered.

"Yes. I have and still do."

She swallowed. "Mom said you were weird."

"*Weird* is a word people use when they are afraid of something they don't understand."

Laurel nodded. "I think I am also weird."

"No, sweetie. You're just sensitive. Can you tell me what you see?"

Her breath hitched. "I see evil."

A ten-year-old girl seeing evil? Leaning against the headboard, I stretched out on the bed and gathered her close. "Tell me."

"In my dream I go to my secret place that no one knows about." Glancing up, she shot me a guilty look.

"Every one needs a special place. Your mother and I would play in the forest behind our house. I can tell you about our games sometime if you like."

"Okay."

"So, what happens when you go to your place in your dreams?"

"A man in a white suit comes after me."

I twirled a curl of her hair around my finger. "White suit, sounds pretty dapper to me. Is he the good guy?"

Slowly, she shook her head. "No, Aunt Eve. He wears a suit like yours and he is *torve,* scary."

I froze. "A protective suit with breathing apparatus?"

"*Oui.*"

Oh my God. Was she dreaming of me? Once I had sent a picture of me working in the field to Maman, joking that she had an alien for a daughter. Had she shown it to Laurel?

"Are you sure it is a man in the suit?"

"Oh, *oui.* I can see his face through the mask."

I relaxed. "How do you know he's bad, Laurel?"

"Because he comes at me with his hands outstretched. He wants to choke me."

Apprehension gripped me. Hadn't I recently had a similar dream? Knowing how strong a nightmare this must have been for Laurel, I hugged her hard. "No one is going to hurt you, baby. I won't let him."

"But, Aunt Eve," she whispered as she burrowed her face against me. "You cannot stop him. In my dreams you are lying in a strange dress on the ground, dead."

Ice shot through my veins. What kind of visions was she experiencing? I kept my tone light. "Well, you know what they say. Forewarned is forearmed. Now that I know about the bad guy in the SBU, I'll have to make sure I kick his butt first."

She sniffed. "I think you can, Aunt Eve."

I pressed my cheek against the top of her head. "Would you like me to stay for a while?"

"Please, if you do not mind." She snuggled closer.

Hearing a slight sound at the door, I looked over and saw Nick standing there. Giving me a thumbs-up, he smiled and shut the door.

"Aunt Eve?"

"Yes, Laurel?"

"Would you like to see my secret place?"

"Very much."

"Okay." She fell silent, and then gradually her tense body relaxed as she drifted to sleep. I closed my eyes to fall into an uneasy sleep where men in white suits chased me through a cave.

The next morning during breakfast, I proposed a trip to Rennes-le-Château. Phillipe didn't look too enthused until

Nick's face lit up. I'd already noticed my nephew hanging on every word Nick spoke and knew he had a case of hero worship. I wasn't about to complain of his model selection. I had a similar bad case going on for Nick.

To the grandparents' palpable relief, we piled into the Land Rover and headed out. My parents would be arriving with Yvette's body tomorrow, and I was sure the Fouquets needed a break before the next onslaught of visitors disturbed their home. After the services, all the guests would be invited to the house for refreshments.

Although the Fouquet estate was only a short distance away as a bird flies, it was a different matter for people, as the infamous village of Rennes-le-Château was perched on the side of the mountain. After parking and purchasing our tickets for the church, I listened with amusement as Nick played tour guide.

"The mystery of Rennes-le-Château stems from its priest Berenger Saunière," he said as we approached the entrance to the Church of Mary Magdalene.

"Why is that, Nick?" asked Phillipe.

"He became unaccountably rich after taking up residence here in 1885. There are a number of theories about how he came by his wealth, the most alluring one being that he discovered a Cathari treasure."

With doubt on her face, Laurel examined the less than impressive facade of the church. "Grandfather Fouquet says that the Cathars were killed many years ago."

"He's right," Nick agreed. "Pope Pious ordered the Third Crusades be held to eliminate the threat of the usurper religion. Before all was said and done, Languedoc was laid to waste and what few Cathars survived left the region or went into deep hiding."

"The Fouquets helped them," Laurel announced with pride.

"What do you mean?" I glanced at her.

"There are ruins of an old house on the estate," she explained. "Grand-père said that pilgrims would hide there."

"But what treasure did the Cathars have?" Phillipe tugged on Nick's arm.

"Legend has it that the Holy Grail and other treasures were held by the Cathars at their last great castle, Montsegur. When the crusaders laid siege, in secret a few Cathars along with Knights Templar descended down the impossible slope of Montsegur and escaped with the treasure."

"Where is it?" Phillipe demanded, but I noticed that Laurel studied her shoes as if she had no further interest in the tale.

"No one knows. Theorists say it's hidden in one of the many grottos or caves around here. Others believe the priest Saunière found it and spent part of it on this village. His crowning achievement was building the Magdala Tower, which housed his library. Others believe the priest found genealogies he used to blackmail the Vatican."

"What are these…genealogies?" Phillipe had trouble pronouncing the word.

I shot Nick a warning glance. I wasn't sure that he needed to go into the details of the rumors concerning Mary Magdalene. He winked at me. "A genealogy traces one's family tree, Phillipe. I bet your father's family has one."

"Do you think…" Phillipe came to a dead stop inside the church, staring at the statue of a horrible, grimacing demon.

I had to admit, after giving a glance at the Latin words, *Terribilis est lows iste,* "This Place is Terrible," the priest had placed over the door, that his choice in statuary also left something to be desired. Of course, if the priest had been guarding sacred treasure, then this was the perfect demon to place at the front door. I made a point of sticking my tongue out at him, and the children laughed and relaxed.

While Laurel did a little hopscotch number on the black-and-white tiled floor, Nick and Phillipe examined the rest of the statuary. I wandered closer to the stained-glass windows.

A woman who had been standing to the side came over. "I heard you speaking to the children. You are American, yes?"

"Yes." I smiled politely but awareness tingled through me. She was a Marian.

"The windows are beautiful, are they not?"

"Yes." They certainly were more my cup of tea than the front entrance decor.

The woman folded her hands. "They have special properties. The glass craftsman made these so that different phenomena can be observed throughout the year. My favorite one comes at the end of March, when light streaming through this window—" she pointed to one showing Christ teaching the apostles "—forms a triangle that becomes so luminous that the whole interior is transfigured by the light."

"Sounds beautiful."

"You will see other examples of their work throughout this region. All have different properties, different mysteries to behold."

"I'm sure I will." I wasn't really planning on a tour, but I didn't want to hurt her feelings. The woman quite obviously was passionate about stained glass.

"Eve?" Laurel spoke from behind me.

"Excuse me a second." I turned around and knelt to Laurel's level. "What is it?"

"Can we leave soon? I do not like this church. It is too—" she lifted her shoulders in an absolutely adorable Gallic shrug "—dark."

Horrified that the woman would be offended by the criticism, I half twisted but she was no longer behind me. Frowning, I rose and scanned the chapel but couldn't spot her. Probably she left through a side door.

I held out my hand. "Come on, let's go roust the boys. I bet there's a café around here with your name on an ice cream cone."

She began to giggle and then, realizing where she was, slapped her hand across her mouth. After leaving the church, we toured the Magdala Tower that the priest had built to house an extensive library. Naturally the kids had to count out loud each and every one of the infamous twenty-two steps of the stairway. Since Nick and Phillipe wanted to explore the cemetery, something neither Laurel nor I had any desire to do, we made plans to meet at the café.

Declining the offer of a glass of the Berenger Saunière wine, I ordered coffee and a dish of chocolate ice cream for Laurel. She was polishing off the last spoonful when she stilled midlick.

Thinking Nick and Phillipe were coming, I turned in my chair. Three tables over at the outer edge of the crowded café sat three men, two of them red-faced as if they were arguing. I recognized two of them immediately—Caleb and Simon Adriano. The third one was familiar but it took a second for my brain to catch up with what I was seeing: Willem van Velsen.

Had they followed Nick and I here? No, that couldn't possibly be it. The ley lines. Were they planning an attack here or…more experiments with the manipulation of power?

I turned around so that my back was to the men and spoke in a low voice as I signaled for the check. "Laurel, do you know those three men over there?"

She glanced over and froze. Her eyes wide with fear, she nodded. "One."

"Which one, sweetie?" I fumbled in my pocket and pulled out a few bills. I needed to get her out of here to safety.

"The man in the tan sweater."

Van Velsen? Stunned, I reached out and clasped her hands between mine. "How do you know that man?"

She swallowed. "He searches, for the Cathari treasure I think. He has come close to finding my secret place."

I relaxed only marginally. Was the scientist into the treasure craze or did he have another reason to be roaming the countryside here? I paid the waiter and declined change.

"Listen to me, Laurel. On the count of three, we're going to get up. When you do, I want you to keep turned away from them and as close to me as you can. Do you understand?"

"*Oui.*"

"Okay. One, two, three." We rose, and keeping my body between her and the other table, I guided her to the other side and headed down the street toward the cemetery. Relief filled me when I saw Nick with his arm casually draped around Phillipe's shoulders. The moment he saw me, though, he went on alert.

"What's wrong?" he asked in a low voice.

"Nick, van Velsen is here with Caleb and Simon Adriano."

"Where?"

"Back at the café. Laurel says she's seen Willem before near her special place."

"Take the kids back to the car." He dug the keys out of his pocket and handed them to me. "I'm going to check it out."

"Be careful."

Laurel and Phillipe both wore frightened expressions, so I smiled. "It's going to be all right. Come on, let's head for the car." When we reached the parking lot, I slid into the backseat with them.

"Aunt Eve, what is going on? Is Laurel in danger?" Phillipe put a protective arm around his sister.

"Not if I can help it," I said, but knew that reassurance wasn't enough. My niece and nephew might be young, but they had already weathered the loss of both parents. They deserved an explanation.

"How much do you know about what happened at Damassine?"

Phillipe glanced at his sister and she nodded. "There was an outbreak of a flu that killed a lot of people."

"That's right. It was the Spanish flu. The last outbreak during World War I killed millions before it ran its course. Some scientists have been playing with its DNA."

My nephew swallowed. "Why would they do that?"

"To see if they could."

"That's stupid." Laurel kicked the back of the driver seat.

"Yes, it is. Some bad people stole the strain from a lab and released it."

"But they killed Maman!" Phillipe clenched his hand.

"They killed a lot of people."

"Murderers," he spat out the word. "I will kill them."

I reached over and cupped his face. "No. We will bring them to justice. That's what Nick and I have been doing. We got the man who released the virus, and now we're after the people behind him."

"They were at the café?" He twisted toward the door.

Realizing what he was doing, I clamped a hand around his wrist. "Nick is there. Let him do his job. Your sister and I need you here."

He looked sullen but nodded. I checked to see if Nick was coming. To my horror I saw the Adrianos and the scientist approaching the parking lot.

"Get down!" I ordered as I scooted off the seat. They followed me. When Laurel opened her mouth, I pressed a finger across my lips, indicating for them to be silent.

In the quiet I could hear the crunch of gravel as the men approached. The footsteps went behind the Rover. I almost had a heart attack when Phillipe raised his head to stare out the window. I grabbed his shoulder, forcing him down again. Car doors opened and closed, and an engine started to life. As tires ground past us, I cautiously rose to see a silver Mercedes turn out of the lot.

I needed a defibrillator for a second time when our driver's door opened but relaxed when Nick slid in. "Are you all right?" he asked with a tense expression.

"Yes." I quickly switched from the back to the front seat. "Get us out of here."

"Yes, madam." Amusement flickered in his eyes as he turned the key in the ignition.

"What happened at the café?"

"I couldn't get too close without drawing attention, but they were having quite a debate." His fingers tightened around the wheel. "My Italian may be rusty, but the Adrianos were quite upset with van Velsen's sojourn to the village. Apparently, he's caught the treasure fever. They wanted him to focus on his work."

"His work? Nick, there has to be a lab nearby within driving distance."

"I'll start a search, particularly for any possible Stelle Consortium holdings."

"Did they mention Scarlet at all?"

"No. I didn't hear her name."

He downshifted for the steep drive away from the village. "I couldn't hear anything about where they were going." Frustration radiated in his voice.

"Nick, we can't go after them."

"I know, *chère.*" He reached out and stroked my cheek. "We will first take the children back to the château."

Phillipe leaned forward between the seats. "Are you worried about losing those bad men because of us?"

I shook my head. "Nick is the best in the business. We'll track them down."

"Aunt Eve, do not be concerned. I can tell you where they are going."

"Phillipe!" Stunned, I stared at him. "What are you saying?"

I didn't know a young boy could have such a grim smile. "Grand-père Fouquet makes me spend an hour every day learning about wines. He's been very upset about a new owner of a neighboring domaine and the money being spent on the vines."

Phillipe pointed at the road. "That car those men were driving? I recognized the decal on the rear window. It is the symbol for Château L'Astral. Take the road to Argues and you will find my mother's killers, *oui?*"

The Star Château. Shaking inside, I reached over and gripped his shoulder. "*Oui.*"

# Chapter 17

Quietly fuming, I stood outside the Fouquet château. Nick had left over an hour ago to do a reconnaissance of the Adriano compound. A quick check with his agency had confirmed that a Stelle Consortium holding owned the Château L'Astral, which was not too far from the Fouquet estate.

Nick had been adamant about my not going with him. In a blunt, no-argument tone, he had said I would only slow him down, before kissing me breathless and then driving off. While I knew he was right, it didn't make the waiting any easier.

"Aunt Eve?"

I turned and found my niece standing uncertainly on the step. "Yes, Laurel?"

"Will Nick be all right?"

"Yes, he'll be fine. He's the best in the business."

She chewed on her lower lip. "Would you like to see my special place?"

I checked the afternoon sun. The plan was to get closer to the Adriano compound once darkness fell. "Is it very far?"

"Just over that hill." She pointed toward the ridge that ringed the estate. She gave me an innocent smile. "We will be back in time for Nick."

Ah, out of the mouths of babes. I held out my hand. "Let's go, then."

We crossed the fertile fields where the scent of earth mingled with ripe fruit. As we walked up the first slope, trees provided leafy shade. Here and there wildflowers still bloomed. We seemed to be following a path meandering along the hill. When we came upon a clearing, Laurel pointed to piles of stones that formed an outline of a small building.

"This is where the pilgrims used to hide. Grand-père said that those fleeing the Crusades would seek shelter here for the night."

"Really?" Fascinated, I circled the rubble. A large moss-covered boulder caught my eye. On closer inspection I spotted a carved letter, a flattened *M.* The same symbol etched in the wall of the Templar castle at Ponferrada.

Excitement hummed inside me. Had the Marian pilgrims I'd seen been here? Had this sign marked their safe passage?

Laurel studied the carving. "Maman said that was an astrological symbol for the fish."

"Pisces?"

"*Oui.* Shall we go, Aunt Eve, before it is too late?"

"Certainly."

With a last look at the boulder, I followed Laurel

down the path. When we reached a denser section of woods, I heard the faint sound of water.

Uneasy at the distance we had traveled, I asked, "Laurel, do your grandparents know where this place is?"

She shrugged. "No."

"Are you permitted to go this far from the house?"

"They only told me not to go off the estate. This is still part of the domaine."

Aha. I was going to have a little chat with the Fouquets when we returned. Obviously, they had underestimated my niece. "Is that a spring I hear?"

"*Oui.* There are several streams and—" she screwed up her face "—grottos? I think that is the word."

Terrific. A tempting playground, for any child, that held all sorts of dangers.

She veered off the nonexistent path toward the sound of water. I had to duck under tree limbs and squeeze between several bushes in order to follow her. "Laurel? Wait!"

I emerged into a minuscule clearing against the steep hillside. A small waterfall trickled more than flowed down the rocky surface to pool at the base where Laurel waited for me expectantly. "It is in here."

"Here? Where here?" I looked around but saw only rock, water and brush.

She slipped behind a bush and disappeared from sight. Stunned, I followed and found a narrow fissure in the rock surface.

*Ohmigod.*

"Laurel, wait!"

"Come on, Eve. It is really quite safe."

Safe for bats, maybe, but humans? Sucking in my stomach and praying that I could get out again, I squeezed through the cool, damp stone. Sharp edges like claws snagged my sweater but didn't hold.

I found myself in a shallow dark cave. The ceiling was so low that I had to keep my head down. As my eyesight adjusted to the dim light, I noticed Laurel stood beside a darker slash at the back, probably another passage.

"Laurel? How did you find this?"

"I was playing one day when a dove flew around my head and then disappeared into the side of the cliff. The bird led me in here."

Uh-huh. I mentally shrugged. Why not? Hadn't I had enough strange experiences lately to fill a book?

I heard the echo of people talking, and for a moment feared that I was slipping into another time and place again. However, Laurel put a finger to her lips and, hurrying to my side, gripped and tugged on my hand. As she knelt on the floor of the cave by the opening, I followed suit.

Over the cheerful gurgle of water as it splashed into the pond, I heard the sound of voices rising and falling. A man and a woman, I thought, and they were uncomfortably near to our hiding place. Unease slithered through me at the sense of evil being present. Next to me Laurel trembled so I wrapped my arm around her, drawing her closer.

Then the man and woman stopped, and the cave's opening acted like a microphone, magnifying their voices. Were they speaking Italian? I concentrated on the words. While I spoke only a little Italian, hopefully my fluency in French would fill in the gaps in interpreting.

The woman's tone was cajoling as if to soothe the man, but I couldn't hear her words clearly. Something about an entrance not being here. Entrance to what?

The moment the man answered, I recognized the cold, arrogant tone. *Simon Adriano.* However, his cadence was so cultured and fluent that I could understand him.

"The parchment spoke of the Land of Oc, and Willem says that the Templars owned much of the land here."

What parchment was he talking about?

"But, Simon…"

"But, Pauline," Simon mocked her. "This would have been a perfect spot for the Marians to hide among the Templars and Cathars. With all the ley lines, this would have been an ideal place for their temple. We are close to finding it, I tell you."

"I think the tales of the Holy Grail and the Ark of the Covenant being hidden in these hills have turned your head," she said in a light, teasing tone. I had to give Pauline credit. If she was angry at Simon's careless disregard, then she hid it well.

They must have moved closer to the spring, for suddenly the zing of recognition quivered inside me. Beside me, Laurel stirred uneasily and I realized she felt the connection as well. My arm tightened.

*Please, don't let Pauline sense us.*

"What is it?" Simon demanded. "You are acting like a dog sensing prey, all tense and alert."

"Do not compare me to a dog, Simon." She precisely enunciated each word. Oh, he had pissed her off. "I thought I felt someone else present."

"Where?" Simon demanded. I could almost see him spinning around to check the brush.

"I do not know. But others are nearby."

*Damn.* Why couldn't we turn off this radar for other Marians?

"As usual," he sneered, "your woman's imagination is getting away from you."

"And one day your superiority may fail you.

However, we should turn back. I want to take another look at that Madonna in the estate's chapel before returning to Naples. There's something about the image that bothers me." They must have turned away, for their voices faded.

After a few long moments I released a sigh of relief. The tension ebbed from Laurel's body. Wiggling loose from my grip, she rose. "The man and woman, they are bad, yes?"

"I wish I knew, sweetie. I don't have all the pieces to solve the puzzle yet."

"They have gone, yes?"

"Yes."

Quickly she moved to the rear passage. "Come."

"Laurel, I don't think this is such a good idea..."

She vanished into the corridor. The child must have the eyesight of a bat and my stubbornness to boot. Apparently, she only listened when it suited her.

"Laurel!" I hurried after her, blinking as my vision adjusted to the even-denser darkness. Although only wide enough for one person to pass at a time, the passage was at least high enough to allow me to walk upright. Lightly I trailed one hand along the wall as the corridor turned and twisted but without forking. I had the eerie sensation that we were walking into the heart of the hill.

Suddenly the passage widened and grew brighter. What the heck? What was the light source?

Ahead Laurel disappeared around a bend, and I picked up my pace. After the twist I came to a dead stop, blinking in amazement at the sight before me. The cathedral-size chamber glowed as if a rainbow were trapped inside.

Bands of reds and yellows striated the limestone

walls with crystal stars of purples, greens and blues. Huge crystal discs, some shaped like milk-glass flowers, clung to the ceiling. Pillars of smooth white stalagmites towered.

Slowly raising my head, I spotted in the vaulted ceiling the opening, with edges fluted like a rose, through which the late-afternoon sun poured.

But even more astonishing was the sight of what filled the cavern. Gold coins and brilliant jewels spilled from bags all around me. I knelt beside one small bag filled with heavy gold jewelry. Nearby on its side was a ruby-and-emerald-encrusted cross. However, an open wood chest containing tubes drew my attention. I rose and walked over. Picking up and opening one tube, I found a rolled-up parchment. Carefully I closed it.

"It is beautiful, yes?" Laurel stood beside a stone altar in the center of the chamber. For a second the cavern fell dark as a cloud moved overhead. Then a sunbeam shot down, spotlighting my niece and the altar. I swallowed, hard.

"The word *beautiful* doesn't even begin to describe this." I gestured at the chamber. "How long have you been coming here?"

She shrugged as she opened a rather plain, small chest on top of the shrine. "I found it last year. No one else knows about it, not even Phillipe. I like to come here to think and dream. You are the first one I have shown."

The trust she had shown thrilled me. Moving next to her at the altar, I had to clamp my fingers around the rough edge as I saw what was in the chest.

"Laurel, do you know what that is?"

She nodded. "But I think it has a different meaning to each person who finds it, *oui?*"

"Yes." With a shaking hand, I reached out and gently

closed the lid. "The Grail represents a different vision quest for each person."

She nodded and then skipped over to a larger chest on the floor close to the altar. "I thought these scrolls might be of interest to you."

I crossed over and squatted beside the chest. These parchments were rolled in leather. Spotting faint markings engraved in the leather, I picked one up. My heart pounding, I realized it was a crude symbol of a snake twined around a staff.

Carefully I unrolled the parchment. Due to my medical training, I could read some of the ancient Latin terms, enough to send my pulse racing overtime.

"Those with certain abilities can journey into another to heal him."

Ancient instructions from an ancient healer—Hippocrates.

Laurel handed me another scroll. "I think this one must be in French, but I can only read a few words."

I examined the careful handwriting. "No, not French, but..." My voice trailed off as I remembered a lecture to which my mother had dragged Yvette and me when we were teenagers. Yvette had been bored, but I had caught my mother's excitement. "This is the language of our ancestors," she had whispered as the lecturer had explained how Occitan had been the language of the troubadours. After that, I had read up on the origins of Occitan.

"Laurel, this may be in Occitan. I can read a few of the words." It appeared to be another medical text of healing potions, but the writing...had a woman written this?

I sat down and began to read both scrolls. When my niece stirred restlessly beside me, I glanced at my watch and, with a start, realized how late it was. Reluctantly I rose. "Come on, we must be getting back."

"You like my secret place?"

"Yes." I scooped up the Occitan scroll and the other medical one. When I had time, I wanted to read these more carefully and take them to an expert.

"Aunt Eve?" Laurel looked at me with a question in her eyes.

"For now I will keep your secret, but—" I turned in a circle, once more taking in the enormous implication of the room and its contents "—you must know that this belongs to the world."

Her shoulders slumped and I tipped her face to meet mine. "We'll talk about this and come up with a decision that you are comfortable with, okay?"

Her smile was sweet with trust and acceptance. "Okay, Aunt Eve."

She took my hand and together we crossed to the passage. With one last look at the legendary treasure, I left.

To keep my mind off the dark cramped exit, I wondered about the one text.

*How could a person walk inside another to heal them?*

Hours later I had more-pressing, less-esoteric matters to consider. Night's cloak crept across the Rennes valley as Nick and I sped along the road. The beam of the car's headlights swept across the discreet sign displaying a familiar logo: two crescents crossed by a bolt of lightning with a star for the center. Around a bend in the road, Nick pulled off and hid the Rover behind a clump of shrubs and trees.

Turning off the lights, he twisted toward me. "Let's go over—"

I kissed him, hard, and then opened the door. "I know the drill, Nick." He muttered about my being headstrong but got out of the car. He did the spy routine with night goggles, but I had to admit to being grateful. Stumbling about in the dark in unfamiliar terrain wasn't within my normal job description.

I kept close as he guided me on a parallel path to the drive before veering up a steep slope. He had detected security measures such as cameras at the front, but minimal effort where the house and other buildings abutted a steep, rocky hill. When he held his hand up in a prearranged signal, I knelt.

Below I saw the mammoth stone château, ablaze with lights. Other buildings dotted the back of the estate, including a smaller stone building with a cross on its pinnacle set apart from the others as if it had been an afterthought. Pointing to a long building, ostensibly one of the wine-storing facilities, Nick murmured in my ear, "That's the one I saw people in protective suits go in and out of."

I nodded. Yet another clue that this was not a typical Languedoc winery was the fancy electronic equipment on the roof. Although it was night, light spilled from the steel-barred windows.

"We'll go down here. Stay low."

I shifted the bag slung over my shoulder. Nick's mouth tightened with irritation but he didn't argue. He hadn't been a happy camper over the amount of gear I'd brought, but I'd been adamant. At my urgent request the Centre had rushed the kit to me. God knows how many strings Frederic had pulled to get the supplies through customs.

Nick led the way along a treacherous trail down the hillside. Suddenly my boot heel skidded on loose rock, and, flailing for balance, I slid into Nick. Grunting from the impact, he steadied me before continuing down.

At the foot of the hill, we paused, checking for any sign of movement. Nick's reconnaissance had indicated that the few guards kept their routes between the road and the château. When Nick gave the all-clear signal, we ran in a crouched position across the yard. I flattened myself against the building as he worked on the door. He shook his head in disgust as it slid open. Apparently, whoever was inside didn't rate security as a high priority.

With Nick going first, his gun out, we slipped inside to another dimension. Rather than wine vats and kegs, Plexiglas cubicles lined both sides of the structure. It was as though the laboratories of the Centre had been transported lock, stock and barrel to southern France.

Most of the minilabs were dim with no workers, but a larger one at the end was brightly lit. We walked toward it, dropping down when a white-suited figure crossed into our line of sight. When he disappeared, we rose. Nick motioned to me that he wanted to check out the office next to us.

He immediately went to the desk and sat before a dimly lit computer monitor. "Good. He doesn't have a time-out feature with password protection turned on. This is like taking candy from a baby." Nick's fingers raced across the keys. "Got it," he softly said.

"Got what?"

"I found his e-mail folder. There's a message dated several days ago from Simon Adriano to van Velsen about a special delivery." Nick pressed a key and the printer next to the computer spat out a page.

Special delivery as in the Spanish flu, or some new bug?

Was it evidence of a diabolical plot against the world health congress? No, but it was evidence of a connection between the scientist and the powerful family. Like DNA, my case against them needed to be built one segment at a time. Taking the paper from Nick, I folded it and placed it in my pocket.

A noise outside in the corridor had us ducking in unison. Peering over the edge of the desk, I watched the white-outfitted man walk up. As he faced the door, I saw his features: van Velsen. Pausing, he shook his head and then continued down the hall. Nick raced across the room and looked through the glass.

"He went outside."

This was our chance. I needed a closer look at the main lab. I hurried past Nick.

"Eve, wait—"

I sprinted down the hall to where protective suits hung from a rack. Grabbing one, I shimmied into it. When Nick reached for one, I stopped him.

"No, Nick. There may not be enough time. I know what I'm looking for. I need you to stand lookout." I thrust my bag at him. "Don't lose this. See that intercom button? Press it if van Velsen returns."

"How about I use the headset that you have on?" he asked wryly.

"Oh. Sure." I slipped on a respirator and entered the interlock. In this world of only hearing the harsh sound of your breathing and the rapid beating of your heart, I was at home. Inside the lab I went straight to the refrigeration unit. Whatever experiments were going on, the results would be there.

I opened the lid, triggering an interior light. As I read label after label in the eerie green glow, my horror grew. Names that could eliminate entire city populations: Ebola, bubonic plague, SARS virus. Carefully lowering the lid, I crossed to the next unit. Inside I found translucent bags—serums.

An opened journal on a lab table caught my eye. I

flipped through the pages. Although the handwritten text was in French, which I could normally read, much of it was illegible due to the cramped scribbling. However, I recognized DNA segments. I turned a page and stared at the drawings of canisters and notations of the spray capacity.

Bingo!

"Nick, I have the proof we need."

"Great, how about getting out of there?"

"In a minute," I said as I surveyed the lab one more time.

My earpiece crackled. "Eve—" Nick's voice broke off with a grunt.

I spun toward the entrance but couldn't see him. "Nick, are you there?"

No answer. Then I saw in the connecting chamber the white-clothed figure holding a gun. I dropped behind the table and moved swiftly one over.

"Do I have the honor of at last meeting Dr. St. Giles?" a man's heavily accented voice called out.

I was going to skip formal introductions. At long last, here was Willem van Velsen. Sweat trickled down my back as I agonized about Nick. Had the scientist only knocked him out? Or worse?

Cautiously I tried to reach out with my senses and heard the sound of Nick's breathing inside my head. He was alive, but…

In my mind's eye I could see an angry red wound in his arm. Even as I watched, the red began to streak through into his body. I had to get to him. Peering around the corner of the table, I tried to gauge Willem's progress through the lab. Fortunately, the guy was a real chatterbox. Must come from being locked up in a lab so much.

"You really have been a pain, Eve." The scientist checked around the first refrigeration unit. "After my successful experiment at Damassine, we were all ready to go forward with the pandemic."

Anger choked me. Successful experiment? My sister had *died* there, along with so many other people.

I spotted a Bunsen burner and several flasks with fluids. Reaching over I turned on the burner. The small click sounded like a clap of thunder, but Willem was too busy listening to himself talk.

"My assistant became obsessed with stopping you. Your name was the source of an ancient wound to him. After all, Eve was the reason man was expelled from Eden. Now another Eve was threatening our work."

The scientist moved past the second refrigeration unit. He was nearing the table next to me.

"Of course, he never knew the true purpose. But Sergio's religious fervor worked well in our scheme."

Sergio. At long last I had a name for the man I had pursued across Western Europe. My fingertips brushed against a cool glass surface and I nudged it toward the edge until I could grip it. Opening the stopper, I tipped it over.

"Fanatics who hate women have proven to be so useful to the cause." The scientist turned to search the opposite end of the row.

I repeated the process several more times, dumping out the contents of every flask I could reach.

"Imagine. I was able to create a flu specifically designed to attack a woman's immune system. If you weren't so dangerous to us, I would use you as a test case for my new and improved Ebola strain."

His voice was closer now, indicating he was moving toward me. "Once we have all our people in place, I will receive the Nobel prize for my work. At last I will have international recognition."

Praying those flasks contained more than water, I sprang up. Gaping with surprise, Willem stood only a few feet away. I grabbed the burner and tossed it into the liquid pool. Turning, I sprinted toward the entrance. After all the years of wearing protective gear, I could run in it at a pretty fair clip.

For a second all the air and sound seemed to be sucked up and then expelled in one long breath.

Whoosh!

I hit the ground. The floor shook as a loud explosion rocked the lab. A wall of fire enveloped the area where I had been hiding. Glass crackled as test tubes and flasks exploded like firecrackers.

Then out of the inferno Willem emerged, shouting, pointing his gun at me. This was it.

I tensed, waiting for a bullet to slam into my body. Shouts drew Willem's attention away from me. As he paused, I scrambled to my feet but kept low. Through the gathering smoke another man appeared.

Not Nick. My hopes plummeted. Then I saw the gun glinting in the man's hand. Over the din I heard the rapid spats of shots. Willem screamed as blood mushroomed across his face and chest.

I didn't wait to see if I was next. I ran forward, placing another bank of lab tables between me and the shooter. All I heard, though, was the swish of the door closing. As more explosions rocked the lab, I couldn't wait.

I raced for the door, wondering if I had been seeing things. If I hadn't, then for some inexplicable reason, Caleb Adriano had just been my savior when I thought he would have been my executioner.

# Chapter 18

Bursting from the decontamination chamber, I glanced around wildly and saw Nick slumped on the floor. I ripped off my head covering.

"Nick!" I shouted and started to race toward him.

A hand clamped on my shoulder. "You bitch!"

I spun around to a horror straight out of a D movie. Half crispy critter, half-*ER* escapee, Willem stood swaying. He had removed his headgear and for the first time I could see the manic expression in his eyes.

"You destroyed everything!" With his bloody hands outstretched, he surged at me. I tried to dart to the left but tripped over Nick's prone body. Willem's forward movement drove us both to the ground. He rolled on top, his weight pinning me.

I fought with every dirty trick I could think of, trying to knee his groin and gouge his eyes out, but two hundred pounds of madman began to prevail. Then his fingers tightened around my throat and white dots exploded in front of me as my vision began to gray at the edges…

*Listening, the healer paused in her task of filling flasks of precious water from the underground river.*

*What was that sound?*

*Years of caring for the ill had given her infinite patience, so she waited. At last she heard the muffled sound of footsteps and metal rubbing against leather.*

*So he had found the entrance. From the moment she had touched him, she had known his intent. When she merged with another in order to heal, she walked away with a part of that person forever as a part of herself. Facing death had not sent him on a new journey toward redemption. Rather, it had only enhanced his hatred.*

*So be it. She had been true to herself.*

*The healer set aside her medical supplies and gripped two other items. Slowly she rose, keeping both hands behind her back. Her heart broke as her assistant entered the chamber followed by the warrior and other men.*

*"You have betrayed your sisters, for what?" the healer addressed the young woman, ignoring the others.*

*"He loves me. He plans to marry me." Her assistant lifted her chin in trembling defiance.*

*Seeing the cold expression in the warrior's eyes, the healer shook her head. "You are a fool. You have forfeited your soul for nothing."*

*The warrior raised his hand and a soldier gripped the assistant's arm. "Take her. She will be someone's prize for tonight's work."*

*Holding out her arms in desperation, the assistant screamed in disbelief, but the warrior never looked at her as she was dragged from the chamber.*

*"So, this is the all-powerful temple." He spat on the ground. "Rock, water. There is nothing to fear here."*

*Her heart pounding, the healer prayed that the others had escaped through the secret entrance. Once outside they would set off a rock slide to hide the main entrance until the new age dawned. However, she could buy them a few more minutes of time.*

*She lifted the sharpened pipe to her lips and blew. The shrill noise echoed through the chamber and into the tunnel behind her. The warning would be heard throughout the temple.*

*Even as the warrior roared with anger and lunged at her, his sword raised, the healer whipped her other hand around. The spike of smoky quartz glittered as she drove it into her attacker's shoulder.*

*She tried to step to the side but her skirts tangled, trapping her. The warrior's sword hissed as it slashed through the air toward her.*

*Pain. Darkness.*

*The healer crumpled to the ground. On her last breath as she began her rise to the beckoning light overhead, she sent out a prayer of love and hope…*

I fought off the consuming darkness. No way was I ready for the light-in-the-sky routine. I had a journey to complete, a madman to stop.

My oxygen-deprived lungs burned. Despite my will, my body couldn't function. My hand fell limply to the side…on something sharp. Summoning strength one last time, I tightened my fingers around the object and swung it toward Willem.

He screamed, releasing me as he grabbed at the glass shard sticking out from his neck. He reared up, but before I could kick free, Nick lurched across me, shouldering the other man off. Suddenly the scientist fell quiet.

Nick lay still across my legs. Dragging the heated air

past my painful throat, I sat up. "Nick," I whispered in a hoarse voice. He groaned and managed to roll off me.

I scrambled to a kneeling position next to him. His eyelids fluttered open. "Go. Leave. Sick."

"Like hell I'll leave you." I grabbed his wrist and pulled. "Come on."

"Stubborn," he muttered but managed to push himself onto his knees.

Spotting my bag, I slung it over my shoulder and got to my feet. All around us flames fed hungrily on the air, seething with heat. It was only a matter of time before the place blew. I had to get us to safety. Fast.

"Come on, Nick. We need to move." As he wobbled up, I slid my arm around his waist and he held on to my shoulders for dear life. I ignored the sprawled body of the scientist, his sightless eyes open, and blood-stained glass spearing his throat.

Nick was so weak that he was almost dead weight, but we staggered down the corridor. The noise of exploding glass crescendoed, rising toward the ultimate conclusion.

Ten feet. Pop, pop, pop! Fat drops of sweat streamed from my temples into my eyes, stinging them.

Five feet. Bam! The small room to our left exploded into flames. Nick swayed but I tightened my grip, practically dragging him.

My breath harsh from exertion, I reached for the door lever and turned it.

Cool night air fanned my face. I gulped in deep breaths but couldn't pause, for I could feel the fire licking at our heels.

No way could I get Nick back up the hill, the way we had come in. Then in the wildly flickering light I saw the small stone chapel.

"Nick, over there." I pointed.

Beneath the soot on his face, his color was ashen, but he merely nodded. Together we limped across the yard. Flames exploded out one of the lab's windows, spewing shards of glass into the air. My muscles burning with numbness, I lifted the latch on the wood plank door but it was rusted shut.

"No!" I steadied Nick against the wall before releasing him. I kicked repeatedly, landing blow after blow right below the latch. The wood groaned. I kicked again and metal scraped. I gripped the latch and it slid up. Grabbing Nick, I shoved him first through the door.

The earth shuddered and the night exploded into an inferno. A wave of energy lifted me up and sent me flying into the interior of the chapel. As the ground rushed up at me, I tried to tuck and roll, but pain racked through me when I landed.

Stunned, I lay still for a few seconds as I listened to the outraged cacophony of bruised body parts. Then I heard Nick moan.

I levered myself onto my knees, and in the dim light saw him only a few feet away. Crawling over, I rolled him onto his back. His eyes were closed and all life seemed drained from his face.

"Nick?" I touched his cheek but he didn't react, not even with a flicker of an eyelid or a curve of his lips. Panic wrapped its icy fingers around my heart.

*No, be calm,* I ordered myself. *Set aside the personal and assume your professional mantle. It's the only way you can save him.*

Releasing a breath, I sat back on my heels and with a clinician's eyes scanned him. No signs of bullet wounds or trauma to the head. Recalling the vision in the lab of seeing red racing along his arm, I first pushed up one sleeve and then the other.

"Oh God, no!" An angry red pustule marked the needle's entry point on his right arm. Willem had injected him with something, but what? In my bag was the special-delivery kit containing a sample of nearly every serum and antidote of known diseases, but I couldn't just do a mass injection of all of them. I had to use the right one, and diagnostic conditions were less than ideal. One wrong conclusion could cost him his life.

*And if you don't act, he'll be dead.*

Right, and repeat my screw-up in Brazil last year. I bowed my head under the weight of the haunting memory.

Without training, without understanding my ability, in desperation I had tried to perform an empathic laying on of hands on a little girl close to death. What I had hoped to do was absorb the sickness into myself because I had been vaccinated. What I had ended up doing was holding the girl as she drew her last breath.

I'd failed so miserably. As I'd connected with the girl, red streams of viral poison had raced toward me. Then suddenly I'd experienced the horrifying sensation of being trapped forever inside the girl's body. Desperate to escape, I'd wrenched my hands free. To this day I heard the child's scream of pain as if the separation had ripped her apart.

Here I was, full circle. Damned if I did, damned if I didn't.

Despairing, I lifted my head and saw the stained glass window.

Glimmers of deep, mysterious light passed through a mosaic of richly colored stained glass painted with the ethereal images of a dark-skinned woman holding a child. More ancient visions mysteriously formed in my mind, uplifting my awareness with a sense of past, present and the hereafter. I felt as if the light passing through the glass penetrated into my eyes, heart and soul.

Then thunder clapped as another explosion seemed to rip the earth apart. A shimmering white line appeared, running from the window across the floor to the other wall. As the light grew brighter inside the chamber, the Black Madonna was projected on the opposite wall. She rose up, following the ley line, only to disappear into Nick's prone body.

I knew what I had to do. Even though my scientist side had fought the unexplainable, my Marian side was ready to embrace itself. My experiences of viewing the past had led me here, to this moment.

I knew now that the reason the healer's emotional imprint had reached out through the centuries to resonate so deeply inside me was that we were linked, by blood and by destiny.

Time to be true to myself and the healing abilities she had passed on to me.

I placed my hands on both sides of Nick's face and relaxed. My rhythm of breathing merged with his; his pulse became mine. I let him flow through me and I through him.

I walked inside him.

*The healer linked herself to the injured warrior. In order to heal him, she needed to be one with him. It was the ancient way, passed down by teachings from one healer to the next. However, even those scrolls detailing the inner walk were secreted.*

*A society bent on tearing itself apart was no place for enlightened wisdom. Such secrets could be used for evil purposes. She was the last practitioner and she meant for this to be her last merging.*

*The blackness she found was so overpowering that she almost tore free.*

*Hate.*

*Fear.*

*Evil.*

*Despite her healing trance, she shuddered in revulsion. How could she save this man who was bent on the sisterhood's destruction?*

*But how long could this struggle go on, generation after generation? If this battle between the Marians and the Adrianos did not end, their children and their children's children would continue to have their lives distorted and destroyed.*

*Hadn't this land suffered long enough from the Crusades and the Inquisition? With the Cathars on the verge of total annihilation by the Pope, the culture that had once enriched the soul now lay as scorched as the fields of death where men, women and children had been burned at the stake.*

*The temple's destruction had already been foretold. If not by this Adriano, then by another. She had to try to stop this cycle of destruction the only way she knew how.*

*By healing.*

*She circled the festering wound with her hands and let the energy of the glowing ley lines fill her.*

I saw the festering virus racing toward Nick's lungs and other organs with every beat of his heart. Strange—always before I'd been removed from the disease, able to observe it only on a slide under a microscope. Now I was seeing it alive, a carnivorous microbe.

A perfect killing machine.

Holding my hands around the injection site, I summoned the ley lines flowing through the earth. Like the fizz of champagne the warm energy filled me, radiating from my fingertips in glowing streams. The pulsating waves surrounded the virus, turning it to gray-colored sludge. As the energy bubbled into a glowing sphere, the virus tracks blackened and withered away. The injection site dissipated.

Okay, now for the tricky part—separation.

"See your body outside of the other person's and go to it," the ancient Occitan text had instructed.

As I allowed the ley energy to flow back to the ground, I saw myself, kneeling beside Nick and walked toward my body.

"Eve?"

I snapped awake to find myself lying next to Nick. Light from the stained glass window spilled into the chapel, but not from the fire.

Dawn.

Fingertips grazed my cheek. I turned to find Nick awake, his gaze intent.

"Hey there, stranger." I braced myself on one elbow to check his appearance. "How do you feel?"

His teeth flashed white against the soot covering his face. "Weak as a baby, hungry as an ox."

His color was good. I wrapped my fingers and felt his pulse, steady and true. I went to rise to get my bag, but his arm snaked around me and tugged me down.

Laughing, I tried to pull away. "You seem all right, but I want to give you a vaccine for good measure."

He shook his head. "The bug, whatever it was, is gone."

"I think the late Dr. van Velsen cooked up a special Eboli."

"So how did you manage to stop its spread? I thought at one point I was a goner and was going toward the light."

Had he seen the ley line? "It's complicated."

"Hmm. I had the weirdest hallucination while I was sick." He watched me carefully.

"Oh." I had to be careful to mask any expression until I could gauge his reaction. "How so?"

"I dreamed you were inside me."

Forcing a smile, I asked lightly, "Did I tickle?"

"No." Man, by the way his eyes focused to laser points, he could have torn secrets from any of the Knights Templar. Not willing to expose myself, I rested my head against his chest. His heartbeat remained strong, measured. So much like the man.

"You don't have to be afraid to tell me what happened last night."

"I'm not sure I entirely understand the process yet. Let's just say I definitely walked on the psychic wild side. However—" I took a deep breath "—to stop the infection I did have to merge with you."

"Whatever you did saved me, Eve." His hand hooked under my chin, tilting my face up. "I love you, woo-woo factor and all."

Yes, he did. Last night when I had been a part of him, I had experienced the depth of love in his heart and soul.

For me.

His love ran as true as his honor and convictions. He no longer feared the lack of normal boundaries between us. Adversity had fused the shattered pieces of our relationship into a stronger, more beautiful mosaic. If we had not journeyed apart, we never would have ended up at this place.

"I love you, too, Nicholas Petter."

Bracing myself against his chest, I slid up his body, intending only to kiss him lightly. However, Nick had other ideas. His hand slid to the back of my head, holding me in place.

His kiss was deep, long, filled with forever types of promises. I had no choice but to open my heart and myself in response. When he finally released me, we both drew in shaky breaths.

Giving him a lopsided smile, I said, "As much as I would love to ravish you, I can't put your religious side at risk here in a chapel."

He blinked and burst into laughter. "Is that where we are?"

Nodding, I rolled away and stood up. Nick's movements were slower as he too got up. Time for that shot. Reaching for my bag, I froze.

"Eve, what's wrong? You look like you've seen a ghost." He gripped my arm.

I pointed at the stained-glass window. Puzzled, he stared at it for a minute. "I don't get it. It's a scene depicting the Madonna and child."

Swallowing hard, I managed to speak. "But Nick, last night she was dark-skinned, like the Black Madonna at Montserrat, Spain. Today she's fair."

He shrugged. "The medieval glass artisans were into symbolism and puzzles. They used the medium to create different illusions, depending on how the light struck the glass."

I remembered the encounter yesterday at the St. Mary Magdalene church in Rennes-le-Château with the woman who had disappeared so quickly.

*You will see other examples of their work throughout this region. All have different properties, different mysteries to behold.*

Oh, yeah. Only, I had done more than see a mystery unfold. I had actually experienced one.

I looked at the serene expression of the lady holding the child and realized the image resembled the woman from yesterday. Smiling, I crossed to the window and, kissing my fingertips, pressed my fingers against the glass.

"Thank you."

Nick rubbed his face. "I'm not going to understand this, am I?"

Laughing, I gripped his arm. "Someday I'll tell you about it."

He ran his thumb over my lower lip. "Going mysterious on me?"

"A woman has to keep some secrets from her man."

"Works for me." He slung his arm around my shoulders. "Let's get out of here before someone comes looking for us."

As we left, I glanced over my shoulder one last time. The light shifted, changed in the chamber, and once more the Black Madonna smiled, waiting for the next soul to enlighten.

# *Chapter 19*

The late-afternoon sun dappled the countryside like a pastoral painting. I stood on the terrace outside the drawing room of the Fouquet château. Inside, mourners from my sister's funeral milled about, drinking, eating and chatting. As is the way with life and death, there was the occasional burst of laughter.

I heard a soft footfall behind me. Nick's arms circled around my waist, drawing me against the hard planes of his body. I leaned back, accepting the security of his strength.

"Nice services," he commented. "Yvette would have appreciated all the people attending."

I had to smile. "Yes, she would have." Even in death my sister would have loved being the star attraction.

"So-o-o—" he swayed me from side to side "—are you going to do it?"

I knew precisely what he was talking about. Earlier,

the Fouquet solicitor had met with me. Both sets of grandparents had agreed with Yvette's written request: that I would be her children's guardian.

Since the meeting I'd been thinking about nothing else. Even during my sister's funeral, I'd stared at her coffin, wondering why she would entrust the care of Laurel and Phillipe to me when we hadn't been able to get along in the last few years of her life.

Was her gesture a sign of trust or guilt?

Nick rubbed his chin across my head. "I can hear the brains at work. You're thinking about this too hard."

"I can't figure out why. She never wanted me alone with them when she was alive so why now, in death?"

"Perhaps her husband's death was a wake-up call. Perhaps this was her way to reach out to you for forgiveness."

A breeze stirred, dancing across the terrace. Hearing the flap of wings, I glanced up and saw a bird take flight from the family graveyard to soar across the translucent blue sky.

A white dove.

Whether or not it was my sister's soul at last at rest, I couldn't say, but I chose to believe.

*Be at peace, Yvette.*

The wind sighed and stilled. I turned to face Nick, linking my hands behind his neck. "Phillipe and Laurel are going to need a father."

"The thought had crossed my mind," he agreed solemnly.

"So-o-o, how about it?" I rose on the balls of my feet and kissed him.

"How about what?" He nuzzled the side of my face, his breath warm against my skin.

"Marriage, you moron." Although I kept my voice light, nerves clenched in a knot in my stomach.

"Ah. Is that a proposal I'm hearing?" His eyes were bright with amusement.

"Fine." I dropped my hands and tried to break free. "I'd rather get a thousand flu shots than ask you again."

My breath whooshed out as Nick tugged me hard against him. He lifted my hand, kissing the palm. "*Chère,* don't you know that you are part of me? I could no longer live without you than I could live without breathing. You have my heart, you are part of my soul."

Relaxing, I linked my fingers with his. "And I carry you inside me."

"Well, then. Will you marry me, Eve St. Giles?"

"Yes."

Nick leaned down to kiss me.

"Does that mean you will be my father, sir?" Phillipe asked from behind Nick.

We turned together. Dressed in a black suit and white shirt, my nephew looked old beyond his years. His skewed tie and his shifting from foot to foot spoke of his nerves.

Nick held out his hand. "If you will have us."

A smile lit his face and he hurried forward. We drew him into our circle and I kissed the top of his fair head. "We have a lot to discuss, Phillipe. Be patient with me. I have loads to learn."

He patted my arm. "I will help you, Aunt Eve." His serious tone brought tears to my eyes.

"Eve!" My mother's urgent call brought me to alert. She hurried through the opened French doors toward us.

"What is it, Maman?"

"I can't find Laurel. She's not in her room, and no one has seen her since she was in the kitchen eating."

That was about thirty minutes ago I calculated. I looked across the estate at the hill bordering the property.

"I know where to find her."

Nick said, "I'll go with you."

"No." I shook my head. "You stay here and do male bonding."

Nick's lips curved. "How do you propose we do that?"

"I don't know. Go watch the soccer game that I know the men have on the TV in the den."

I patted my mother's cheek and hurried down the stone staircase that curved from the terrace to the lower level. I struck out across the field and within short order entered the forest at the base of the hill. Finding the thread of a path that wasn't a path, I followed it until I could hear the trickle of water.

I didn't have to worry about stumbling across a stray Adriano. There was a reason no one had come to find Nick and I at the chapel last night. In the aftermath of the explosion and the whirlwind of official investigation, I had learned that, allegedly, none of the family had been at the château last night. They had left in their private jet earlier in the day. The Adriano representative had expressed outrage when advised of what had been in the lab.

Dr. van Velsen had been hired to develop new strains of disease-resistant grapes and to devise fertilizers that would replenish the farmed-out land. The family members had complied with the eccentric scientist's request to never enter the lab. The family would gladly furnish documents to back up their innocence in the affair.

Already the investigation's focus was shifting to the Men for Men Societies across Europe. A possible money trail linking van Velsen to the society had been uncovered.

An Adriano apology expressing shock, concern and an offer of financial aid had already been sent to the Centre and the Swiss government. Nick's client Janssen Pharmaceutical had also been contacted. The Adrianos' extensive resources would be made available to help Janssen get back on track to manufacture the Spanish flu vaccine.

Plausible deniability.

While the authorities had my statement concerning van Velsen's ravings in the lab before his death, the Adrianos had the money and clout for a whitewash of their involvement. Too early to call, but I suspected the family knew how to get off the hook without breaking into a sweat.

Whatever had been the end goal of the Adrianos' role in the Spanish flu outbreaks, the game was over. A connection had been made to them, and they would be foolish to continue down the viral path.

The Adrianos were no fools.

And they were no quitters. They'd been playing powerball since the beginning of civilization. They would simply find a new game.

To stop them once and for all and bring them to justice, I would need the help of a few good women.

The Marians.

Hearing a child's sobs, I broke into a run and rushed into the clearing. The waterfall was all but obliterated by fallen rock. My niece lay curled in a ball by the now-muddy pool.

"Laurel!" Hurrying to her side, I scanned her for any signs of trauma even as I knelt.

"Sweetie, are you hurt?" I touched her shoulder.

She sat up and then threw herself into my arms. I held her close as sobs racked her small body.

"It's gone!"

I stroked her tangled hair. "The cave?" She nodded against my shoulder.

I considered the hillside where rock had scored the surface with fresh scars. Recalling how the earth had moved during last night's explosion, I realized the small quake must have triggered a rockslide.

"I'll never get to see my special place again!" Laurel whimpered.

Placing a finger under her chin to lift her tear-stained face up, I smiled. "Laurel, do you understand the special treasure that cave holds?"

Or held, I thought. A very skilled climber or determined protector could easily access the chamber through the opening and spirit away the treasure to a new secret location.

My niece swiped her nose on the sleeve of her black dress. "Yes. It's what all those people have been looking for."

"Yes. And why haven't all those clever people with all their resources and theories been able to find the treasure?"

She shrugged.

"Because they weren't meant to." I flicked a finger along her nose. "But you were. For a short time you had the honor of keeping one of this world's greatest secrets."

Her lower lip trembled. "I would have kept the secret. They didn't need to take it from me."

"Laurel, the Grail legend is revered and shared by the world. I choose to believe that a very special person's need summons the Grail's appearance." I tightened my grip.

"Even now, somewhere, another soul awaits the Grail magic. Perhaps it's your time to let go as a keeper and move forward with your life."

I pressed a kiss to her forehead. Here goes everything.

"Your mother named me your guardian. Nick and I are going to get married. If you like, you can live with us and be a family."

She looked at me with solemn eyes. "And Phillipe?"

I smiled. "He and Nick are bonding over a soccer game."

Laurel wrinkled her nose. "Men."

Her expression sounded so adult that I laughed. "You're right. I need another woman to help balance the odds."

Nodding, she wrapped her arms around my neck. "I would like that."

Tears flooding my eyes, I held my precious gift close and looked skyward. "Thank you, Yvette."

*One last time, her heart breaking, the healer held her most precious gift close.*

*"I cannot leave you," her younger sister cried. "When will we see each other again?"*

*The healer looked over the head of her sister at the former Knight Templar standing silently at the edge of the clearing. She knew the hours of darkness were passing and they needed to be far away from this place when dawn broke.*

*She tilted her sister's chin and brushed the silky dark curls from her face. "You must be strong. Evil is all around us."*

*Last night, the healer had seen a vision of her own death. Had felt the slashing pain of the sword and floated above her own crumpled body. She did not know if she could change her destiny, or that of the Marians, but she could save her sister.*

*Wrapping her sister's fingers around the bag, she urged, "You must get these tiles out of harm's way.*

*The people who seek to destroy the power of the Goddess will stop at nothing to get these. You must hide them. You must pass on our legacy so that it is not lost to time."*

*She cupped her sister's cheek. "Your abilities are strong, different from mine. You will remember the past and the present as will your children and their children. It is your gift, your responsibility."*

*She stepped away, feeling the loss of her sister already. "Promise me that you will hide the tiles and not come back here."*

*Although tears ran freely, the girl nodded. "I promise."*

*So young for such a burden, but these troubled times dictated it. The healer kissed her. "Once this war is over, if I am able, I will find you."*

*Drawing her sister to the waiting man, she studied him. Once he'd been her patient, needing her touch to cure an infection. Unlike the Italian knight, this knight had a heart that beat strong and true. His was a protective nature. He would die before allowing harm to come to her sister.*

*Still, she had to say the words. "Take care of her, sir."*

*"With my life." Then he startled her by bringing her hand to his mouth and kissing it. "May the Goddess's grace be with you. Your healing has been a blessing in this cursed blight of war."*

*Her sister and the knight disappeared into the darkness of the hillside, heading east toward a neutral country. The healer fell to her knees and looked skyward. "May the Goddess's light be with them on their journey."*

Snow covered the stone circle outside Damassine, Switzerland. Understanding that I needed to complete this journey alone, Nick remained outside the ring. For a moment I stood in the center, wrapping myself in the silence of the snowfall. It was here that I began experiencing the past and here was where I would end it.

Grief engulfed me. My friend Scarlet was dead. Found brutally murdered in a hotel room in St. Tropez. Nick had gathered me close to him as he gave me the horrible news during our flight here. I could barely breathe past the sorrow.

I'd lost both my sisters. Although Scarlet may not have been a blood relative, she had understood and accepted me like no friend I'd ever had before. I raised the bouquet of the Madonna Lily to my face, taking comfort in the sweet fragrance, before I laid the pristine white flowers on the ground.

"Goodbye, my friend. I love you." While one circle of my life had ended, another awaited me.

After I closed my eyes, I sought to join myself with the power all around me. When the tingling rushed through my body, I opened my eyes. Despite the white blanket, I could see the shadow lines forming a pulsing grid within the circle. One line in particular glowed brighter than the others as it ran to the largest standing stone.

Crossing to the stone, I knelt and, using a small shovel from my backpack, began to dig at the base. Amazingly, the earth wasn't frozen in this spot. Scooping aside dirt, I saw the leather pouch.

Setting aside the shovel, I reached for the pouch. My heart racing, I opened it, put my hand inside and brought out tiles of every imaginable size and hues of silvers and grays.

The gleam of hammered silver, the sparkle of smoky quartz, the glitter of sphalerite crystal. I didn't recognize all the materials of the tiles, but when I put together a few of the larger ones, the outline of a sword began to emerge.

The image of the Lady in the temple. Had she worn a sword?

Carefully, I rebagged the tiles. I didn't comprehend the meaning of all my visions, but I knew where I had to start. That morning I had called an equally grief-stricken Catrina Dauvergne and arranged for a meeting. Scarlet would have liked that.

I was about to start a new journey, but this time I would be open to the full extent of my abilities.

I rose and went to where Nick waited. He glanced at the bag. "You found what you needed."

"Yes." I wrapped my arms around his waist. Strong, steady, protective. Nick was my foundation. He would allow me to soar and explore myself.

"Yes, I most certainly have." I kissed him, allowing all the love I felt to flow from myself into him.

Behind Nick, two figures appeared in the circle. The knight linked his fingers with the young woman. She glanced over her shoulder, and for a moment her face was Scarlet's. Scarlet gave me a reassuring smile before her image faded. The young woman turned back to her knight, and together they walked from the protective circle to a new life.

* * * * *

*The Marians' work is not yet done.*
*Come back next month for the thrilling*
*continuation of* THE MADONNA KEY,
*HIDDEN SANCTUARY*
*by Sharon McClellan.*
*On sale November 2006.*

*And don't miss Carol Stephenson's*
*next exciting romantic adventure story,*
*COURTING DISASTER*
*on sale April 2007.*

*Only from Silhouette Bombshell!*
*Available wherever Silhouette Books are sold.*

RUN, ALLY! Don't be fooled by him. He's evil. Don't let him touch you!

But as the forbidding figure came through the mists toward her, Ally knew she couldn't run. His features burned with dark malevolence, and his physical domination of everything around him seemed to hold her like a net.

She'd heard the tales. She knew all about the Wolverton legend and the ghost that haunted The Willows, an elegant old mansion lost by Micha Wolverton nearly a hundred years ago. According to folklore, the estate was stolen from the Wolvertons, and Micha was killed, trying to reclaim it. His dying vow was to be reunited with the spirit of his beloved wife, who'd taken her life for reasons no one would speak of, except in whispers. But Ally had never put much stock in the fantasy. She didn't believe in ghosts.

Until now—

She still didn't understand what was happening. The figure had materialized out of the mist that lay thick on the damp cemetery soil. A cool breeze and silvery moonlight had played against the ancient stone of the crypts surrounding her, until they joined the mist, causing his body to thicken and solidify right before her eyes. That was when she realized she'd seen this man before. Or thought she had, at least.

His face was familiar. . . so familiar, yet she couldn't put it together. Not with him looming so near. She stepped back as he approached.

"Don't be afraid," he said. His voice wasn't what she expected. It didn't sound as if it were coming from beyond the grave. It was deep and sensual. Commanding.

"Who are you?" she managed.

"You should know. You summoned me."

"No, I didn't." She had no idea what he was talking about. Two minutes ago, she'd been crouching behind a moss-covered crypt, spying on the mansion that had once been The Willows, but was now Club Casablanca. And then this—

If he was Micha, he might be angry that she was trespassing on his property. "I'll go," she said. "I won't come back. I promise."

"You're not going anywhere."

Words snagged in her throat. "Wh-why not? What do you want?"

"If I wanted something, Ally, I'd take it. This is about need."

His words resonated as he moved within inches of her. She tried to back away, but her feet were useless. "And you need something from me?"

"Good guess." His tone burned with irony. "I need lips, soft and surrendered, a body limp with desire."

"My lips, my bod—?"

"Only yours."

"Why? Why me?" This couldn't be Micha. He didn't want any woman but Rose. He'd died trying to get back to her.

"Because you want that, too," he said.

Wanted what? A ghost of her own? She'd always found the legend impossibly romantic, but how could he have known that? How could he know anything about her? Besides, she'd sworn off inappropriate men, and what could be more inappropriate than a ghost? She shook her head again, still not willing to admit the truth. But her heart wouldn't play along. It clattered inside her chest. The mere thought of his kiss, his touch, terrified her. This wildness, it was fear, wasn't it?

When his fingertips touched her cheek, she flinched, expecting his flesh to be cold, lifeless. It was anything but that. His skin was smooth and hot, gentle, yet demanding. And while his dark brown eyes were filled with mystery and wonder, there was a sensitivity about them that threatened to disarm her if she looked too deeply.

"These lips are mine," he said, as if stating a universal fact that she was helpless to avoid. In truth, it was just that. She couldn't stop him.

And she didn't want to.

* * * * *